POTLATCH

I0541110

POTLATCH

a comedy by

Bruce Hartman

Swallow Tail Press

Potlatch

Published by Swallow Tail Press
Philadelphia, PA, USA
www.swallowtailpress.com

ISBN-10: 0-9889181-9-6

ISBN-13: 978-0-9889181-9-1

Also available in library paperback and ebook format

Prologue

Being Ray Coggins's daughter hasn't exactly been easy. Your friends don't want to come over when they find out your Dad's serving a life sentence under house arrest. He takes up the whole living room, stretched out on the Barcalounger in his sleep apnea mask, scratching under his electronic ankle cuff with a bent coat hanger as he passes the time watching Phillies games, Eagles games, Flyers games, Sixers games, NASCAR races, even golf and pro bowling, or listening to one of his hundreds of vinyl Frank Sinatra albums. For the rest of the family—my Mom, my sister Tiffany and me—it's been like serving a life sentence of our own, praying for the day they'll wheel us in for a lethal injection.

As far as I know, my Dad never did an honest day's work in his life. Not that he's been lazy or unambitious. He devoted twenty-five years to various scams, ponzi schemes, insurance frauds and all kinds of other rackets before he came up before Judge Rotundo for the last time. Facing life behind bars as a career criminal, he called in his favors from Desmond Gallaher and the political machine that runs the city. Like most complicated apparatus, the Gallaher machine needs a lot of guys in greasy jumpsuits to keep it running. That's what made my Dad so valuable. He knew Philadelphia like the back of his hand, and he could tell at a glance what needed to be fixed. So when he was convicted that last time, it was the Boss himself, Desmond Gallaher, who arranged for him to serve his sentence under house arrest.

If we had a more normal family, it might not be so bad. My Mom isn't under house arrest but she never leaves the kitchen. She hates my Dad, even though he's crazy about her. It's nothing personal—she hates everybody, except our cat Rizzo and my sister Tiffany. My Grandma, who lived here until they stuck her in a nursing home, says my Mom loves me, but I've never noticed any sign of it. I guess that's why I've developed a pretty thick skin.

Tiffany is 26, two years older than me and definitely thinner, especially in the bust line (all right, pretty much everywhere except her feet). She's a bottle blonde, while I've kept my natural color, a reddish brown which (she likes to tell me) would look better on a cocker spaniel. Her handicaps, though she doesn't know it, are her face and her brain. Neither of them is a pretty sight. She and Mom want me to go out with Judge Rotundo's son Kyle, whose IQ hangs in the low double digits, depending on how many Jägermeisters he downed the night before. Kyle is my Dad's probation officer. He has a fat face, a drooping chin and eyebrows that make him look like a dog. They hope that if I sleep with him he'll persuade the judge to reduce Dad's sentence to time served. "Face it, Alice," Tiffany tells me, "if you don't lose fifty pounds, Kyle's the only boyfriend you're ever going to get."

"Unless you go out with that Hector who lives on the next block," Mom adds. "He tells everybody he wants to marry you. But Kyle would be a better catch."

"The guy's brain dead," I tell them.

"You don't have to marry him," Tiffany says. "Especially his brain. Just sleep with him so we can get some peace around here."

"What daughter wouldn't do that for her father?"

At least my Dad hasn't tried to pimp me out so he could get his sentence reduced. Mom has no sympathy for him, especially when he complains about the ankle cuff.

"I'm itching to death!" he hollers from the couch about once an hour.

"Don't get my hopes up," she yells back from the kitchen.

"I mean it. This thing's killing me."

"It's working, then. Just give it a chance."

Dad's always been crazy about me, maybe a little too crazy. Back when he was drinking, he used to smack Mom and Tiffany around a little, but he never laid a hand on me. That made my Mom so angry (I guess you could say she was jealous), she'd slap my face when she knew he wasn't looking. All that domestic violence stopped when Dad quit drinking (though Mom still threatens to slap me if I happen to mention that Tiffany is a slut). When he went under house arrest, he pulled some strings to get Mom a no-show job in the Motor Vehicles Department. I guess he pictured himself lounging in front of the TV while she waited on him hand and foot, but that's not how it worked out. He didn't foresee how dedicated she'd be to her no-show job. On weekdays from eight to six she sits at the kitchen table working crossword puzzles and drinking coffee. On weekends she does the same thing, claiming it's mandatory overtime. She even stays in there during her breaks.

"Hey," he shouts, "come on in the living room and join the human race!"

"That's the last place I'd look."

"You're supposed to be spending more time with the family. That's why I got you this no-show job."

"It's a government job," she tells him. "So get in line like everybody else."

Actually the part about joining the human race is a sore point in our family. Most of the people on the block are Irish or Italian, but I've never been sure what ethnic group we belong to. My parents never talk about it, either because they don't know or they don't want to get in a fight. When my eighth grade class visited Ellis Island, we had to type into a computer where our ancestors came from. Since I didn't want to look stupid, I typed in "Finland." I was the only Finnish kid in my class.

My parents disagreed about what I should do when I finished high school. Mom thought I should take a no-show job like hers, possibly in the law enforcement industry, but Dad wanted me to follow in his footsteps in what he called the "organization." It was time I learned the political ropes. Whenever he could get permission from Probation to leave the house, he'd take me with him to the seedy clubhouses where the organization plots its strategy for the next election. He longed for some political turf of his own, a low-level city appointment or at least a party office, but his ambitions were blocked by an obvious handicap, which also hindered mine. It's hard to follow in the footsteps of a man who's limping along in an ankle cuff.

One night after I'd cooked and served dinner, cleared the table and washed the dishes (those are my jobs; Tiffany is in charge of her hair, nails and makeup), I sat down at the kitchen table to catch my breath. Dad pulled out a Q-tip, asked me to open my mouth, and took a swab of DNA from inside my cheek to send to the National Geographic ancestry project. "You might find out you belong to some group that's entitled to benefits," he explained. "Maybe you could open a casino."

"Or live in a refugee camp," Mom added.

The report we received in the mail was disappointing. I guess I expected something more elaborate, like a genealogical chart going back to Adam and Eve. Instead it was a couple of pages with a list of categories, some percentages and a map with circles that included everything between Ireland and the Black Sea.

"It's basically like we thought," Dad said as he eyeballed the list. "We're white people."

"But look at this," I said. At the bottom of the list I'd found a disturbing statistic. "It says I'm 2.6% Neanderthal."

"You didn't get that from me," Mom said sharply.

"Then it must've come from you," I told Dad. "That means you're 5.2% Neanderthal."

"Practically a pureblood," Mom agreed.

As Dad squinted down at the list, his forehead looked a little more sloped than I remembered. "Maybe that's not so bad," he finally said. "Politically, I mean."

Mom and I exchanged worried glances. We were afraid he was having one of his brilliant inspirations, like the time he tried to convince the City Council to annex Las Vegas. "Let me guess," Mom said. "You're going after the Neanderthal vote."

"Why not? Every other ethnic group has its own community, its own politicians, even its own neighborhood.

The Chinese have Chinatown, the Germans have Germantown..."

"The fish have Fishtown," Mom added.

"Right. So why shouldn't the Neanderthal-Americans have their own pressure group?" You could almost hear the pressure rising as he envisioned his ascent to power. "Why shouldn't it be based right in this house?"

"I think it already is," Mom said.

When I was seventeen—that was seven years ago—I came home from school with my backpack full of college catalogs and brochures, which I spread out on the kitchen table. Mom sat there working a crossword puzzle while a pizza sizzled in the oven. Dad lounged on his Barcalounger in the living room, yelling swear words as he watched Judge Judy on TV. All I could think about was what my guidance counselor had told me that afternoon: that if I applied to college, she would write a strong recommendation. When my Dad shuffled in, complaining about the itching under his ankle cuff, I came right to the point. "Dad, I need to talk to you about college."

"College?" Mom snorted without looking up from her puzzle. "I didn't go to college. Your father didn't go to college. Your sister didn't go to college. Nobody in this family ever went to college."

"That's the point, Mom. I want to be the first."

"Why don't you just get a job?"

"There aren't any jobs. The jobs all went to China."

Dad wrapped his arm around my shoulders. "You don't need college, sweetheart. All they do is put a lot of ideas in your head. And you don't need a job. Just stick with the family business."

"The family business?"

"What I do every day." He tapped the side of his head with his finger. "Living by my wits."

"And he's only got half of the usual amount," Mom said.

"Yeah, I won't deny it. I'm no Einstein. I wouldn't have graduated from Cardinal Dougherty if I hadn't cheated on the Theology exam. But that taught me a valuable lesson. If you can cheat on Theology and get away with it, you can do anything."

"But Dad—"

"The main thing is, I've got connections. Desmond Gallaher personally asked the judge to keep me out of prison. He knows I can make things happen."

"You could get a government job like mine," Mom told me. "You won't even have to leave the house."

"With all due respect," Dad said, with a quick glance at Mom, "jobs are for losers who can't do anything else. They're not for the movers and shakers like us."

All this time, he had been flipping through the college brochures I'd left on the table. "Look at this!" he finally shouted. "Women's Studies. Gender Studies. _Queer_ Studies! Create your own major! They don't even teach you anything at these places. And look at the price tag!"

At that moment there must have been parents all over the country choking with rage as they read those brochures. But I doubt if there were many who reacted the way my Dad did— with the awe and admiration of a true connoisseur.

"I think I just found what I've been looking for all my life," he said in a hushed voice. "I think I found the perfect scam."

A few days later Dad got permission from Kyle Rotundo, his probation officer, to leave the house on a mission for the Boss. He asked me along and in a few minutes we were cruising through South Philly in his baby-blue Cadillac to meet some unlucky dog who owed a loan shark named Baby Boy Barkocy half a million dollars. The whole thing was hush hush, very confidential, because of who the guy was. Dad didn't even know his name, just his code name, which was "Half Nelson," and that he was a college president with a compulsive gambling habit and a poor choice of lenders. He'd done everything humanly possible to raise the money he owed to Baby Boy, Dad said. He'd embezzled the tuition payments and the scholarship funds and the room and board accounts, but with interest and late fees it still wasn't enough to pay off the debt. Baby Boy ran a butcher shop equipped with cleavers, meat axes, hacksaws and mallets that he used on people who fell behind in their payments. The university, which started as a Gallaher operation, was pretty much out of business—the faculty had fled and the classroom buildings were being foreclosed by Gallaher's bank. But Gallaher didn't want to see it shut down, and he asked my Dad to convince Baby Boy to back off.

"How are you going to do that?" I asked Dad.

"This Half Nelson has been running a college, right? The perfect scam. He ought to be able to figure something out."

We were supposed to meet "Half Nelson" outside Baby Boy's butcher shop at 22nd and Wolf at five o'clock. Naturally we were late—Dad is always late when he drives the Cadillac. He doesn't like anyone calling his Cadillac "old," but it is old, old enough to have tail fins and twin D-cup protrusions on the front bumper. Floating along in it, you feel like the mayor in a Columbus Day parade, honking and waving to cheering crowds of old ladies on their stoops, kids on their bikes, bald guys in wife-beaters waxing their cars. Dad piloted south on 7th, jogged on Washington to 11th, then down past Pat's Steaks at 9th and Passyunk to avoid the Italian market, then south on 6th and across Broad on Tasker—cruising warily down the narrow streets and lurching through the stop signs at the end of every block. He talked and talked, like he always did, about the neighborhood and the people who'd lived there all their lives, and by the time we got to 22nd and Wolf, I knew more than I wanted to know about Baby Boy Barkocy. His parents were a couple of gambling hustlers, Dad told me, who pushed their luck a little too hard and made the wrong enemies. They were gunned down on Oregon Avenue the day after he was born—and before they'd had a chance to name him or fill out his birth certificate. In the box for "First Name," the nurses had written "Baby Boy" and that was the only name he ever had. At St. Peter's Orphanage, they called him Baby Boy even after he was six feet four and weighed 280 pounds. He started loansharking as an altar boy, filching money from the collection baskets and loaning it back to the priests to buy porno movies. Hoping he'd forget what they owed him, they apprenticed him to a Polish butcher in Port Richmond, where he learned to tenderize meat with a big wooden mallet. "In a few years he opened his own shop," Dad chuckled, "but he never forgot the priests of St. Peter's. To this day most of them walk with a limp."

The butcher shop was a front for his loansharking business. Eventually he opened a branch "downtown"— meaning in South Philly—where he could expand his customer base. "South of South," Dad said, "you're in Gallaher territory. Baby Boy's clients know what they need to do to keep their lines of credit open. At seven a.m. on Election Day they line up outside the butcher shop like they've got a sudden craving for kielbasa. But even though it's raining cats and dogs—it's always raining on Election Day—they don't come inside and take a number. They pile into hearses and limousines from Gallaher Funeral Services Inc.—I used to drive those around myself—and memorize obituaries as they make the rounds to the polling places."

"Isn't that a subversion of democracy?" I asked naively.

"Far from it," Dad laughed. "You remember all that talk a few years ago about issuing voter ID cards?" We were on Wolf, about two blocks from Baby Boy's butcher shop. Some teenagers waved from the sidewalk, probably admiring the Cadillac. Dad assumed they thought he was somebody important, so he waved back and missed a stop sign. "They claimed dead people were voting, but trust me, nobody in Philadelphia'd ever thought of that. In those days, nobody was voting anymore. We had elections that were decided by one vote because only three voters showed up at the polls. That's how cynical people had become. So the Boss got the idea of using his funeral service to help get out the vote. You could argue that he saved democracy."

"You could," I conceded. When it comes to Gallaher, you could argue anything.

We sailed through the next stop sign.

"That's when I started driving for Gallaher on Election Day," Dad said. He laughed as he recalled the scene at the polling places. "I remember one poor guy who had to pose as somebody he knew. The guy didn't even know his friend was dead until he read the obituary in the hearse. He climbed out and walked into the polling place with tears in his eyes.

"'What's your name?' asks the clerk.

"'Dennis O'Mara,' he says, 'may he rest in peace.'

"'You're looking well, Denny,' the clerk says, 'taking everything into account. Good of you to come in from the cemetery to vote on a nasty day like this.'"

It was funny, but—like most of Dad's stories—he probably made it up. "That's what I don't like about politics," I told him. "Dead people voting and all that."

"Dead people are the fastest growing segment of the population," he said. "Why shouldn't they be treated like everybody else?"

"But they're not really like everybody else, are they? Aren't they, like, dead?"

We drove past the butcher shop, where we could see Half Nelson standing outside the door, sweltering in a gray suit. "It's like being handicapped, only worse," Dad went on, still talking about dead people. "They don't get out much, so on election day they're anxious to get to the polls. We make sure they have a ride, that's all. It's a question of respecting their last wishes, doing what they would've done if they were still alive. And you know what?"

He turned a sly smile in my direction as he eased the Cadillac up to the curb. "They always vote the straight Gallaher ticket."

Half Nelson leaned against the shop window smoking a cigarette, which he tossed down as we climbed out of the car. Not my image of a college president—no jaunty tweeds or horned-rim glasses, just a nervous old Waspy guy with stooped shoulders and hollowed-out eyes—but not my image of a compulsive gambler either. Sixty years old if he was a day, with a face as gray as his suit. He seemed glad to see my Dad, but suspicious of me, demanding to know what I was doing there. "She's my bodyguard," Dad told him, and led the way into the butcher shop. There was only one customer ahead of us, but Dad tore the top sheet off the Take-A-Number pad and handed it to Half Nelson, who clutched it like a lottery ticket he hoped would win the jackpot.

Baby Boy had a huge bald head, bloated cheeks and wide, penetrating eyes. I could see why the name stuck: looming behind the counter with his cleaver, he looked like an enormous baby dismembering a loin of pork. Across from him slouched his only customer, a fat man in a cheap suit who clearly identified with the pork, emitting an audible grunt each time Baby Boy whacked the cleaver down on the carcass. The butcher's assistant Howie hulked beside him in a psychopathic daze, pounding thin strips of meat into submission with a wooden mallet. The three of them were discussing a certain sum of money owed by the fat man, who had apparently requested an extension of the time for repayment.

"Do I look like the Federal Reserve Bank?" Baby Boy demanded.

Actually, he did look like the Federal Reserve Bank (at least the way I imagined it), with his massive front porch, the staircase of double chins, the glistening dome over a granite-hard facade. Somewhere he probably had a printing press that churned out money and a stash of unmarked bills that backed up his loansharking operation like the gold in Fort Knox.

Pork chops flew in every direction as Baby Boy went to work with his cleaver. "You think I'm in business to increase the money supply?"

"No, of course not," the fat man mumbled. "I never thought that."

Baby Boy wrapped a fistful of kielbasa in white butcher paper and laid it on the scale, waving aside the fat man's attempt to pay for it. "I'll give you a week to settle up for all the money you owe me," he said, "including the cost of this kielbasa, with accrued interest and late fees. If you show up with one penny less than that, you won't be driving home."

"Or walking," Howie added, flattening a medallion of beef with his mallet.

"Such a stickler for details!" Baby Boy laughed. "That's Howie for you!"

The fat man mopped the sweat off his face with his necktie. He seemed like he might pass out.

"Look," Baby Boy said, shifting to a friendlier tone, "I'm a businessman. But Howie here is more like what you'd call a criminal. In fact, just between you and me"—he lowered his voice—"the guy's sort of nuts. Loves the sound of bones splintering, eyeballs popping, kneecaps cracking, that sort of thing. Isn't that right, Howie?"

Howie nodded sullenly.

"Like I said, Howie's a little crazy," Baby Boy said. "Sometimes I can't control him. But you know what?" He leaned forward with a smile that was more like a snake's than a baby's. "Sometimes I can."

He aimed his smile at Half Nelson as the fat man vanished out the door. "Next!"

When you're seventeen, you think graduating from St. Maria Goretti is a big deal. You spend your summer at the shore, putting on weight and sleeping with every guy you meet. By the time you come back your girlfriends are going to beauty school, looking for jobs, getting pregnant. None of that's for you. You're unhappy but you don't know why. Is it because your Dad can't leave the house? Because your Mom treats you like a servant girl, your Grandma's locked up in a nursing home, your sister's everything you'd never want to be? You pine for a little understanding—maybe life would be bearable if anyone seemed to care what's going on in your head. In this family, Rizzo the cat comes closest to being a normal human being. You never get any dates. Your Mom wants you to marry Kyle Rotundo to get Dad out of the house. Nerdy Hector around the corner peeks out his window every time you walk by. Your sister Tiffany expects you to polish her shoes and pick up her dry cleaning. The only neighbor who'll talk to you is an old black homeless guy named Randolph, who stops by every day with his shopping cart to chat with Dad on the front stoop. When you need a sympathetic ear you visit Mr.

Reddy, the Indian man who runs the little store on the corner. He listens to everybody and agrees with everything they say. Sometimes you wish your ancestors never left Finland.

Surprisingly, Dad has found some followers for his Neanderthal-American movement. The economy's in a shambles; people feel disaffected, distrustful, disoriented. They worry that our society, if not our species, has taken a wrong turn, maybe as long ago as the Early Pleistocene. Randolph, the homeless guy, thinks the problem may go back even farther than that. For every crackpot theory Dad comes up with, Randolph has two—fully documented by the newspapers, magazines and books he hauls around in his shopping cart. When I tell him I can't find a job, he suggests that I try the WPA.

"The WPA?" I assume it's a kind of craft beer.

"Works Progress Administration," he explains. "Dates back to the New Deal."

"The idea was to keep people working," Dad adds, "even if it meant raking leaves in a forest. Digging holes and filling them back in. That kind of thing."

"That's how I found my job," Randolph says. "Been at it fifty-three years this August."

I glance down at his shopping cart brimming with old clothes, discarded newspapers, *National Geographic* magazines, broken appliances. "This is a job?"

A sly smile lights up his wrinkled face. "You think I'd do this for nothing?"

Dad pops open two cans of Coke and hands one to Randolph. He knows I don't want any.

"Most folks have the mistaken notion that the WPA ended long ago," Randolph says, sipping his Coke. "That's just what the government wants you to think."

"Then how can they help me find a job?"

"Oh, they'll help you. You just wait." He downs the rest of his Coke and tosses the can into the shopping cart. The smile sneaks back over his face as he turns the cart around and heads down the sidewalk. "They're an equal opportunity employer," he says over his shoulder. "Probably got a special program for Neanderthal-Americans."

As you look back, you know what you always wanted, but you didn't know it then. What you always wanted was to get away from where you were, and when you got to the next place, to get away from there. Just make a run for it, like in a movie, and keep running. But that's not what you do. Instead, you find an internship at a pizza place called Pinocchio's, where you have to wear a silly hat and apron that makes you look like a marionette.

My parents still can't understand why I don't leap at the future they envisioned for me. "I want my life to be more than a racket," I tell them, and they both laugh.

"Well, la-de-da!" Mom hoots. "Listen to the Queen of England!"

"A racket?" Dad says, probably wondering if I've thought of one he hasn't tried. "Like what, for instance?"

"Like scams, no-show jobs, rigged contracts, politicians elected by dead people. I want to do honest, productive work, and make the world a better place."

Mom laughs again. "At least it's not just us," she tells my Dad. "The whole *world's* not good enough for her!"

"It'll never fly," Dad says, shaking his head. "You're talking about something that's never even been *attempted* before. At least not in Philadelphia."

"There's always a first time."

"What you're calling a racket is how everybody makes a living."

"She's better than everybody," Mom explains.

"Just look around," Dad says. "Does the world look like it's crying out to be a better place? The kids don't finish school, and if they did, there's no jobs for them anyway, and even if there were jobs, they wouldn't show up for them, and if they did show up, they'd rob the place or go on strike or sit around not doing any work. Without what you're calling rackets, nobody would get out of bed in the morning. Nothing would happen. People would starve."

"We would starve," Mom adds.

"Sure, the world could use some improvement," Dad says. "But how likely is it that you're going to be able to fix it? This is the real world we're talking about, not some kind of a fairy tale world."

Sometimes I think the world I've been brought up in is a fairy tale world. Not the kind where you live happily ever after, but a world ruled by malignant dwarfs who've enchanted us into forgetting who we are. Living in this world is like going around in a dream. Why else can't my parents see what's going on?

"What do you want out of life, anyway?" Mom asks, looking serious all of a sudden.

I don't answer because I can't stand to hear them laugh again. But I know what I would say. What I want is what everybody wants—to find my own kind of happiness, even in a totally screwed up world. I could go into some racket, like my parents want me to do, marry Kyle Rotundo and console myself with zombie novels and fattening desserts. Or like Tiffany, turn my whole life into a racket.

What do I want out of life, anyway?

Independence and connectedness, freedom and security, to love and be loved without making too much of a commitment. Adventure. Romance.

Is that too much to ask?

When the fat man stumbled out of the butcher shop, all eyes—Baby Boy's, Howie's, Dad's and mine—were on Half Nelson or whatever his name was. Baby Boy smiled at him and said "Next!" and he staggered backwards as if he'd been whacked with the meat cleaver. The blood was in such a rush to drain out of his face I thought it might end up on the floor, even without any help from the butchers. He looked like he expected to be slaughtered on the spot: astonished eyes, flyaway hair, collapsing chin—which only collapsed farther when he turned over his Take-A-Number and found a big fat 13. His hand trembled as he reached it over the counter.

"Lucky thirteen!" Baby Boy grinned. "What'll it be today? How about some split pig knuckles? Or some nice head cheese. You like head cheese?" He waved a slimy, pinkish loaf in his customer's face. "It's really not cheese, more like sausage, made from chopped-up parts of a head. Cheeks, tongue, lips—that sort of stuff. Only six ninety-nine a pound."

"I think I'll pass," Half Nelson gagged, revolted by the smell.

Dad reached across the counter and shook the butcher's enormous hand. "Great to see you, Baby Boy. The Boss thought maybe I could help, you know, facilitate communications a little. For the sake of the organization."

The butcher squinted at me as if he was sizing up a side of beef. "Who's the young lady?"

"This is my daughter. Could we do this in your office?"

Baby Boy laid down his cleaver, removed his apron and led us into his office, where he sat down behind what looked like a child's desk. "OK, let's cut the crap," he said to Half Nelson, forming his kielbasa-like fingers into the shape of an inflatable tent. "You owe me a lot of money. I'm waiting to be paid."

"I apologize," Half Nelson said, his voice cracking. "I'm truly sorry for the delay. I intended to pay you back as soon as the tuition money came in, but with applications down, enrollment falling, the classroom buildings being foreclosed—"

"Just a minute!" Baby Boy reached under his desk and pushed a buzzer summoning Howie into the office. "I thought you might want to hear this, Howie. You're the Wharton graduate. Go on."

"If you could just have a little patience—"

"Patience? I'm famous for my patience—right, Howie?—especially when I'm losing it."

"—you'll be able to collect *multiples* of what you're owed."

"Multiples! When I hear 'multiple,' I think of multiple fractures, multiple contusions..."

"Multiple personality disorder," Howie added sullenly.

Baby Boy cracked a smile. "I told you he was a Wharton grad. So what's all this got to do with me getting paid?"

Half Nelson was hyperventilating, unable to speak. Dad took the opportunity to jump in. "Baby Boy," he said, "let me try and facilitate the discussion a little. This gentleman is being modest. Far too modest, in my opinion. For years he's been sitting at the top of the biggest scam in America, and he's here because he wants to cut you in. It's called a university. You get that? A university?"

"Are you messing with me, Ray?"

"A university is a money machine, Baby Boy. All you need is a tiny piece of it and you'll be raking in the cash like there's no tomorrow."

"I don't want a tiny piece of it. I want a big piece of it."

"Sure, and that's what you'll get. Right?"

Half Nelson looked like he might be sick. Everything Dad said had come as a complete surprise to him. "What choice do I have?" he mumbled.

Baby Boy still wasn't buying it. "You're gonna have to connect the dots for me, Ray. I went to parochial school."

"OK," Dad said. "At a university they've got something called financial aid. It's like what you do, Baby Boy—basically a loan sharking operation—only on a grand scale and with a higher interest rate. The college charges the students whatever it wants for tuition, room and board and all that, and the students have to borrow whatever they need to pay for it, at any interest rate the college wants to charge. And get this: *it's all completely legal!*"

Baby Boy laughed. "When do Santa Claus and the Tooth Fairy come into the story?"

"Believe me, Baby Boy. This is for real."

"Have I ever heard of this university?"

"It used to be called the Philadelphia School of Embalming," Half Nelson said. "A few years ago we added a gym, a student center and a football stadium, and renamed it UCLA."

"UCLA?"

"University on the Corner of Lancaster Avenue."

"Didn't you say the place was going broke?"

"Well—"

"It was going broke," Dad broke in. "But we know how to turn it around. I've talked to the Boss about this. He sees UCLA as an asset to the organization. We don't want it to close its doors."

"To be clear," Half Nelson mumbled, "currently the university doesn't have any doors. Just sheets of plywood nailed—"

"Exactly what are you proposing?" Baby Boy interrupted.

The college president sat with his head bowed, as if he wished he could make his whole body recede as completely as his chin. "We'll put you in charge of Financial Aid," he finally said. "No questions asked."

"I told you I don't just want a piece of the action!" Baby Boy thundered. "I want to run the whole scam!"

Half Nelson took a deep breath before he replied. "All right, it's yours. I'll make you the Chief Financial Officer."

"You won't regret this, Baby Boy," Dad said.

And that's how it came about that Baby Boy Barkocy was named Chief Financial Officer of UCLA. He never regretted it, but plenty of other people did. It was a momentous event, not just for the university but for the whole city, and eventually for me, though none of us knew it at the time.

And we owe it all to my Dad.

I.

Seven years later...

1. Mail

Mail everywhere. Mail waist deep in canvas bags and castered bins. Mail in bundles lashed with twine or stuffed in plastic bags. Mail thundering in on trains from Chicago and New York and Washington, forklifted into the Central Post Office by grim-faced civil servants in hardhats and leather gloves. There to be weighed for postage due, tested for anthrax, scanned for explosives, sniffed for drugs, then sorted and trucked to a hundred branch post offices throughout the city. And then to be hauled in shoulder bags—heedless of snow or rain or heat or gloom of night—up a hundred thousand steps, stoops and elevators to the condominiums of the rich and the houses and apartments of the impecunious, where it will be crammed into mailboxes, slipped under doors or tossed down on the steps—all in all, a feat of human energy and organization rivaled only by the construction of the Egyptian pyramids.

Mail everywhere, engulfing the city like a vast mudslide. Measured by bulk, it consists chiefly of catalogs printed on slick, heavy paper, colorful brochures offering views of women in dresses, men in plaid shirts, dogs in snug woolen vests, sportswear, loungewear, sleepwear, underwear, running shoes, walking shoes, snow shoes, Caribbean vacations, computers and phone accessories. And there are letters, millions of them, advertising phone companies, health insurance, car insurance, life insurance, burial insurance, pet insurance, and insurance against identity theft, offering membership in museums, theater companies and political groups, soliciting support for charities and victims of all kinds.

Mail everywhere. By noon the mudslide has reached crisis proportions, overflowing every mailbox and doorstep in the city. The inundated citizens resort to violent and drastic action. They scoop up their mail by the armful—with scant regard for its contents or the superhuman efforts of the postal service in delivering it—and throw it in the trash without a glance.

Does anyone care what's in this immense midden of wastepaper? For Tiffany Coggins, age 26, who lives and dies by her phone, mail is an evil omen that presages parking tickets, collection notices and unwelcome solicitations from the charities she pretends to support. Her sister Alice, 24, never checks the mail because she never gets any. Their father, Ray Coggins, serving his tenth year of a life sentence under house arrest, worries that his electronic ankle cuff may have gone out of style. He flips through the catalogs in the vain hope of finding the current fashion, and makes a mental note to launch his own line of designer ankle cuffs with endorsements by celebrities like Lindsay Lohan, Martha Stewart, Michael Vick....

Twenty blocks to the north, at the Federal Reserve Bank, the day's mail delivery is subjected to minute inspection by women in moon suits with Geiger counters and ricin-sniffing dogs, after which it is hauled away in special trucks, there being no conceivable circumstance (the Board of Governesses has determined) in which information delivered at less than the speed of light could be relevant to the instantaneously mutating global economy.

Exactly one mile west, at the exclusive Walden Tower Condominiums, the building concierge, Mike Malatesta, assists the mail carrier in discarding flyers and catalogs and stuffing the residents' boxes with bills. His eyes linger on an item addressed to Patti Ogleby (19th floor), which appears to be a bill from Dr. Theophile Eisengrim, a cosmetic surgeon famous for his attention to the rich and famous. Patti Ogleby—tall, blonde and comfortably under forty—is the trophy wife of David Ogleby, the white-haired, blue-blooded elder statesman of the local non-profit community (a Trustee of the new Museum of Homeless Art, Chair of the upcoming March to Stamp Out Plantar Fasciitis). His dramatically younger wife Patti, a realtor specializing in high-end condominiums, is a recognized mover and shaker in her own right and by far the hottest woman in the building. The concierge, Mike Malatesta, who is a mover and shaker of a different sort, has set his sights on her as a potential conquest (which should be easy, he reasons, since she's at least thirty years younger than her husband). When he sees the letter from Dr. Eisengrim, he wonders if the beautiful Patti has been the recipient of cosmetic surgery. What is she hiding?

The Oglebys' mailbox is just below that of Bob Baskerville, owner of the most luxurious unit in the building, the two-story penthouse with a private elevator to the parking garage. Bob Baskerville is another giant of the non-profit world, rumored to be up for this year's Man of the Year award. A bachelor and a ladies' man, he undoubtedly also has his eye on Patti. How to handle the plastic surgery letter? the concierge asks himself. He considers steaming it open and reading it, but that would be unethical. Instead, as if by accident, he slips it into Bob Baskerville's mailbox.

Mail everywhere, quickly morphing into trash. No sooner are the day's deliveries thrown away than an army of garbage collectors, trash haulers, recyclers, street sweepers and scavengers fans across the city, first gathering millions of bottles and cans which have been painstakingly separated by the patriotic citizenry into clear glass, green glass, brown glass, clear plastic, green plastic, white plastic, steel and aluminum, then unnumbered tons of letters, bills, envelopes, newspapers, magazines, catalogs, flyers, advertisements, carefully sorted into a dozen categories so they can be mixed back together, shredded, boiled to a pulp and reformulated into the paper stock needed for the next round of mail. In this mountain of trash (weighing 27 tons and requiring landfill capacity of 47 acre feet), there is one item—a Sotheby's catalog about an upcoming art auction in New York—that is destined to topple the mighty and bring a momentary semblance of justice to the world.

The Sotheby's catalog is fished out of the gutter on East Passyunk Avenue by an elderly homeless man named Randolph wearing red high-top sneakers and a torn Burberry raincoat. He leafs through the catalog and stashes it under a moth-eaten Oriental rug, a broken electric skillet and the rest of the junk in his three-wheeled grocery cart.

2. Stark Raven

Andrew Ogleby—David Ogleby's 26-year-old son by his first marriage—smiled at Mike Malatesta as he walked through the lobby of the Walden Tower Condominiums and headed out to the sidewalk. He had recently passed the bar exam, and today would be the first day of his legal career. Like many in his generation, he rejected the greed and social irresponsibility of the corporate world, and accordingly his father had secured him an unpaid internship at Stark Raven, the city's premier law firm dedicated solely to non-profits. He felt awkward in his suit and tie—what he called his "lawyer costume"—and as he strolled to his new office he wondered if the people he passed could tell he was a lawyer. Everyone liked Andrew—he was a good-looking, easygoing, almost innocent young man, with his twinkling eyes, his bashful smile and his wavy brown hair—but he could be evasive and stubborn in his pleasant way, especially with his father's wife, Patti, who insisted on calling herself his stepmother (sometimes, jokingly, his wicked stepmother) in spite of being only a dozen years older than he was. Andrew dealt with Patti the same way he dealt with the rest of the world. On whatever issue she tried to discuss—the status of his engagement to Melissa Forepaugh, for example—he'd smile and said "Yes," and go on his way.

As he stepped off the elevator at Stark Raven, he was met by the office manager, an angular, middle-aged woman who introduced herself as Miss Burge and escorted him to his office, next to that of his new boss, Mr. Peter Wolf, a senior partner in the firm. His office was surprisingly plush for a non-profit, with leather upholstery, mahogany paneling and a spectacular view of the city. A young woman who seemed to consist mostly of cleavage sat in a nearby cubicle staring at her phone. "Clea is interning as a secretary," Miss Burge said. "You'll be sharing her with Mr. Wolf."

Without looking up, Clea pushed a buzzer to open the door to Mr. Wolf's office, and Andrew stepped inside. A thin, balding man with furtive eyes stood talking on his cell phone beside a naked woman who stretched beside him on a waist-high stone pedestal. The woman was about thirty years old, with strawberry blonde hair, blue eyes and pale freckled skin. Her breasts (as Andrew couldn't help noticing) were round and well-formed, her lips thin, her smile sly and enigmatic. She didn't flinch when he walked in, and she didn't seem to care how much he stared at her. In fact, though she looked perfectly lifelike, down to the moles on her arms and the hair follicles on her legs, he realized as he edged closer that she was not a woman at all, but a full-scale, full-color replica of one.

"Her name is Hildegarde," Mr. Wolf said without lowering his phone. "You can touch her if you like. She doesn't bite."

"It's a statue?" Andrew asked.

"A sculpture," Mr. Wolf corrected him. "Vassily Plescinski, 1985. An enormously valuable tax write-off for one of our clients. "

He smiled and gestured Andrew toward a chair in front of his desk. "Very pleased to have you on board," he said, still holding the phone to his ear. "Tonight at six—the usual place. The work is demanding, and there's plenty of it. What? Under

501(c)(3)?" His fingers danced around on the phone. "Where's the nearest Chinese restaurant?"

This must be a test, Andrew decided. "I think there's one right around the corner."

"Thank you, Steve. I appreciate that."

"Actually, my name is Andrew."

"Are you insane?"

It took Andrew a moment to realize that Mr. Wolf, with the aid of his phone, had four conversations going at once: one with a lawyer named Steve, which had something to do with Section 501(c)(3) of the Internal Revenue Code, another with a woman he hoped to meet at a bar called the Red Rooster at six o'clock, another with the phone itself (which he addressed with exaggerated politeness), and least significantly one with Andrew, who passed the time, while Mr. Wolf talked to the others, stealing glances at Hildegarde. After Steve had clicked off in anger, and the woman agreed to a tryst at the Red Rooster, and the phone downloaded a map locating the nearest Chinese restaurant, Mr. Wolf—constantly poking the screen, reading and tapping in messages, monitoring the headlines, managing his Twitter feed—sat down across from Andrew and welcomed him to the firm.

"Let me give you an example of the work we do here at Stark Raven," he said. "The client builds up a collection of something—it doesn't matter what; the more apparently worthless the better. We have the collection appraised and the client donates it to a museum. Better yet, he starts his own museum, as Bob Baskerville has done with the Museum of Homeless Art, so there can be no question about the museum accepting the donation. What have I told you about that?" he added sharply.

This sudden aside was evidently prompted by an incoming text message. "How many times do I have to tell her?" he chuckled as he smiled at Andrew. "Not during working hours. By the way, this idea of 'sharing' Clea. Don't take it literally."

"No, sir. Of course not."

He set the phone on his desk, his eyes darting back to the screen. "Stock market down a hundred points! Now where was I? Ah, yes, Bob Baskerville. He acquires his collection of homeless art at soup kitchens and shelters, has it appraised, and donates it to his own museum, taking a deduction for the appreciated value. Even though it started out as junk—*because* it started out as junk (and between you and me, it's still junk)—it's way more valuable from a tax standpoint than Hildegarde, for instance, who was a pretty pricy piece of plaster even when she was new. And if he defers the gift into his estate plan, not one penny of capital gains tax will ever be paid. Are you following this?"

"Sure," Andrew lied, his mind boggling.

"The bottom line is," Mr. Wolf said as he herded Andrew out of the office, "at Stark Raven, we do well by doing good."

He shook Andrew's hand and opened the door, signaling to Clea to put her phone down and come inside. "It's all about helping people," he said. "Helping them get rich and stay rich."

Andrew's head was spinning. "But... I thought this firm only represented non-profits."

"That's right. That's all we do."

"I don't get it. If it's all about money, why do we represent non-profits?"

The lawyer shrugged as a sly smile crept over his face. "That's where the money is."

During his lunch hour Andrew bought a turkey club on whole wheat toast in the food court at the Third Millennium Center and carried it back to his office at Stark Raven. He ate at his desk, trying to tell himself that he was happy with his new job, his new career. Of all the people he'd met at Stark Raven so far, he liked Hildegard the best, and she wasn't even alive. He dreaded spending the evening with Melissa Forepaugh, his fiancée, but he knew he would probably marry her. What did he want out of life? he asked himself. He wanted what everybody wants—to find his own kind of happiness, even in a totally screwed up world.

3. Like a Virgin

Across town at the Federal Reserve Bank, Andrew's best friend Hector Lopez had just completed the third week of his unpaid internship as a junior economist. To be sure, Hector's internship was not completely unpaid—he was paid just enough to cover the deductions for Social Security and Medicare, unemployment, and dues to the Interns' Union. That's how all internships work, and Hector felt lucky to have one, even if it made no net income and meant living at home with his grandmother on a diet of rice and beans. Most of his first three weeks on the job had been spent studying the Bank's 900-page Compliance Manual, a compendium of every error or infraction that might conceivably be committed by a Bank employee. His boss was a woman named Gwendolyn, whose boss was a woman named Maureen, whose boss was a woman named Joan. The economists (he quickly realized) were all women, the secretaries were all women, the security guards were all women—astonishingly, due to a glitch in the Bank's affirmative action program, every single person who worked at the Bank was a woman (even the Board of Governors had been renamed the Board of Governesses in recognition of this fact), except for one shadowy figure, a man known only as Arbuthnot (the "h" was silent), who could sometimes be seen hunched over a styrofoam coffee cup in the back of the employee cafeteria. If Hector glanced in his direction, Arbuthnot would lower his eyes, as if any contact between the

Bank's only two male employees might be construed as a conspiracy.

As the first in his family to attend college (they had immigrated from the Dominican Republic), Hector was determined to succeed at the Bank. His upbringing was traditional: he attended Catholic schools and his devout grandmother (who had raised him after his mother died) steered him toward the priesthood. He enrolled at UCLA planning to major in embalming, with a minor in medieval theology, but on his initial visit to Financial Aid (unfortunately, soon after Baby Boy Barkocy's takeover of that office) he was persuaded to take out enormous loans, sufficient to build a medium-sized aircraft carrier. He signed the papers and opted for a double major in medieval theology and economics, with a minor in embalming. Hector was naive and shy but unusually handsome, with medium-dark skin, a high forehead and wavy black hair. He projected a purity of heart that made him highly attractive to women, but he resisted their charms. Only one girl had caught his eye, and that was Alice Coggins, who lived in his neighborhood. During high school he had often seen her on the bus, and sometimes they chatted at Mr. Reddy's store on the corner. He fell in love with Alice and promised himself that one day he would marry her. That was the happiness he envisioned for himself in his most unguarded moments.

On his first day at the Bank, in the cafeteria with a few of the secretaries, the subject of sex came up. Hector made the mistake of mentioning that he was saving himself for marriage, hopefully to Alice if she would have him. This sparked a roar of laughter that spread like wildfire through the cafeteria and beyond. Even Arbuthnot could be seen chuckling into his styrofoam coffee cup. By the end of the day Hector had acquired a nickname: "Virgin Mary." Wherever he went in the office, the secretaries danced like Madonna and sang, "Like a Vir-ir-ir-ir-gin," as he walked by.

4. The Health Care Industrial Complex

No one could remember the precise moment when health care took over the city. It had mutated and divided a thousand times before anyone noticed the warning signs: the incessant health warnings and reminders in the media, the hand sanitizers at every doorway, the dietary restrictions imposed on the healthy (an increasingly suspect group) in the name of preventing diseases they were unlikely to get, the replacement of "citizens" by "patients" in political debate, the harrowing schedule of doctor visits every patient was required to adhere to, the proliferation of service dogs, service cats and even service parrots (to remind patients when to take their medications), and finally, after it was too late, the telltale lumps and thickenings, clots and blockages in the city's vital organs that never seemed to go away. There had always been health care, of course; its recent efflorescence had been triggered by the discovery that patients would pay any amount of someone else's money to stay alive for another fifteen minutes. Hospitals grew like tumors, replacing whole city blocks, then entire neighborhoods, appropriating arteries or constructing new ones for their own sustenance, replicating themselves as medical centers, health complexes, health campuses— monuments to the power and beneficence of health care, larger and more sumptuous than the pyramids of Egypt or the cathedrals of the Middle Ages, though alike in their promise of immortality and salvation. The scourges of mankind were conquered one after the other, but addictions, obsessions, compulsions, phobias flourished as never before, and the man or woman who claimed to be healthy was assumed to be suffering from a psychotic delusion and immediately hospitalized. Health came to be viewed as a kind of grace that could be conferred only by the health care system, which was increasingly perceived as omniscient, omnipotent and infinitely good.

The Dwight D. Schopenhauer Memorial Health Center had relocated from its original site in Northeast Philadelphia to occupy several city blocks along the Schuylkill River in central Philadelphia. It was what used to be called a nursing home, an enormous warren of rooms and wards where patients lay immobile beside their IV poles, breathing with the aid of respirators. Alice Coggins's Grandma had lived there for ten years, ever since her stroke. Thanks to Ray's connections, she had a private room, with a splendid view of a toxic waste dump leeching into the Schuylkill River. Alice visited her as often as she could.

To all appearances, the Health Center was a beehive of life-affirming activity. But beneath its happy surface, it harbored a secret so shocking in its implications that even Alice, who was the first to uncover the truth, could not believe what she had found.

5. Seven Years An Intern

Alice Coggins

How long have I been an intern at Pinocchio's? Seven years? I can hardly believe it.

The food there is a little too good for somebody who's trying to keep her weight down. As an intern you have to study the menu and taste everything on it so you can describe it to the customers. Unfortunately I'm not a very quick study. I had to sample the tiramisu about a hundred times before I could find the words to describe it—two words, actually: delicious and fattening. After a few weeks I looked like Miss Piggy in a Tyrolean hat.

Tiffany gives me all kinds of advice calculated to make me as big a slut as she is. Hair, makeup, clothes, shoes, jewelry, even how to smile and what apps to download on my phone. The idea is to be as fake as humanly possible. "And stop reading those stupid zombie novels," she says (I read about five zombie novels a week). "You don't want guys to find out what a wack-job you are."

"What you don't understand," I told her one day, "is that I don't want to be you. I want to be me."

"Alice has low self-esteem," Mom explained.

"Only if you consider wanting to be me a sign of low self-esteem," I pointed out.

To my sister, that was a no-brainer. (A lot of things seem like no-brainers to Tiffany, since she doesn't actually have one.)

"Your self-esteem has a lot to be low about," she said. "That's what I'm trying to fix."

Tiffany has been a part-time intern in the file room at Third Millennium Life for the past four years, meanwhile trying to meet rich men at charity fundraisers. In her opinion I would be much better off quitting my internship at Pinocchio's and switching to food service in the non-profit sector. "First of all, they have horrible food at fundraisers. No pepperoni pizza, no cannoli's, no tiramisu. Nothing you'd ever want to eat. Rich people are all vegetarians or vegans or something. They won't eat anything that's ever been alive."

Dad wandered into the kitchen, scratching under his ankle cuff with a coat hanger as he sang along with Frank Sinatra, *"I've got you under my skin..."*

"They're afraid that if they eat a cheese steak," Tiffany went on, "that's one less cheese steak some kid in Africa is going to get. They lose sleep over that kind of stuff."

"So what do they eat?" I asked.

"All they eat is arugula and broccoli rabe and organic, locally-curdled tofu. Trust me, you won't be getting fat on that!"

"So what should I do then?"

"Use your mentality," Dad sang. *"Face up to reality."*

"You need to make the transition to non-profits," Tiffany said. "You can even stay in food service. There's a company that does the catering at all these fundraisers, I forget their name. The waitresses wear cute black uniforms—they might even have one you could fit into."

"But why non-profits?" I pressed her.

"That's where the money is." She gave me a big sisterly smile. "Don't worry, I'll show you the ropes."

There were those ropes again. Whatever you do, there are ropes that somebody has to show you, or you might get tripped up in them or maybe even strangled. At least these were different ropes than the ones Dad showed me when he wanted me to follow his footsteps into crooked politics.

"I know that company," Dad said. "Gallaher Catering. I can get you in there."

Come to think of it, maybe they *were* the same ropes. "You can?"

"Sure," he winked. "All I gotta do is ask."

Sometimes I visit my Grandma at the Dwight D. Schopenhauer Memorial Health Center, where she's lived for the last ten years. One day when I arrived there was a shriveled old man in a wheelchair next to her bed, leaning sideways at an impossible angle. He was trying to get closer to Grandma, but his wrists and ankles were strapped to the wheelchair. He was drooling a little and had a crazed expression on his face. A friendly nurse with a West Indian accent named Ms. Jenkins was straightening the bed. She introduced me to the old man in the wheelchair. "This is Armand," she told me. "Armand used to be a famous artist. Now he and your Grandma have quite a little romance going— considering that neither of them can talk!"

"What's wrong with my Grandma, anyway?" I asked the nurse.

"Aphasia. That means she can't talk."

"They said she had a stroke ten years ago. I was fourteen."

"It was probably a stroke," the nurse nodded. "But some people just stop talking. We don't know why. Maybe they've just said everything they had to say."

Ms. Jenkins smiled and walked out, and as soon as she closed the door behind her, Grandma began to talk. Armand must have heard her too, because he repeated the last few words of everything she said. When her breath faltered I told her about Tiffany and my Mom and all the problems I was having because I couldn't keep my weight down working at Pinocchio's and how I needed to find a different job where they didn't serve tiramisu or I'd end up marrying Kyle Rotundo and spend the rest of my life listening to him talk about fantasy football, and how I was considering going into the non-profit sector to work for Gallaher Catering. After about ten minutes I felt light-headed and I think I was hyperventilating and maybe even crying a little, because suddenly Grandma interrupted and made me stop. "You're a much prettier girl than Tiffany," she said. "I've always thought so. All you need is to believe in yourself. You have a good heart."

"A good heart," Armand echoed.

"And you're not fat."

"Not fat," Armand agreed.

"Hang on to the best in yourself," Grandma said, "and you'll drive all the young men crazy."

"Crazy." Armand let out a choking sound and his head rolled sideways as if he'd been strangled. Then he suddenly sat bolt upright. "Get out of here," he gurgled, his eyes widening in desperation. "Get out of here!"

His head rolled around again and his wild eyes fastened on me. "Get the hell out of here!"

My sister laughed when I told her Grandma had talked to me. "That's just one of your wacko fantasies," she said. "Grandma can't talk."

"She can," I insisted, "when nobody's around. And so can Armand."

"Armand?" Tiffany hooted. "Who's that? A little old man who lives in Grandma's room?"

I couldn't repeat what Grandma said, so I had to let Tiffany think I was crazy. The old lady was all wrong about me, anyway. She wouldn't have said I have a good heart if she knew what I thought. For example, I hope Tiffany will catch one of her stiletto heels in a grate at one of those fundraisers and fall face-down in a platter of miniature hot dogs wrapped in bacon with toothpicks sticking out. Well, not really. Just one of my wacko fantasies.

This isn't a good time for people my age. Everybody still lives at home and nobody expects to get a place of their own. You'd need a paying job for that, which nobody has, except in China. Nobody expects to get married either, except Tiffany, who's determined to snag some rich guy she meets at one of her charity balls. "It doesn't matter who you go out with," she told me one night as we sat at the kitchen table, "as long as they've got money. You can find their financial statements online if you know where to look. Then you research the charity they're involved with—it's usually some stupid museum or a hospital or a band with a lot of violins in it—and you can find out how much they donated. The idea is to get them to spend so much money on you that it would be cheaper to marry you. You can always fake a pregnancy if you have to."

"But then what?" I asked. "I mean, if it's fake, won't they find out?"

"It doesn't matter—you're not going to stay married for long. Six months to a year, max. Then you file for divorce and take him to the cleaners. It's as simple as that."

"Sounds pretty grim," I said.

Mom smirked at my innocence. I had on my Pinocchio's outfit, Tyrolean hat and all, so I guess I looked a little more ridiculous than usual.

"Hey, it's a living," Tiffany said. "Unlike these internships we all have, it might actually put money in your bank account."

"That sounds like a pretty good scam to me," Dad said, hobbling in from the living room. "I wonder why nobody ever thought of it before."

"Dad, this is *marriage* we're talking about," Tiffany laughed. "It's the Big Con."

Dad was shocked, not at Tiffany's cynicism—we were all used to that—but at the idea that he'd been on the wrong end of the Big Con. All these years he'd thought the Big Con was the city government and he was part of it. Could it really be marriage? He smiled at Mom in the fond hope that she would spare him this indignity. "Hey, Hun," he murmured—and when a Neanderthal-American calls his wife "Hun," you know he's appealing to her most tender emotions—"you didn't marry me for my money, did you?"

"Yeah, I was short cab fare," Mom said. "I should have taken the bus."

Tiffany and I laughed, but Dad blinked in embarrassment. I felt sorry for him. In the heart of every con artist there's a core of innocence that enables him to lull his victim but clouds his own eyes when he's on the wrong side of the scam. And to lose your heart for such low stakes! "See that, Dad?" I said to comfort him. "How much could cab fare have been? She must have married you for love."

Tiffany couldn't let it drop. "But Mom, would you have married him if you knew he'd spend half his life under house arrest?"

"It's not so bad," Mom shrugged. "As long as he doesn't ask for conjugal visits."

6. Conspicuous Consumption in the Twenty-First Century

Patti Ogleby was a woman of obscure origins and many secrets, some so shocking that she would rather have leaped off her 19th-floor balcony—or more likely, thrown someone else off—than allowed them to be made public. Privately, her goals were simple: to preserve her secrets, advance her social standing, and sell as much real estate as humanly possible. On a more public level, her focus was on philanthropy. When not organizing and attending fundraisers, she dedicated herself selflessly to maintaining the lavish lifestyle required for serious philanthropists.

After seeing Andrew off to his new job at Stark Raven, Patti reluctantly turned her attention to her husband. David Ogleby came from the right family, grew up in the right neighborhood, and went to the right schools, but unfortunately didn't end up with the right amount of money. His once-brilliant career in business and academia had ended prematurely, which, for unexplained reasons, he blamed on Bob Baskerville. This had happened six or seven years ago, before he met Patti, and for a while he managed to keep up appearances. She married him for his money, only to discover that he didn't have any. After four years as his trophy wife, she looked forward to the next championship bout. In due course the trophy would pass to a younger, fitter contender (possibly Bob Baskerville, if all went well), and when that time came, she needed to be ready for the awards ceremony.

Now she needed to show David the new dress she'd bought for that night's gala reception at the Museum of Homeless Art. He'd been called out of town and would be unable to attend, and it was essential that he see the dress (plus the matching shoes) before he saw the Neiman Marcus bill. There was no chance that she would return these items, no matter how much he might protest. She needed to look her best for Bob Baskerville, Founder and Chairman of the museum, who would be giving the keynote address.

She slipped into her new dress, poured a mug of coffee and waited on the balcony for David to complete the interminable regime of personal hygiene he indulged in every morning. To pass the time, she dusted off her 300-year-old pet tortoise, Achilles, who lived on the balcony and doubled as the breakfast table. (Achilles was more a piece of furniture than a pet, since he never moved, and as furniture he was one of Patti's most prized possessions, having once belonged to Marie Antoinette.) She set her coffee mug on his back and stretched out on the chaise longue to complete her reading of the current bestseller, *Conspicuous Consumption in the Twenty-First Century: or, How to stop worrying and start living beyond your means,* by Thorstein R. Veblen. This book, by the great-grandson of a famous economist she had never heard of, had opened her eyes with the force of a revelation. Of course she knew what conspicuous consumption was—that was what other people did to show off their wealth. But Veblen (she wasn't sure which one) had demonstrated that conspicuous consumption goes much deeper than that. For people of adequate means— for anyone, actually—the primary purpose of spending money is to prove that you can afford it, and therefore *that you're the right kind of person.* Consumption isn't about spending money, it's about who you are. To show that you're a worthy person, you must prove that *you don't care about money.* And to prove that you don't care about money, if you really want people to respect you, you have to spend it on things you don't really need, things that are *wasteful,* even stupid. Who else but a high-minded, non-materialistic person can afford to do things—*must* do things, openly and shamelessly—that are utterly wasteful and stupid? This was the secret of life which, until now, had eluded Patti.

Some of these ideas came from the elder Veblen's book entitled *The Theory of the Leisure Class,* to which the new book was a sort of sequel. That book obviously didn't apply to Patti—she worked like a dog—but if there was a leisure class it included every one of her real estate clients, whether they admitted it or not. Melissa Forepaugh's parents, for example, seemed to have a different home for every set of GPS coordinates. That was why, when David finally emerged from his bathroom and she showed him her new dress (she didn't have the heart to show him the shoes) and he objected to the extravagant sum she'd paid for it, she didn't cry and stamp her feet as she might have done before she read the book. Instead she took the high moral ground. Didn't he realize that her very essence and value as a human being was at stake?

"It's a waste," he sputtered, "to spend that kind of money on a dress you're only going to wear once. A colossal waste of money—"

"Of course it's a waste," she interrupted. "That's the whole point."

"—when there are things we actually need."

She silenced him with a gaze of withering superiority. "To spend money on necessities would only show how shallow and materialistic we are," she said. "Anyone can do that."

On her way down to the Fitness Center, Patti ran into a young couple, Rick and Rosemary Wurlitzer, to whom she'd recently sold a three-bedroom unit on the twelfth floor. Naive, *nouveau riche* and unsure of themselves, they were anxious about how they fit into the building. Patti unhesitatingly took them under her wing. She felt sorry for them—to have all that money and yet be clueless about how to spend it! She gave them pointers on color schemes, rugs, furnishings, even art works for their unit (this was especially important—the selection of art works could make or break a new resident), as well as tips on locally-grown arugula, organic house plants and gluten-free shampoo. As their realtor, with access to references and credit reports, she probably knew more about the Wurlitzers than they knew about themselves. Rosemary was an aspiring teacher, hoping to land her first job in one of the local schools. Rick, though his background was distinctly lower class, had already retired from a successful career in whistleblowing. After graduating from college with a dual major in pet care and industrial espionage, he'd landed an internship in a cat food factory, and within a year was awarded an astronomical sum when he informed the FDA that the cat food was contaminated with mouse hairs, rat whiskers and other rodent parts. ("This is one of the cat food factories owned by the Forepaughs," Patti noted in her file. "Don't *ever* let them find out you sold a condo to these people!") She understood why the Wurlitzers didn't want anyone to know where their money came from. Not that there was anything wrong with whistleblowing—it was practically the only high-paying job that hadn't been sent to China—but if they wanted to last more than fifteen minutes in this building, it would have been a serious *faux pas* for Rick to admit that he made his fortune working in a cat food factory. The Wurlitzers were young and inexperienced, a pair of rubes who had no idea what was expected of them in a building like this. Apparently they were having problems with the other residents. People turned away from them in the elevator, ignored their dinner invitations, shunned them in the Fitness Center.

"Is it because I want to be a public school teacher?" Rosemary asked desperately.

"Don't be absurd!" Patti said. "People know you won't be living here on your teacher's salary."

"Or is it because I made my money the old fashioned way—by working for it?" Rick demanded.

"This isn't that kind of place," Patti lied. "It doesn't matter where your money came from. All that matters is how much you have, and how you spend it."

The Wurlitzers lowered their eyes, embarrassed by their ignorance. "Do you think...?" Rick began, and his voice trailed off.

"Do you think," Rosemary finished the question, "you could give us some pointers on that? On how to spend our money?"

"Of course I can," Patti reassured them. She didn't want to seem patronizing or arrogant or holier-than-thou; after all, she was only their realtor. But based on her own experience, and fortified by her reading of *Conspicuous Consumption in the*

Twenty-First Century, she felt she was in a position to give the couple some badly-needed advice. "I won't be able to do it today," she said, squeezing Rosemary's hand. "I've got to get ready for the gala—but some other afternoon, the two of you can come down to my office and we'll talk about it. We'll see if we can figure this out together. Right now I've got to get to the gym."

At the Fitness Center, Patti fitted her shapely, spandex-bound gluteus maximus onto the seat of a rowing machine and adjusted the electronic settings to simulate the experience of a sixteenth-century galley slave. Before she began to row, she sensed the hulking presence of Bob Baskerville on a nearby treadmill. Bob was the most eligible bachelor in the building and indeed in the whole non-profit world, a towering hunk of masculine flesh, almost literally larger than life. As the founder of the new Museum of Homeless Art, he would be honored that night at the gala opening reception. Patti had been hoping she'd run into him in the Fitness Center. "Hi, Bob," she exhaled, as if she'd already run a mile.

"Hi, Patti," he answered with a broad smile. He reached in his waist pouch and pulled out an envelope. "I have something I've been meaning to give you." He stepped off the treadmill and handed her the envelope. "This was in my mail box. I think it's for you."

They exchanged a meaningful glance as she eyed the return address. The envelope was from Dr. Theophile Eisengrim, the famous cosmetic surgeon and TV star whose reality show *Silk Purse From A Sow's Ear* had some of the Fox network's highest ratings. In one hour on live TV, Dr. Eisengrim could transform a seriously under-bitten, bug-eyed, bent-nosed file clerk from Jersey City into a smokin' hot babe.

"Just a piece of junk mail," Bob Baskerville suggested gallantly.

Patti ventured a coy smile. "I was afraid you'd think it was a bill for my last operation."

"I'm sure you don't need Dr. Eisengrim."

"Don't be so sure. I'm sort of a cougar, you know."

"You go for younger men?"

"Not younger than me," she giggled. "Just younger than my husband!"

Baskerville laughed out loud. "That covers a lot of territory."

"More every day," she winked, pulling back on the oars.

It was almost three o'clock. Patti swabbed down her rowing machine, said a warm good-bye to Bob Baskerville— "I'll be seeing you tonight!"—and glided into the locker room, where she enjoyed a long, soothing shower. It had been a hectic, stress-filled day, emblematic of the life a woman in her position becomes inured to, but it was only half over. In view of her responsibilities at the gala reception, she couldn't spend any more time flirting with Bob Baskerville. She needed to have her hair coiffed, her nails manicured, her eyelashes adjusted and her makeup pasted on. Shortly before seven o'clock, after enjoying a quick cocktail, she would slip into her new dress, select some suitable jewelry and ask the concierge to call her a taxi. Although the Museum of Homeless Art was less than two blocks away, it could not be reached on foot in the shoes she'd bought to go with her new dress.

7. Civilization And Its Discontents

Like most young people, Andrew Ogleby was burdened by an amount of student debt that would have sunk a small Central American republic. Though his parents were obviously rich, they never seemed to have any money. They donated every spare dime to the Affluenza Research Institute or the Dwight D. Schopenhauer Memorial Health Center or the March to Stamp Out Plantar Fasciitis. It irked him that they could afford to make extravagant gifts to UCLA to support its fantasy football program and yet require him to take out enormous loans to finish his law degree. But this wouldn't be a problem, he told himself, because as long as he worked as an intern in the non-profit sector (Stark Raven being a non-profit law firm), the required payments on his student loans would be a percentage of his take-home pay, which was zero. His friend Hector Lopez, who came from a poor family in South Philadelphia, faced the same dilemma when he graduated, which was why he'd taken an internship at the Federal Reserve Bank. Under their financial aid packages, they would both be indentured to the university until they repaid their loans, which—thanks to the magic of compound interest—could never happen in their lifetimes. "But at least you have an internship," Patti reassured Andrew. "You can be thankful for that. And when you marry Melissa, the first thing the Forepaughs will do is pay off those loans."

That reassurance—delivered by Patti the week before Andrew started his internship at Stark Raven—cleared up the mystery of why she had insisted on his taking out the student loans in the first place: it was to render him insolvent so he would have no choice but to accept a bailout by Melissa's fabulously wealthy parents, which of course would be on condition that he marry her. Patti had plotted the nearest thing in the modern world to an arranged marriage. After she'd delivered him to the Forepaughs, selling them a unit in the Walden Towers would be a walk in the park.

Melissa, like anyone else, had her plusses and minuses. Standing four feet ten inches tall, she had stringy brown hair, a light moustache and a pair of glowing amber eyes that were set too far apart. On the minus side, she was argumentative and scheming, a bulimic raw vegan with a dandruff problem and an inflated opinion of herself shared only by her Jack Russell terrier, whose name (this was one of the minuses) was Pickles. Andrew had occasional bouts of weakness, typically alcohol-induced, when, despairing over his crushing debt load, his feelings toward Melissa grew warm and fuzzy. But in his sober, lucid moments he would have gnawed off his arm before he'd marry her.

"What time are you picking me up?" she squawked into the phone, apparently beside herself because he'd been ignoring her text messages. It was his first day at Stark Raven and he was trying to get some work done. His boss, Peter Wolf, after his paean to non-profit money-grubbing, had redeemed himself somewhat by offering him a plum pro bono assignment. In addition to his work for millionaires like Bob Baskerville, Andrew would be handling the case of an indigent young African American, Eric Johnstone, who had been arrested for no apparent reason but remained in jail after four months of fruitless effort by the Public Defenders Office. Reading through the file was an unnerving experience, like a glimpse into a parallel universe where everything was the opposite of what you expected. And now Melissa was wrenching him back to the real world, where everything was normal, so she could finagle a ride to the reception at the Museum of Homeless Art.

"I don't know," he hesitated, "I'm sort of—"

"I need to get there early so I can rehearse my lecture a couple of times," she interrupted. "I want you to be there for that."

Melissa was giving a talk on Buster McCoy, one of the homeless artists in the collection Bob Baskerville had donated to the museum. Having already been forced to listen to her rehearse it a dozen times, he'd made up his mind that if he ever met Buster McCoy he'd refuse to give him any spare change. Arriving at the reception early was not on his agenda. His plan was to arrive late, when Melissa was tied up with her talk, so he'd have a chance to meet other women.

8. Shades Of A Conspiracy

Alice Coggins

Sometimes I'm tempted to forget about food service and just become a charity whore like Tiffany. Instead of serving hors d'oeuvres at fundraisers in the plain black uniform of Gallaher Catering—that's where I'm interning now—I'd be slinking around the refreshment table like Tiffany in a zebra-striped cocktail dress, sipping white wine out of a clear plastic cup, dragging gluten-free tofu chips through the guacamole dip, and yakking about somebody's plan to install hand sanitizers in every hut in Africa. But how much of an improvement would that be? Everything Tiffany said about fundraiser food is true—it's so lean and tasteless that I'm losing about a pound a week—and as for the men I'd meet there if anyone would talk to me, most of them seem as vain and greedy as she is. They may be rich, but that doesn't mean they have any money. They still live at home, just like we do, and they're loaded with student debt. They work at unpaid internships (it seems our whole generation has been interned, like refugees or prisoners of war) at other non-profits, where they pad their resumes with valuable experience at doing nothing. Is that where I want my life to be going? I'm trying to hold on to the best in myself, like Grandma said, and not be taken over by morons, including my sister (who, I know, when she suggests Botox injections or stomach-stapling or electroconvulsive shock therapy, is just trying to be helpful), but live instead on my own terms in the body I was born with.

Every morning my Dad carries a styrofoam Eagles cooler loaded with ice-cold Coke out to the front stoop (that's as far as he can go without setting off alarms at the Probation Department) to shoot the breeze with Randolph, the old homeless guy who's practically his only friend. Sometimes Mr. Reddy wanders over from the corner store with a pack of cigarettes or a lottery ticket. My Dad welcomes the free cigarettes but always insists on paying for the lottery tickets. You can't win, he says, unless you pay for the ticket. You've got to have skin in the game. Right now there's one of those Mega Millions lotteries going on, with the jackpot rising about fifty million dollars a day. My Dad asked Mr. Reddy to bring him a ticket and he made a big show of paying for it, just in case Lady Luck happened to be spying on our front stoop. Still he only bought one ticket. "Your luck's the same with one ticket or a thousand," he told Mr. Reddy, who'd suggested that he buy more. "If your ticket's the one that's going to win, you'll win. And mine's the one that's going to win."

"How d'you know that?" Randolph asked.

"I feel it in my bones."

"Then I should have kept that ticket," Mr. Reddy said.

"It wouldn't have won if you kept it," Dad laughed, chugging back his Coke. "I'm the one with the luck."

The last time I visited Grandma was sort of a creepy experience, maybe because I'd been reading so many zombie novels. No nurse was in the room, only Grandma and her friend Armand, leaning out of his wheelchair beside her bed.

Luckily he was drooling or I wouldn't have known he was still alive.

Grandma, pale and wasted, lay with her eyes closed. She looked like she'd seen a ghost—or was a ghost. "Grandma, are you OK?" I asked her.

No answer, not so much as a twitch. Maybe she was afraid one of the nurses was listening. "The door is closed," I told her, "so it's OK for you to talk. Are you afraid of something?"

"It's the Potlatch," she whispered, without looking toward me. "I heard the nurses talking about it."

"Talking about it," Armand echoed.

"The Potlatch? What do you mean, Grandma? What's the Potlatch?"

"It's what keeps us alive," she said. "Whether we want to live or not."

"Live or not," Armand muttered.

I'd heard about how old people in nursing homes often sink into despair. "You want to live, don't you, Grandma?"

"I want to get out of here," she said.

"Get out of here," Armand grumbled. It sounded more like a command than an echo.

He lifted his head and noticed me for the first time. The sight of me seemed to infuriate him. "Get out of here!" he shouted. "Get the hell out of here!"

What's this "Potlatch" that Grandma is so paranoid about? It's a word I've heard my Dad use without ever explaining what it meant. I wanted to ask him, but I sensed I shouldn't bring it up in front of Tiffany or my Mom. The next morning I got my chance, when I heard him on the front stoop with

Randolph debating the reasons for the decline and fall of the Roman Empire. Dad can be quite eloquent when Mom isn't there to shut him up.

"The Romans had a pretty good scam going," I heard him say as I stepped outside. "Basically a massive loan sharking operation. After they conquered a country—Greece, for instance—they'd loan them way more money than they could ever pay back, and those poor saps, unless they wanted their kneecaps broken, had to grow huge amounts of food—wine, olive oil, pasta; you know, Italian food, even though they were Greeks—and send it to Rome to pay their debts." He whistled with admiration. "You gotta hand it to the Romans. They had a great civilization while it lasted."

Randolph looked skeptical. "How could they eat all that food?"

"God love 'em, they did their best," Dad said. "They gorged themselves at feasts, orgies, saturnalias and whatnot, and when they couldn't eat any more they'd stick feathers down their throats and start all over again. You know, for the sake of the economy."

"Got to keep those imports streaming in," Randolph agreed.

"But the problem was, with all that free food from the provinces, nobody in Rome had to work anymore." Dad drained the last few drops of his Coke and tossed the empty can into Randolph's shopping cart.

"Except the slaves," Randolph pointed out, nodding to thank him for the can.

"Sure"—Dad glanced at Randolph, then at me—"but as time went on even the slaves worked shorter hours and started putting on weight—no offense, Alice—and pretty soon the barbarians were streaming over the border and lining up for the jobs the slaves wouldn't do."

I felt like dragging him down to the zoo and throwing him to the lions. "Tell me something, Dad," I asked. "What's the Potlatch?"

The question caught him off guard. "It's... a word I've heard the Boss use sometimes," he stammered. "It means the organization—you know, the Gallaher organization. The well-oiled machine that keeps us all alive and well."

Randolph laughed out loud. "You don't know what a potlatch is, do you, Ray?"

"Sure, like I say, it's the organization."

"No, it ain't."

"What is it then?"

"It's something the Indians out West used to do, until the white man put a stop to it. I read about it in *National Geographic*. It was a kind of pow-wow where the big chief gave lots of stuff away to keep the tribe happy."

"Well, there you go," Dad said, sighing with relief. "In this town Desmond Gallaher is the big chief."

Randolph grabbed his shopping cart and shoved off down the sidewalk. "He never gave me nothing," he muttered over his shoulder. "But then again, I ain't exactly a member of the tribe."

9. Stimulus Package

After three weeks at the Federal Reserve Bank, Hector was summoned to a conference room to discuss a new work assignment with his boss, Gwendolyn, and her boss, Maureen. The two bankers could hardly have been less alike. Gwendolyn was a tall, attractive black woman in her early thirties who (it was said) had been unlucky in love, resulting in a vendetta against the male sex. Maureen, a Vice President, was white and pale, in her mid-sixties, and so short that her puffy coiffure seemed calculated to double her height. The two of them sat across from him at the conference table, studying a folder that turned out to be his personnel file. He could hear Gwendolyn humming "Like a Vir-ir-ir-ir-gin" as he walked in.

Gwendolyn stopped humming and asked Hector to sit down. She held a laser pointer that functioned as a remote control, conjuring a slide presentation on a huge screen that occupied the wall at the end of the table.

"As you may have heard," Maureen began, "last year the Bank did a major study of the sex industry."

Gwendolyn aimed her pointer at the screen and the title slide flashed up on the screen—*Sex: Where Does It Go From Here?* The laser beam lingered on the word Sex, highlighting it for special attention. Hector felt his facial muscles contracting into an embarrassed grin. Talking about sex with a woman Maureen's age—she was old enough to be his grandmother— or with Gwendolyn, who could have squashed him like a bug, made him want to run out of the room.

"The issue is how to include sex in our measurement of the economy," Gwendolyn said.

"You mean... pornography?" Hector mumbled, striving for a professional tone. "Strip clubs, sex toys—that type of thing?"

"Actually, no," Maureen said. "Those things have always been included. In this study we've added a new element: illicit sex."

"You mean, like, prostitution?"

Gwendolyn clicked to the next slide. "Hookers, streetwalkers, call girls, escorts," she read aloud from a bullet list. "*Sex workers,* we prefer to call them."

"Pimps?" Hector chirped involuntarily, strangling the word on its way out.

"*Sex supervisors,*" Maureen corrected him, smiling. "Of course they're included. It turns out that sex workers and their supervisors give a huge boost to the economy. Previously they stayed off our radar screen by operating outside the law. But now we're measuring the sex industry the same way we measure food service, entertainment, and all the other segments." The next slide showed a pie graph with explanatory notes. "As of the beginning of this year it accounted for 27% of the overall economy."

"Cheating, too," Gwendolyn added in a bitter tone. "You forgot to mention cheating."

"Extra-marital affairs," Maureen nodded. "We view them as a type of outsourcing."

Sweating profusely, Hector did everything in his power to affect an air of nonchalance. "But extra-marital affairs aren't part of the economy, are they?"

"They're a huge part of the economy," Maureen assured him. "Twenty-five percent of the hotel industry, twenty percent of alcoholic beverages, fifteen percent of tourism. The impact is magnified if the sex consumers get caught. In that event enormous sums can change hands—legal fees to divorce lawyers, property settlements, alimony and the like. Those payments alone account for 12% of the economy, roughly the same as the public schools."

"But how do you know all this?" Hector demanded.

Maureen gazed back at him with a Delphic smile that conveyed supreme self-confidence, as well as the tiniest hint of annoyance that he would ask such an idiotic question. Obviously the Bank knew everything.

He sat with his eyes cast down, biting his fingernails (a bad habit he developed at St. Agnes Elementary School). Gwendolyn came to his rescue. "I get the feeling Hector is wondering why we called him in to tell him all this," she said to Maureen.

"I do feel a little that way," Hector agreed, looking up. "Didn't you say it was for a new assignment?"

Gwendolyn wielded her pointer and the next slide appeared: a set of graphs with lines declining sharply toward the x-axis. "Frankly, we're worried, Hector," Maureen told him. "The most recent data show a sudden drop-off in activity. Slower traffic at pick-up bars, sex worker unemployment hitting 15% in some areas, hourly hotel rentals down 30%. These are depression-level readings."

He hazarded a guess. "Maybe more people are sleeping with their spouses."

Maureen chuckled condescendingly. "Well, that doesn't do the economy much good, does it?" she said, snapping back into her serious mode. "What if everybody suddenly decided to eat dinner at home three nights a week instead of going out? What would that do to the restaurant industry?"

Gwendolyn pointed her clicker to bring up the next slide, which showed a crowd of impoverished sex workers in halter tops, mini-skirts and high leather boots slouching in an unemployment line.

"We're facing a humanitarian crisis," Maureen said. "Obviously we can't just sit back and let a quarter of the economy go limp on us."

Gwendolyn clicked back to the display of sagging performance graphs. "Not just limp," she smirked. "Downright flaccid!" Whistling like a downed fighter jet, she drooped her pointer toward the floor to illustrate the severity of the slump.

"It seems to be a symptom of a more general malaise," Maureen explained. "Entropic deceleration. Abbreviated 'ED.'"

"And there's evidence that the effect is spilling over into the general population, affecting not only illicit sex, but all sex between consenting adults."

"The Board of Governesses met this morning to discuss the crisis," Maureen told Hector. "In a few days we'll be announcing a new stimulus package."

"Stimulus?" Hector gulped.

"More cleavage on prime time TV," Gwendolyn smiled.

"Topless waiters and waitresses at leading restaurants," Maureen added.

"More aggressive outreach by sex workers."

Each element of the stimulus package was illustrated—in explicit full-color photographs—on the next few slides. The program was already working on Hector: his mouth was dry, his pulse racing. Before he could think, he was on his feet, backing toward the door. "What do you want me to do exactly?"

Maureen fixed Hector's eyes in her steely gaze. "I need you to be my eyes and ears," she said.

Gwendolyn offered more practical guidance. "Get out in the community and sniff around," she told Hector. "Get some hands-on experience. See what's going on out there."

Maureen stood up to signal that the meeting was over. "We'll expect weekly reports on how the stimulus package is working."

Hector fled through the door and clicked it behind him. He was back in his cubicle—and well out of earshot of the conference room—before the two women burst into uproarious laughter.

10. Urban Legend

Alice Coggins

Tiffany made me do her hair for the big reception at the Museum of Homeless Art. That was after helping her slip into her zebra-striped cocktail dress and then struggling for fifteen minutes to squeeze her fat feet into the matching stiletto heels. "You'd never fit your feet into these," she taunted me as she limped around the bedroom with her heels sticking out (she didn't know I'd already tried them on and they fit me like a glove). "But it doesn't matter, does it? You're not going to the reception."

"I am, actually," I said.

"What are you talking about?"

I explained that I had signed up to work at the museum that night.

Her angry scowl rearranged itself into a smile. "What are you wearing?"

"The same thing I always wear," I told her. "My black Gallaher Catering uniform."

"Oh, did they find one you could fit into?"

Dad appeared in the doorway with his remote, as if he wanted to put us on mute. "What kind of guy are you hoping to meet at this thing?" he asked Tiffany.

"A lawyer," she said. "I'm going with my friend Clea. She works at Stark Raven, the law firm that set up this museum."

"Tax dodge?"

"I guess so. Why else would somebody start a museum?"

Dad nodded approvingly. "And you're trying to con them into what? Marrying you?"

"Sure. Why not? I told you, it's the Big Con. Why not go for the gold?"

"Then you've got to go through all the right steps for a con," he said. "First you lay the foundation, gain the mark's confidence. Give him a series of small payoffs so he stays in for the long game."

"She knows how to do that," I said.

"Laugh at his jokes," Mom called out from the kitchen. "Agree with everything he says, even if it's stupid."

"Right," Dad agreed. "But don't make it all about him. He needs to think you've got some skin in the game."

"Flesh, anyway," I said. "That should be easy."

"Then pull back, put the outcome in doubt before the big hurrah. That's how you stay in control."

"You're talking to an expert, Dad," I told him. "The only difference is, she usually charges by the trick."

"We're not paying for this wedding, by the way," Mom yelled.

I've been so busy with work I hardly gave another thought to the Potlatch question until one afternoon I saw Randolph pushing his shopping cart down the middle of East Passyunk, with a honking, swearing, fist-shaking traffic jam massing behind him like a hostile army. He ignored the abuse and concentrated on nudging the cart forward without spilling any of the junk he'd piled on it.

"Hey Randolph!" I called out to him. "What are you doing in the middle of the street?"

"I told you I work for the WPA, didn't I?" he shouted back. "What those fools back there don't understand"—he gestured toward the mob of vehicles behind him—"is if they don't slow down, they're going to put the whole country out of work. Folks got to learn to slow down!"

Truck drivers, cab drivers, little old ladies in Subarus, all yelled obscenities and leaned on their horns. I stepped out beside him, triggering a new wave of abuse from the drivers, who blamed me for their plight. "They're just trying to get somewhere," I told Randolph. "Maybe they have appointments—"

"What if time could be speeded up so everything happened twice as fast?" he glared at me. "Would that do the world any good? No, it wouldn't. Folks'd get where they're going in half the time, but there'd be nothing for them to do when they got there, because everybody else would have already left."

At the first corner I was able to steer him into a side street. "And the economy would collapse," he added. "I'd be out of a job, you'd be out of a job, the whole country'd be out of a job."

That made me wonder: "Does this have something to do with the Potlatch?"

"You bet it does. I wasn't just blowing smoke signals when I told your Dad about that Indian pow-wow. You come on over to my office and I'll show you."

"You have an office?"

"Hell, yes," he said. "That's where my files are at. You think I can keep all this stuff in my head?"

Randolph's office was a boarded-up garage along an alley near Moyamensing, accessible by prying open a plywood-covered window in the back. "It looks awful dark in there," I said.

"No problem." To my amazement, he pulled out a cell phone and plugged in a power cord that made it light up.

"You have a cell phone?"

"Can't live in this world without a cell phone."

On one end of the garage stood some shelves and a workbench, buried under a jumble of auto parts, tools, appliances and indistinguishable junk. At the other end, the wall was covered with blotchy sheets of cardboard, probably tacked on as insulation. The rest of the place was stacked floor to ceiling with old newspapers and magazines, phone books, religious tracts, financial records and random scraps of paper. "Don't worry," he said. "I know right where everything is." And after a few seconds he held up an issue of *National Geographic* magazine from 1955 with a totem pole on the cover that contained just what he was looking for: an article on the Tlingit Indians of the Pacific Northwest.

"These Indians lived right along the Pacific Ocean," he told me, holding the magazine under the phone so he could squint at the article. "All they ate was salmon, which it took them about a hour a day to catch. This left them with so much leisure time, they started getting on each others' nerves."

"Leisure time? I didn't realize Indians had leisure time. I mean in the old days."

"Sure they did. And they had nothing to fill it with, which is a recipe for disaster. So the big chief told them: Catch as many fish as you can, even though we don't need 'em, and pick up shells off the beach to make trinkets."

"Trinkets? What were they going to use trinkets for?"

"Nothing. That's the whole point of a trinket, ain't it? You can't use it for anything, all you can do is give it away or trade it for something. When they'd caught about a year's supply of salmon and made about a million trinkets, the chief invited the neighboring tribes over for a feast. They fed them the salmon and showered them with trinkets, and let me tell you, those neighbors were impressed—and grateful to the chief."

This was starting to sound crazy. "Even though the trinkets were useless?"

"*Because* the trinkets were useless," he laughed. "That's what it says here: Because the trinkets were useless. You see, this proved that the tribe that gave out the trinkets was high class and the chief was a big man."

"Why?"

"You've got to be pretty rich, don't you, to have all those useless trinkets to give away? Naturally the neighbors had to start making trinkets and throwing feasts of their own, even bigger than the first tribe's. And then their neighbors had to throw a bigger feast, like a backyard barbecue with ribs and sausage and grilled chicken, potato salad, the works. And this is what they called a potlatch."

My mind was spinning. This was a potlatch? Obviously it had nothing to do with whatever my Grandma was so upset about. I'd thought of Randolph as a crackpot like my Dad, but now I suspected he was something worse. What was I doing in this dingy garage with a crazy person?

"'Course the white man put an end to all this," he chuckled, "just like everything else the Indians did. The white man didn't want those Indians giving away trinkets to each other. He wanted them to sell the trinkets to the white folks who gambled at the casino."

My wary eyes lighted on the sheets of cardboard he'd tacked to the wall. The cardboard was covered with dark blotches, like oil had dripped on it, and as I stared at those blotches in the dim light I imagined that I was seeing things in them, figures and patterns that weren't really there. Maybe they're like Rorschach blots, I told myself, where you see whatever you're looking for. Still I could have sworn they were human faces, or fantastic birds, a lot like the faces on a totem pole.

"Are these things pictures?" I asked Randolph.

"Those are some of my paintings," he beamed back at me. "That's how I spend my leisure time."

"These are paintings?"

"You like 'em? I got a lot more on my website."

11. The Museum of Homeless Art

Andrew felt a little ashamed of himself as he left the office and
walked to the gala opening reception at the Museum of
Homeless Art. The Museum, Mr. Wolf had explained, was the
brainchild of the Stark Raven tax department, conceived and
executed as "Operation Shelter" for Bob Baskerville, one of
their most important clients. The shelter in question was a tax
shelter, not a homeless shelter (although, as Mr. Wolf
emphasized, if the client could have enjoyed the same tax
advantages by founding a soup kitchen, he certainly would
have done so). Bob Baskerville had started collecting homeless
art at a time when other collectors literally turned up their
noses at it. Now his collection was appraised by Gallaher
Appraisal Services LLP at over $100 million. By donating it to
the Museum, he would earn a tax write-off equal to the newly
appraised value, not the nominal amount he'd paid for the art
works (typically the price of a hot meal and a bottle of rubbing
alcohol).

Outside the Museum—attracted, perhaps, by the lure of
artistic renown—a crowd of homeless men were held at bay by
a small army of security guards. Some of the men displayed
scrawled signs asking for help, reciting their life histories or
warning of an impending Armageddon. One—an elderly black
man wearing a Burberry raincoat and red high-top sneakers—
held up two cardboard rectangles, one covered with greasy
blotches and the other inscribed with the words:

WILL AUTOGRAPH FOR MONEY.
ACCEPT VISA, MASTERCARD,
AMERICAN EXPRESS.

Andrew had timed his arrival to coincide with the end of Melissa's lecture. His plan was to make sure she noticed him in the audience, and then avoid her as long as possible so he could concentrate on meeting other women. This would require avoiding her parents as well, and his step-mother Patti, who would be buttering up the Forepaughs in hopes of selling them a condominium. Luckily his father was out of town and would not be attending.

The lobby teemed with art lovers, including an astonishing number of attractive women in slinky cocktail dresses, eager to make their way in the selfless world of non-profits. Andrew slipped through the crowd into the auditorium just in time to hear the last part of Melissa's talk. She was discussing a painting entitled "This Side Up" by one of the nation's most eminent homeless artists, Buster McCoy, which to Andrew's untutored eye looked like a refrigerator box scrawled with stick figures in various obscene poses.

"...reminiscent of Cézanne," Melissa was saying, "with the same sure grasp of the materials, the same bold re-envisioning of the picture plane. And the subtle irony of the title—'This Side Up'—a phrase which indeed appears *à l'envers* near the bottom of the painting, along with the iconic 'Frigidaire,' also upside down—one can only ask, how many unhomed artists have endured the 'frigid air' of artistic neglect while—"

"If I might ask a question?" an older woman interrupted (Andrew later learned she was Lydia Poffenbarger, a board member and moderator of the lecture). "You said McCoy's paintings were created using 'available media.' What does that mean, exactly?"

"Well, primarily soot, spittle and crankcase oil. Urine, occasionally. And in rare instances—"

"Thank you, Melissa," Mrs. Poffenbarger cut in sharply, turning toward the audience. "Are there any other questions?"

Andrew waved to Melissa and disappeared into the crowd before she could follow him.

Circulating through the gallery, he inadvertently landed next to Patti, who was deep in a profoundly shallow conversation with Mr. and Mrs. Oscar Van de Kamp ("...the baked bean Van de Kamps," she whispered in his ear), on topics ranging from their daughter to their son. Mrs. Van de Kamp looked as if she'd been built from the ground up over an extended period, with ample support in the lower stories, possibly from reinforced concrete. Her husband was a red-faced, triple-chinned man who devoured hors d'oeuvres at a breathtaking pace.

"And how's your daughter?" Patti asked Mrs. Van de Kamp. "She went to Princeton, didn't she?"

"Oh, yes," Mrs. Van de Kamp said proudly. "Lucinda graduated *summa cum laude,* with a double major in Tasmanian gender studies and Albanian gender studies, and minors in Mongolian gender studies and Nigerian gender studies. From Princeton she went on to Yale for her Ph.D in seventeenth-century Navajo gender studies."

"Do you realize how many beans we had to sell to pay for that education?" Mr. Van de Kamp grumbled.

"Maybe you should ask one of your bean counters," Mrs. Van de Kamp sniped back.

"How complicated can it be?" the husband persisted. "There are only two genders, aren't there?"

"Obviously," Mrs. Van de Kamp sniffed, "it's a lot more complicated than that."

Mr. Van de Kamp clearly felt more comfortable talking about beans than gender studies. "We have a whole staff of bean counters at the plant," he confided to Andrew. "If you don't count the beans, they've been known to walk out the door."

"I didn't know beans could walk," Andrew observed. He would do anything, even affect idiocy, to extricate himself from this conversation.

"And what about your son Oliphant?" Patti asked. "Is he still in Hollywood?"

"Oliphant has written fifteen unproduced screenplays," Mrs. Van de Kamp beamed. "All on the theme of mother/son incest."

"You must be very proud of him!"

Andrew feigned a coughing fit and escaped into the crowd, keeping an eye out for Melissa as he threaded his way toward the back of the gallery, where the priceless Baskerville collection was on display. The guests avoided looking in that direction, and for good reason. The paintings were just what you might expect in a museum of homeless art: sheets of cardboard and scraps of wood or sheet metal smeared with coal dust, cough syrup and axle grease in primitive patterns and designs. He found himself standing beside a young woman in a black Gallaher Catering uniform, who had paused in her waitressing duties to inspect one of the paintings, described on its plaque as follows:

Wm. Randolph Hearse
American (born 1950 ?)
HELP WANTED (ca. 1997)
Sterno, urine and pigeon guano on Help Wanted section, Philadelphia *Daily News*.
15" x 27"

The girl was a cute redhead, though a little plump, which to Andrew's eye, jaded by the bulimic vegan Melissa, gave her the freshness and beauty of a Botticelli angel.

"I can't believe this!" she said under her breath. "It's Randolph!"

"You know the artist?"

"No," she hesitated. "Not really. I recognize his style, that's all."

Andrew had to laugh. "Is he that famous?"

"Oh, he's incredibly famous. You've heard of Picasso, right? Listen, I've got to get back to work."

She took a step away and he followed her. "Wait a minute. What's your name?"

"We're not allowed to use our names," she smiled, turning to face him. "Just fake ones."

"What's your fake name, then?"

"Amber."

"Do you work here at the Museum?"

"No, for the caterer. I'm just an intern."

"What's your real name?"

"I've got to get back."

Andrew had invited his friend Hector, without expecting him to show up. Hector was socially awkward, shy around women, and hopelessly in love with some girl he'd met in high school. Apart from that, all he seemed to care about—though he talked about it in vague, mysterious tones—was his internship at the Federal Reserve Bank. Yet there he stood, alone beside the cash bar in sunglasses and a dark suit, peering around suspiciously like an undercover cop.

"Hector," Andrew greeted him, stepping close. "What are you doing around all these hot women?"

"Investigating sex," Hector confided in a low voice.

Andrew laughed. "How old are you? Twenty-five? Twenty-six?"

"Twenty-seven next month."

"And you're just now investigating sex?"

"You don't understand," Hector said, glancing around to make sure no one was eavesdropping. "I'm doing this for my job. It's a top secret investigation."

"What's the Federal Reserve Bank's issue with sex?"

"Why there's so much less of it than there used to be."

Andrew laughed again. "You need to get out more, Hector." He motioned toward a woman reconnoitering in front of the bar, who turned out to be Clea, his secretary. She had arrived with Peter Wolf. Andrew said hello and introduced her to Hector. "Hector," he said, "this is my secretary, Cleavage, I mean Clea"—a gaffe which she ignored in her umbrage at being called his secretary.

"I'm not your secretary!" she growled (a statement that proved all too true: as long as she worked for him, she would never do one iota of secretarial work). "I'm your administrative assistant. Anyway I'm here with Peter." Without looking at Hector, she muttered something that sounded like Pig Latin.

"Excuse me?" Andrew said.

"I was talking to my phone." In fact she'd sent a voice-activated text message to another woman hovering nearby—a slender blonde in a zebra-striped cocktail dress—who wriggled up beside her in less than ten seconds. In tandem, the two women lurched forward, backing Andrew against the wall. "Tiffany, Andrew; Andrew, Tiffany," Clea announced. "And this is—what was your name again? Hector?"

Clea pulled Hector away, leaving Andrew face to face with Tiffany. "You work with Clea?" she asked with an over-eager smile. "Are you an attorney?"

"Um, yes," he mumbled (unsure, after his first day at Stark Raven, whether it should be a boast or an admission). "Just started today. Non-profit work only."

"I'm so impressed with attorneys," she said, edging closer. "Especially non-profit attorneys. They're the smartest people I know."

He glanced around to make sure Melissa was nowhere in sight. At four feet ten, it was easy to lose her in a crowd. "One of our clients started this museum."

"I *love* homeless people!"

"It's a very good cause," he agreed, a little hesitantly. "But there are other charities I'll be working on. Like"—he tried to think of one—"Friends of the Lesser Prairie Chicken."

"I *love* chicken!"

"And the March to Stamp Out Plantar Fasciitis."

"I *hate* fascists!"

Tiffany flicked her eyelashes, and it was clear to Andrew that she would agree with anything he said. How much of her eager-to-please attitude stemmed from the impression that he was a rich, successful attorney, and how much of it would survive when she found out he was an unpaid intern? Before he had a chance to ponder these questions, something happened that would change his life forever. The waitress he'd chatted up earlier in front of the masterpiece of sterno, urine and pigeon guano on the Help Wanted section of the Philadelphia *Daily News*—how could he ever forget that?—appeared beside him and thrust her hors d'oeuvres tray in the narrow space between him and Tiffany, level with Tiffany's somewhat disappointing bust line, forcing her to take a step backwards. "Stuffed shrimp?" the waitress smiled, aiming a pair of lustrous emerald eyes in Andrew's direction. How had he missed those eyes? She was much more attractive than Tiffany.

Tiffany's obliging blush had reddened into a fury. "What are you doing here?"

"Catering."

"Get away!" Tiffany pushed her away with the tray. "Go back to the kitchen where you belong!"

Andrew reached for a shrimp, hoping to hold the waitress there for another brief moment, but she quickly backed away as if Tiffany were a force that must be obeyed. "Now," Tiffany gloated, thrusting her torso into the space left by the tray, "where were we?"

As he watched the waitress vanish into the crowd, Andrew sensed a new presence encircling his elbow and clinging to the lower right half of his body like a boa constrictor. It was Melissa, greeting his new friend with a feral smile. "Ah, Melissa. This is Tiffany."

"More like Zale's," Melissa sniffed. "Or Target. Let's go. They're about to start the program."

"May I have your attention, please!" came an announcement over the P.A. system.

As Melissa tugged him toward the podium, Andrew lost sight of Tiffany and quickly forgot about her. All he could think of was the waitress with the emerald eyes and his determination to see her again. He would watch for her during the speeches, and find her as soon as they were over, even if it meant tracking her down in the kitchen.

When Clea jostled Hector away from the bar in order to leave Andrew alone with Tiffany, Hector had followed her a few steps before she located Peter Wolf and draped herself around his sticklike form, turning her back on Hector as if he'd never existed. Earlier in the evening, shortly after he arrived, Hector had been astonished to encounter Alice—the love of his life, at least of his fantasy life—dispensing tiny hot dogs wrapped in dough from an hors d'oeuvres tray.

"Hey, Alice," he'd stammered.

"Hector! What you are doing here?" She speared one of the hot dogs with a toothpick and handed it to him.

"Talking to you!" he laughed, but she didn't seem to notice what he said. She was smiling at everybody the same way she smiled at him. She had no idea what a thrilling moment this was for him.

"Mustard?" was all she'd said before twirling back into the crowd. Now he stood alone for a moment, hoping for another glimpse of Alice, when a slender dark-haired woman, thirty or thirty-five years old, glided up beside him and touched his arm. "I couldn't help overhearing what you said about your investigation," she said with a slight Spanish accent. "About there being less sex than there used to be. I might be able to help you with that."

Hector blushed and looked away. "No, you don't understand, I—"

"I understand completely." She lowered her voice. "Do you know about the Potlatch?"

"The Potlatch?"

"Shhh! Not so loud. They're listening. They're always listening."

"Who?"

She spun around to face him and bored her dark eyes into his. "If there's less of something," she whispered, "or more of something, it's because of the Potlatch, do you understand? Not a sparrow falls from the sky without them knowing about it."

Not a sparrow falls from the sky. That phrase sounded familiar, but as usual, owing to his checkered college career, Hector couldn't pinpoint whether it was in the study of medieval theology, economics or embalming that he'd acquired any particular piece of knowledge. Did it refer to the workings of Fate, the Invisible Hand of the market, or Divine Providence? Wherever he'd heard the phrase, it was surely about something there was no point in opposing. "Then the Potlatch must be a good thing," he said, testing the woman's reaction, "and you must be working to advance it."

"No," she hissed. "We're dedicated to destroying it."

We? Apparently she wasn't just speaking for herself. "But," Hector hesitated, "who *are* you?"

"*Somos pero no somos,*" she murmured in Spanish.

Hector understood the words: *We are but we are not.* But what were they supposed to mean?

"The speeches are starting." She squeezed his hand—"We'll meet again"—and disappeared into the crowd.

For Alice, the speeches offered a chance to tidy up while everyone's attention was on the podium. She had waitressed at enough fundraisers that she'd stopped noticing what the speakers said, or what they looked like; there were never any surprises. As she made her way around the gallery collecting empty cups, wadded-up napkins, shrimp tails and half-eaten pastry puffs, her thoughts kept coming back to the only dramatic moment of the evening, her near cat-fight with Tiffany over the guy she'd met in the gallery. She gloated at how angry Tiffany was, and hoped she'd spoiled her attempt to lure the mark into her con game. She'd pay the price the next morning, when Tiffany woke up in her own bed. But it would be worth it—that guy was definitely too good for a charity whore like Tiffany. What was he doing there anyway?

Alice had plenty of time to clear the tables and pick up the trash. The first belabored introduction was just reaching its climax. "And so I give you," Mrs. Poffenbarger declaimed, "without further ado, tonight's distinguished guest of honor, the Founder and Chairman of the Museum of Homeless Art, past President of one of our great universities and visionary supporter of so many other worthy causes, without whose generosity none of us would be here tonight in the midst of this marvelous collection—Mr. Bob Baskerville."

Applause rippled through the gallery as the Museum's benefactor stepped to the podium, an enormous man in a dark suit who beamed his broad smile over the crowd. As Alice caught a glimpse of him, strange thoughts swirled through her mind: he reminded her of a side of beef hanging in a meat locker. Next to him stood a misshapen man in a shiny gray suit, staring directly at her, with a mottled face that looked like a pounded veal medallion. He muttered something out of the corner of his mouth and Bob Baskerville peered over the crowd to search out her gaze, gesturing with one of his beefy hands as if chopping with a cleaver. She imagined a string of kielbasa flying apart as he chopped. Their eyes locked for an instant in a lethal flash of recognition—it had been seven years, but there could be no doubt about who he was, or who she was, or how they knew each other. She whirled around and ran back to the kitchen, where she tore off her apron and bolted for the door, her mind reeling in terror.

Bob Baskerville was Baby Boy Barkocy!

II.

12. Law

Law everywhere. Law seeping out of the courts and the law firms and the police stations to swallow the city in a fog. Law oozing like mud out of the Mayor's office and the City Council chamber and the regulatory agencies over the streets and sidewalks, miring the citizens (increasingly called "suspects") in ten thousand violations a day. Law adding new deposits to the crust upon crust of mandates, orders, regulations, procedures and penalties known to past generations, as the sins of the fathers are visited tenfold on their sons and daughters.

Law everywhere. Law elaborating itself in the majesty of civil proceedings, administrative proceedings, class actions, arbitrations, mediations, depositions, discovery conferences, settlement conferences, trials and appeals. Law working out its ineluctable destiny in summonses, arrests, arraignments, bail hearings, investigations, suppression hearings, jury selections, continuances, writs of habeas corpus, plea bargains, jury verdicts, sentencings, incarcerations. Law commanding an army of good cops, bad cops, detectives, correction officers, parole officers, probation officers, police chiefs, judges, marshals, magistrates, bailiffs, clerks, prothonotaries, paralegals, district attorneys, assistant district attorneys, defense attorneys, public defenders, bail bondsmen, process servers, addiction counselors, psychiatrists and social workers.

Law everywhere. Omnipresent, omniscient, omnipotent: single-mindedly devoted to good, and yet (for that reason) beyond good and evil. In the belly of this beast lands Eric V.

Johnstone, Jr., black male, age 22, who finds himself held without charge in a pre-trial detention facility in Northeast Philadelphia.   Since, after four months, he has not been charged, he cannot be tried, bargained with, sentenced or released.   It gives him small comfort to learn that his case has been accepted, on a pro bono basis, by a first-year intern at Stark Raven named Andrew Ogleby.

13. Free Lunch Day

Alice Coggins

I raced out of the museum in a panic, past the security guards and the crowd of homeless guys who'd camped outside, and ducked into the shadows under the trees. In the doorway I could see Baby Boy's pet weirdo—Howie? Was that his name?—peering out as he searched for me in the darkness. I crouched behind a low wall near the street and dashed around a corner. Then I ran for my life, though I knew there was no way I could escape from Baby Boy. He knew who I was and where I lived. I was afraid to use my phone—I considered smashing it and throwing it in a trash can like they do on TV—so I hopped on the first bus that came along and went winding all over the city until I found my way home. My parents were in bed, Tiffany out sleeping around (I just hoped it wasn't with the guy I'd talked to in the museum). Rizzo the cat welcomed me by sinking his fangs into my big toe when I crawled in bed. By the time I woke up, Mom was in the kitchen, working hard at her no-show job, and Dad was out on the front stoop for his morning briefing with Randolph and Mr. Reddy. I poured myself a cup of coffee and stumbled outside to join them.

Today's topic was "Free Lunch Day," an annual holiday created by the city to show its appreciation for the voters' support in the last election. On Free Lunch Day, every city resident is entitled to a free lunch at the restaurant or take-out counter of their choice. Families crowd in from the neighborhoods to wait in line at Jim's Steaks, Pat's Steaks,

Geno's Steaks, Phil's Steaks, Sonny's Steaks and all the other popular eateries. When those places are filled to overflowing, the crowd trickles down to lesser venues like Mr. Reddy's store, where they are offered hummus and cucumber on naan bread, with a small plastic cup of tap water. Mr. Reddy's frugality hasn't endeared him to the populace. Last year on Free Lunch Day some of the local teenagers spit out their cucumber sandwiches and grabbed armloads of snack foods on their way out the door.

Even before I got outside I could hear Mr. Reddy's voice droning as he complained bitterly about Free Lunch Day. He had walked over with my Dad's daily pack of free cigarettes, saving me the trip. Randolph stood grinning at the foot of the stairs next to his shopping cart.

"You don't have to participate in Free Lunch Day," Dad was saying. "It's completely voluntary."

"Technically yes," Mr. Reddy admitted. "But if I don't participate, they won't pick up my trash, they'll tow my car away, give my children impossible homework assignments, and send overdue notices for books we didn't check out of the library. Eventually the health inspectors will pay a visit and shut down my store, upon the orders of your Mr. Gallaher. Free Lunch Day is a bad thing. A very, very, very bad thing."

Dad never tolerates criticism of the Boss. "Desmond Gallaher is a great man," he said. "He's just spreading the wealth a little. What's wrong with that?"

"All the wealth your Mr. Gallaher is spreading around has been confiscated from its rightful owners," Mr. Reddy said. "His entire program is an illusion. Mr. Gallaher is not a great man. He is just another politician stealing the taxpayers' money."

Dad lit up one of the free cigarettes Mr. Reddy had brought him and tossed the match on the sidewalk. "What do you think, Randolph?" he asked.

Randolph already had his shopping cart in motion. "It's all part of the Potlatch," he laughed, and shuffled away.

After Mr. Reddy had returned to his store, Dad finished his cigarette and put his arm around my shoulders. I stiffened with fear since I had a good idea what was coming next. "I had a call from Baby Boy this morning," he said. "Nothing too serious, he was just surprised to see you at the museum last night, that's all. Told me to tell you hello. Said you ran out before he had a chance to chat with you, which maybe gave him the wrong impression. At least I told him it was the wrong impression."

"I was hoping he wouldn't recognize me." My voice crackled.

He shook his head. "How long has it been?"

"Seven years. I was still in high school when you took me to the butcher shop."

He lit another cigarette and leaned over the railing so he wouldn't have to look at me. "A lot's happened to Baby Boy in the past seven years. That Financial Aid job I fixed him up with opened a lot of doors. First he was Chief Financial Officer, then President of UCLA. Now he's in all kinds of non-profits. Up for Man of the Year."

"You've known about this all along?"

"Sure, I keep on top of things."

We stood next to each other like we were watching something in the street. There was nothing to see but the usual junk cars and a few stray plastic bags tumbling along the curb. "It's hard to believe," I finally said.

"When Baby Boy took over the university," Dad said, "he did everything he could to save it. He raised tuition, laid off the faculty, leased the library out to Starbucks, and switched the place over to the cooperative model of education."

"What's that?"

"It's a hands-on approach. You know, learn by doing. Instead of wasting their time sitting around in classrooms and reading books, the students clean the toilets, mow the lawns, serve the food—let's face it, that's what they're going to be doing when they graduate—and in their spare time they work on converting Gallaher's run-down apartment buildings into dorms, which rent out rooms for twice as much as the Ritz Carlton. That's no problem for the students—there's plenty of financial aid available, which they don't have to start paying back until they graduate. That keeps them in school, usually seven or eight years, and when they graduate they get internships at one of Gallaher's non-profits."

"Unpaid internships," I pointed out.

"Sure. What do you expect? It's not like these kids know how to do anything."

There was something wrong with this picture. "How can they pay back the loans?"

"That's the beauty part," Dad laughed. "They can't, and never will. The loans stay permanently on the books of Gallaher's insurance company, Third Millennium Life, which uses them as collateral for bonds they sell on the stock market. Every day I ask myself: Why didn't I think of this?"

And I'm asking myself: How does he know all this? Is this what they talk about on those "conference calls" he dials into every morning? I always thought they were phone sex. "I still don't get it," I said. "How did Baby Boy Barkocy turn into Bob Baskerville?"

Dad chuckled to himself as he tossed his cigarette butt on the sidewalk. "Did I say he got rid of the faculty? Well, he kept some of them around—'useful idiots,' he calls them—until he completed his makeover. Kept a theater professor to teach him how to sound educated, an art historian to explain the collecting racket, a psychologist to work with him on anger management—that was the hardest part. And now he's moved on to bigger and better things. Living at the swankiest address in town, running every charity you could name, starting his own museum with pieces of junk he picked up from bums on the street. It's the kind of old-fashioned success story that makes you proud to be an American."

"But hasn't anyone else figured this out? Am I the first one who ever noticed that Bob Baskerville is Baby Boy Barkocy?"

"You think those high-society types ever set foot in South Philly? In this city the rich people and the normal people like us live in two separate worlds. It's like Philadelphia and Pittsburgh. You ever met anybody from Pittsburgh?"

"I guess not."

"Nobody knows Bob Baskerville used to be a butcher in South Philly. And that's where you come in, sweetheart. Nobody—and I mean nobody—can ever find out about that."

"I sort of figured that out. What happened to the other guy we saw down there? Half Nelson."

Dad lowered his eyes as if he wanted to change the subject. "He left the university to pursue other interests."

"Is he pursuing them under an exit ramp?"

"Not yet. Believe it or not, he still works for Baby Boy."

I started shaking, then sobbing uncontrollably. Dad wrapped his arms around me and kissed my forehead. I thought he was going to take me inside, but I guess he didn't want Mom to start asking questions. "I'm afraid, Dad," I told him. "I don't want to be part of Baby Boy's world. I'm afraid of what he's going to do to me."

"Don't you worry, sweetheart. Me and Baby Boy go back a long ways. Trust me, he's not going to hurt you. Just make sure you don't mention anything to anybody. Ever."

"What about that other weirdo? Howie."

"Howie's a psycho, but he does whatever Baby Boy tells him to do."

That made me feel a lot better. "What about you, Dad?" I asked him. "You know everything I know."

He tried to laugh, I guess to reassure me, but it sounded more like a turkey being strangled. "Like I said, me and Baby Boy go back a long ways. I got him to agree to a little something extra on account of you and me keeping all this to ourselves. He's not in the loan sharking business anymore, so I asked him if he minded if I did a little lending myself. You know, just in the neighborhood."

"Lending what? Do you have any money?"

"Well, not yet." For the first time I could see a glimmer of the usual hopefulness in his eyes. "But when the lottery pays off I'll have money coming out the wazoo. Until then I'm going to have to lend on credit."

"Lend on credit? What does that even mean?"

"Lending out money you don't have."

"How can you do that?"

A smile crept over his face, that sly smile I dreaded more than anything in the world. More than Mom's sarcasm, more than Tiffany's scorn, even more than getting carved up into loin chops by Baby Boy Barkocy. If you grew up in our house, you knew, when you saw that smile, there was no turning Dad back from whatever insane idea had just hatched in his brain.

"Don't worry, sweetheart," he said. "People do it every day. It's called a bank."

14. Lucky To Have A Job

"A fundraiser? For a law firm?"

Andrew had kept his opinions to himself since joining Stark Raven, but his jaw dropped when Peter Wolf asked him to organize the firm's annual fundraiser. They sat in his boss's corner office, Mr. Wolf behind his spacious desk and Andrew across from him next to Hildegarde.

"Of course," Mr. Wolf replied, smiling at Andrew's greenhorn incredulity. "Didn't I mention that the firm is a non-profit, 501(c)(3) organization, like the March of Dimes?"

Andrew wondered if Mr. Wolf was playing a joke on him. He glanced at Hildegarde, who obviously wasn't the non-profit type (Clea had informed him that Vassily Plescinski, the sculptor, recruited all his subjects from a high-end Manhattan call girl service). In fact, Andrew had assumed that her prominent (and supine) position in Mr. Wolf's office was meant to symbolize what most people thought of lawyers. But no, his boss seemed to be dead serious. "Fundraisers play a key role in our business model," Mr. Wolf went on. "We also run a Beg-A-Thon as part of the United Way campaign, during which interns man the phones while the clients call in with their donations."

"Donations?" Andrew blurted. "Surely the clients pay hourly fees?"

"Don't be ridiculous. They make tax-deductible contributions. What do you think we're running here?"

Andrew knew he was lucky to have a job, even if it didn't come with a paycheck. The sad truth was that Stark Raven, being a non-profit law firm, was unlikely ever to have enough money to pay the interns. Peter Wolf explained the firm's economics one afternoon over a glass of sherry (grape juice for Andrew) in the partners' lounge. The only source of income was cash and property donated by clients at the annual fundraiser or during the United Way campaign ("Interns are strongly encouraged to contribute to the United Way campaign," Mr. Wolf observed). After paying necessary business expenses—club memberships, stadium boxes, yoga instruction, first class air travel, and above all, partners' compensation—there was barely enough left over to pay for plain cheese pizza at the semi-annual intern lunches, let alone anything resembling a salary. "We're thinking of eliminating the pizza," Mr. Wolf confided, sipping his sherry. "We really can't afford it."

The plight of the interns troubled Andrew, and not just for his own sake. Some of them—emaciated law graduates of indeterminate gender who huddled in tiny cubicles like chickens at a factory farm, scratching out memos and briefs that no one would bother to read—had been at the firm ten years or more. In their spare moments they tinkered with their resumes, hoping to build on their experience at Stark Raven to find a paying job. But no other firm would ever hire them. A seismic shift had occurred in the job market, owing to the glut of experienced interns: to have been an intern was now viewed as a blot on their records, sufficient to disqualify them from gainful employment. Some saw that as a lucky stroke: at Stark Raven the only thing worse than being an intern was being an associate. Associates (it was rumored) were forbidden to venture more than ten feet from their desks except in case of terrorist attacks or natural disasters. They walked around (when they were allowed to walk around) with a hollow-eyed, zombie-like stare reminiscent of fish who've gone blind from living in caves. Again there were rumors—unconfirmed, and probably exaggerated—that in extreme cases (e.g., urgent court filing deadlines) they had to be kept alive with respirators and feeding tubes until they finished their work.

Andrew realized that he'd been hired because of his father's connections (it was David Ogleby who'd brought Bob Baskerville to the firm). His record in law school had been abysmal, partly because he never cracked a book. Now he was expected to master the Internal Revenue Code, or at least Section 501(c)(3), which was bad enough. Fortunately, his boss rarely gave him any legal work to do. Apart from organizing the annual fundraiser, his only duty was to stand guard while Clea was in Mr. Wolf's office "taking shorthand." Apparently Miss Burge had once been caught cackling with her ear against the door. The lack of work assignments allowed Andrew to devote more time to his pro bono case. His client, Eric Johnstone, had been arrested for no apparent reason. That fact alone—which to one unversed in the law might have made the case seem an obvious winner—was precisely what made it so challenging, since none of the usual defenses was available. Innocence, for example, could not be raised as a defense when the client had not been charged with a crime (indeed, the claim of innocence would imply awareness of a crime and thus cast the client in a suspicious light). For this reason Andrew knew he had to tread carefully. He did hours of patient research and scheduled a series of meetings over the next few weeks in hopes of finding out why his client was in jail.

His personal life was even more frustrating. It consisted of humoring everyone he knew—his parents, Melissa, Melissa's parents, even Melissa's dog Pickles—that he would marry Melissa (to which he would always add, "when the time comes," which Melissa took to mean when the right church, country club, caterer, band and DJ would be available, though what Andrew meant was somewhat different, i.e., when she was the last woman left on earth after a nuclear disaster and he had only a few days to live). Every weekend she dragged him to her parents' beach house, mostly for the purpose of bonding with Pickles. The little mutt had become insufferable ever since he was on Good Morning America, and even more so after hitting No. 3 on *US News & World Report's* "Most popular dog" rankings. Pickles was a typical celebrity: all smiles (if you call the baring of teeth a smile), but dangerous when ignored. If Andrew curled up on the couch and fell asleep, he would awaken to find the dog nipping and snarling at his face. "Isn't he adorable?" Melissa would chirp as he leaped up and struggled to shield his ankles from attack.

"Yeah, he's adorable. Like Hannibal Lecter. Or Hitler. Why didn't you name him Hitler?"

"Insult him if you want to," Mr. Forepaugh glowered at his future son-in-law. "He's only a defenseless animal. But I'll tell you something: that little dog has sold more dog food than there is gold in Fort Knox."

Back in the city Andrew prowled charity galas, fundraisers and receptions—any affair serviced by Gallaher Catering—in search of the waitress he'd met at the Museum of Homeless

Art. There were so many such events that he despaired of ever finding her. His spirits rose when he was put in charge of the firm fundraiser. He hired Gallaher Catering to provide the refreshments and asked Clea to invite her friend Tiffany, implying that he was interested in her. In fact he was hoping to question Tiffany about the waitress (it seemed obvious that they knew each other). Having taken these steps, he felt optimistic that the fundraiser would be a success, both personally and professionally. He had a chance of finding the waitress—and this time holding on to her—and organizing such an important affair for the firm could only help his career. Unfortunately he had yet to learn the most important lesson of a novice lawyer: Never drink at firm functions.

15. The Curse Of The Leisure Class

Patti Ogleby applied a fresh coat of makeup before she caught the elevator down to the lobby. Since her business dealt almost exclusively in condominiums at Walden Towers, she maintained an office on the ground floor, adjoining the sumptuous lobby. It was here, at three o'clock, that she took time out of her busy schedule to meet with Rick and Rosemary Wurlitzer, to help the young couple understand the lifestyle choices required of new residents and the expenditures needed to display those choices. She often told her clients that they weren't buying a condominium but a way of life. Even that was an understatement—what they were committing themselves to was a philosophy, a philosophy she'd absorbed and elaborated over a lifetime and which now, thanks to *Conspicuous Consumption in the Twenty-First Century*, she was in a position to impart to the rising generation.

The Wurlitzers sat perched in front of her desk, each with a yellow legal pad on which to record her recommendations. They fidgeted anxiously and avoided her eyes, as if they'd come for marriage counseling instead of financial advice. Patty understood how they felt. She'd had similar conferences with new residents before; such sessions were in fact a kind of therapy, in which the couple was called on to re-examine their deepest preconceptions. Unfortunately, as much as Patty wanted to help the Wurlitzers, she knew she'd have to keep the meeting brief. She had a massage scheduled at the Fitness

Center at 3:30. "Do you have any children?" she began, perhaps a little too abruptly.

"Well, not exactly," Rick said. "We have two Abyssinian cats—"

"Aden, 5, and Jaden, 4," Rosemary added.

"—and a Portuguese water dog."

"Caden, age 3."

"And we're seriously considering having two kids," Rick said.

"A boy named Hayden and a girl to be named later."

"We've already enrolled them in the best pre-school in the city."

"It's a feeder pre-school for Harvard and Yale."

"And they're on the waiting list for their first ten years of pediatric appointments. But after researching the cost of strollers in *Consumer Reports,* we've been having second thoughts about kids."

"We're not quite ready to give up our beach vacations."

Patti's mind had wandered to her schedule for the rest of the afternoon. What time was her hair appointment? Did she have time for a pedicure after her massage? She found listening to people talk about their children, even their potential children, only slightly less boring than hearing about their dogs and cats.

"So what do you think?" Rick asked her, as if sounding her out on a color scheme for the drapes. "Should we have kids, or just adopt a more exotic pet?"

"A tortoise, for instance," Rosemary hinted. She had heard that Patti kept a Galapagos tortoise on her balcony.

"I would definitely suggest investing in a tortoise," Patti said, her eyes brightening at the mention of tortoises, "or even better, a pair of tortoises. They're incredibly expensive, and utterly useless. I don't think I've ever seen Achilles move."

Rick brought her back to his question: "But should we have kids?"

Annoying as he was, Patti gave Rick credit for asking her advice on this point. Far too many young people acted as if deciding to have children was a personal choice they could make without regard to its impact on their neighbors. "This building has high standards," she said. "I assume you've read the bylaws of the Homeowners Association. Once you live here, you can't just live any way you please."

"Then we're not allowed to have kids?" Rosemary asked anxiously.

Patti smiled and shook her head. "What it comes down to is whether you can afford to have kids, *really* afford it, and still maintain our standards."

"We can afford it," Rick said decisively.

"I'm sure we can afford it," Rosemary agreed.

"You might think you're rich," Patti said, "but will you still be rich after you spend all your money on kids? The nannies— you'll need at least three of them, each from a different country—and the Mercedes Benz strollers and the ergonomic car seats and the gluten-free pacifiers and the Norwegian organic soy milk and the locally-grown arugula sticks. And that's just when they're babies. After that you'll have the trilingual day-care centers and the birthday parties at *Charles de Fromage* in Paris and the private schools and the summer camps in Maine and the Olympic-level swimming teams that do their winter training in South Africa. Will you be able to pay for all that and still maintain the lifestyle a resident of this building is required to maintain?"

"I think so," Rosemary said, her voice weakening.

"The lavish entertaining, the European vacations, the luxury cars, the art works, the clothes and the jewelry and the theater tickets and the charitable donations—especially the art works and the charitable donations?"

"We've done all right with Aden and Jaden," Rick said.

"And Caden," Rosemary sniffed.

"Kids are different from cats and dogs. You don't have to have kids. They're an added expense which, frankly, not many people can afford."

"But most people have kids, don't they?" Rick objected. "Even rich people?"

"Especially rich people," Rosemary added defiantly.

"They're a problem even for those who can afford them," Patti explained. "If you have kids you'll be spending a disproportionate share of your money on low-status consumer items, and people will notice. Put yourself in the neighbors' shoes. They've paid in the high seven figures to live in this building. Do you think they'll want to share it with people who spend their consumer dollars on diapers and baby formula and peanut butter sandwiches?"

The color had drained from Rosemary's face as she followed Patti's argument to its logical conclusion. "Then there aren't any kids in the building?"

Patti smiled. "Have you noticed any?"

The young woman buried her face in her hands and sobbed. She tore at her hair and dug her fingernails into her cheeks, emitting a steady moan. Rick reached out to comfort her but she pushed his hand away.

Patti was afraid she'd been unduly harsh. "Not to imply that it has to be that way," she said cheerfully. "You could have kids here, as long as you still spend enough on the right types of things."

Rick squinted at her warily. "What types of things?"

"High-end things, of course. Things the average person couldn't afford."

"Such as?"

"Well," Patti said, "for example, if you must have children, you should conceive them through in vitro fertilization."

"No," Rosemary said, "we don't need to, we—"

"It's very expensive—and not covered by insurance. People will notice how much you're spending on it."

Rick tried to change the subject. "If you don't mind, I think we'll stick with the tried and true—"

"IVF is practically mandatory in this building," Patti cut him off. "Be sure to post selfies of every step of the procedure on Facebook and Twitter. And after the kids are born, they'll be expected to have food allergies, rare metabolic disorders and psychological maladjustments, so they can go to expensive specialists and special camps. Above all, *you must send them to private schools.*"

"But the public schools around here are supposed to be very good!" Rosemary objected.

Patti glanced at her phone and realized that she was due at the Fitness Center in five minutes. "All the more reason to send them to private schools," she said, gathering the papers on her desk. "It's not the money you spend on necessities that people judge you by—it's the money you throw away! Do you think the Pharaohs really needed all those pyramids?"

"But I'm going to be a public school teacher—"

"Nobody in this building—and I mean *nobody*—would send their kids to public school, if they had any kids, which of course they don't. The idea is positively indecent!"

"We want Hayden and his sister to go to Harvard or Yale," Rick said.

"Or maybe Princeton," Rosemary agreed. "Whatever gets the highest ranking in *US News & World Report.*"

Patti closed her office door and led them into the lobby. "The only difference between those schools is which decals you put on your car," she said. "When people see the decals, they'll know you're spending hundreds of thousands of dollars a year on colleges. Isn't that what you want for your children?"

16. Monster Rally

Alice Coggins

My Dad's so sure he's going to win the Mega Millions jackpot, he's got the money all spent. "I'm going to build the biggest house in Philadelphia," he told me one day. "More like a mansion, or a castle even, with servants, cooks, gardeners, the whole nine yards. Fifty rooms, Olympic-size pool, ten-car garage, helicopter pad, tennis courts—"

"Where are you going to find a lot big enough for a castle?" Mom called out from the kitchen.

He gestured grandly toward the street. "Up in the Northeast."

"How about a moat? You going to have a moat?"

"Sure. A moat's included." He winked at me, like it's my Mom who's crazy. "You ever see a castle that didn't come with a moat?"

Now he's on the phone all day making the arrangements. He found the blueprints for a castle online, and his cronies at the clubhouse are lining up the licenses and inspections he'll need to build it. "I've got a big receivable coming in," he tells them (meaning the Mega Millions jackpot), and on the strength of that he's signed up stonemasons, bricklayers, framers, roofers, plasterers, plumbers, electricians, even a steel fabricator to install the portcullis. Yesterday he met over the kitchen table with the moat contractor, who looked like the type who'd bury his mom under an exit ramp if she asked him to clean his room. The building trades are ecstatic: there hasn't been so much work since Hurricane Sandy. With all this activity, credit hasn't been hard to come by, and Dad is spreading it around. Suppliers ship to him on credit—marble from Italy, granite from Vermont, lumber from Idaho—and he borrows against the shipments to make loans to the guys at the clubhouse at astronomical interest rates. The word is out: Ray Coggins is back in the game.

"What kind of a scam are your running?" I asked him when the moat contractor left the house.

"This is no scam. It's a sure thing."

"Aren't you messing with the wrong people?"

He looked me in the eye and laughed. "Sweetheart, you've got it all wrong. I'm messing with the *right* people."

Is he crazy? Or does he know something I don't?

Last week Dad asked me to go around the neighborhood handing out flyers for the big rally he planned for the Neanderthal-American Party, to be held at 2:00 o'clock Sunday afternoon on the sidewalk in front of our house. Not the ideal place for a mass meeting, but Dad couldn't step off the stoop without tripping an alarm at the Probation Department. On the day of the rally I picked up a couple of large pizzas from Pinocchio's and set them out on a card table, along with some cans of cold Coke. Old Mrs. Tomai next door must have caught a whiff of the pizzas. She and Mr. Tomai came out for a free slice and sat in their lawn chairs, unaware that they were joining the ranks of the Neanderthal-Americans. By two o'clock a dozen people stood in front of the house, helping themselves to pizza and Coke and enthusiastically shaking hands with my Dad. Most of them looked Irish or Italian, but there were a few blacks and Hispanics, even the Vietnamese couple who live up the block. Everyone seemed to be welcome as far as my Dad was concerned. I didn't see anyone who looked like a cave man.

Dad delivered a speech that was surprisingly fiery and eloquent, though nobody in the crowd (including me) had a clue what he was talking about. He said Neanderthal-Americans—"who built this country"—were sick and tired of being treated like second-class citizens. "I refuse to call us a minority," he declared, his voice rising. "We're the majority, but the victims of a discrimination so long-standing that the Cro-Magnons" —that's what he calls everybody else—"have forgotten that we exist. There was a time when we ruled a big chunk of this planet, and ruled it well. Not to boast, but we were human before a lot of other people were. And now we've been marginalized, all but invisible. Well, I'm here to tell you, we're mad as hell and we're not going to put up with it any more! This time around"—he waved his clenched fist over his head—"the Neanderthal's not going down without a fight!"

"What's Neanderthal?" the Vietnamese woman asked me. "Is that some kind of cheese?"

"Yeah," I told her. "It's what's on the pizza."

After the rally, I sat with Mom and Dad at the kitchen table eating what was left of the pizza. "There's something I've been meaning to ask you," I said to Dad. "Were the Neanderthals white?"

He shoved a giant slice in his mouth so he wouldn't have to answer. Mom and I waited. "Well," he finally said, licking some tomato sauce off his fingers, "they were hairy. I picture them with brown hair and brown eyes, like your mother."

"Leave me out of this," Mom warned him.

"But were they white?"

"They lived in Europe, didn't they? So they were white."

"Underneath the hair?"

"Right. That's what counts. You gotta look under the hair."

He opened the refrigerator, popped open a tallboy of Bud Light, and escaped into the living room. I followed him, wondering if he had any idea what he was talking about. "What if it turns out their skin was black underneath?" I asked. "That would mean Neanderthal-Americans are black."

He stood at the window, sipping his beer as he gazed outside. There was nothing out there but the usual—neighbors' cars along the curb, row houses across the street, garbage piled on the sidewalk—so I assumed he was looking at the big picture, which is what he's always telling me to do. In view of the light turnout at the rally, maybe he saw the need to rethink his strategy. "Hey, I've got nothing against blacks," he shrugged. "Look at Randolph. If only everybody was like him."

"A bum prowling around with a shopping cart?" Mom cackled from the kitchen.

"He's smart, knowledgeable—"

"And a total nut job."

"You've got Randolph all wrong," Dad said, shaking his head. "He and I think alike on just about everything."

17. Girls Can Do Anything

Even though Dad assured me I'd be all right as long as I kept my mouth shut, I still worry about Baby Boy Barkocy. He and Howie are probably just as good at keeping people quiet as they are at making them pay their debts. Sometimes I have the feeling I'm being followed, usually when I'm coming home from work late at night. Walking down some deserted street, I pretend to take a sudden interest in a passing car so I can sneak a glance behind me. No one's there, but the sight of the empty street is almost as scary as whatever I was afraid of finding. No, I take that back: a deserted street with Howie in it would be ten times as scary.

Tiffany's been flying high ever since she was invited to a fundraiser at Stark Raven. One of their attorneys is the guy Tiffany chased me away from at the Homeless Art Museum. His name is Andrew, and his secretary, Clea, is my sister's best friend. Apparently she charmed him, because he asked Clea to bring her to the fundraiser. I guess that's the end of it for me. I wouldn't even mind if Tiffany didn't spend all her time gloating about it.

"Can you imagine?" she asked Mom. "He specifically asked Clea to invite me. Just me," she added, smirking in my direction. "Nobody else."

"Have fun," I said.

"The only problem is, I don't have anything to wear."

"What about your zebra-striped cocktail dress?"

"No way," she laughed. "I had that on the last time I saw him."

Dad shuffled into the kitchen, pulling a wadded-up $100 bill out of his ankle cuff. "Here, honey," he told Tiffany. "It's a picture of Ben Franklin. Go buy yourself a new dress."

He held out the bill but Tiffany wouldn't touch it. "Thanks, Dad," she said. "Do you have a clean one? And while you're at it, could you spare two or three? I can't buy a decent dress for a hundred dollars. And I'll need shoes."

"Maybe I could wear the zebra dress," I sighed, hoping to attract a little sympathy from my Dad.

Tiffany laughed so hard she almost choked. "First of all"—she jabbed her thumb into the air—"you'd never fit into it. And second of all"—she added her forefinger, as if I wouldn't be able to follow her reasoning without it—"you can't just walk in off the street. You have to be invited."

"And third of all?"

"What do you mean?"

"Since you're counting on your fingers, I assumed the count might go higher than two."

She glared back as if she didn't know I was teasing her. "There are plenty of other reasons," she said, "which I'm too nice to mention."

I knew a way to go without being invited. I scoured the Gallaher Catering job postings and signed up for the Stark Raven fundraiser. Of course I'd have to wear my waitress uniform, but I couldn't resist the temptation, the next time Tiffany was out sleeping around, to try on her zebra-striped cocktail dress. By then she'd bought a new one—it was a slinky black affair with a neckline so deep you could probably catch shrimp in it (crabs, definitely)—and shoved the zebra dress to the back of her closet. Unfortunately, on the question of whether it would fit me, she'd been right for the first time in her life. I couldn't squeeze it halfway on, and I didn't have enough money to buy a dress of my own. Dad never gave me a hundred dollars for a dress or anything else. I was so depressed I considered posting an exposé of Bob Baskerville on the internet in hopes that he'd send Howie over to whittle me down to a size eight. Instead I jumped on a bus to the Health Center to visit Grandma.

She was lying in bed, as always, with her friend Armand (who seemed to be dozing) beside her in his wheelchair. Ms. Jenkins, the nurse, leaned over her, spoon-feeding some sort of gruel, which mostly dripped out the side of her mouth and down her bib. I told the nurse I'd be happy to take over the feeding if she needed to do anything. She stuck the spoon in my hand and disappeared out the door.

Grandma opened her eyes as soon as the nurse was gone. She spit out the rest of her gruel and asked me to bring her a cheese steak from the cafeteria, which I did. As she wolfed it down, I told her all about my frustrations with the Stark Raven fundraiser and Tiffany's dress.

She said, "Don't worry, dear. You can fit into that dress. I know you can."

"If Tiffany finds out I borrowed her dress, she'll go ballistic."

"She'll never miss it."

With only two days to go before the fundraiser, I didn't know what to do. How was I going to fit into that dress?

Peering into the full-length mirror, which (though not exactly my friend) never lies, I realized that a crash diet wouldn't get the job done. An actual crash would probably be necessary, ideally with a freight train or a steamroller. Then I remembered what the boys on the wrestling team at Neumann-Goretti did when they needed to cut weight: they went around in full-length rubber suits that were designed to sweat the pounds off at a superhuman rate. Hadn't I heard that some of them sweated off twenty pounds in one day?

I called a wholesale athletic supply store on North Broad to ask if they sold rubber suits. The guy who answered didn't seem to know what I was talking about.

"You know," I said, "for wrestlers?"

"They got girls wrestling now?"

"Sure. Girls can do anything."

"OK, come on up. What's your weight class?"

Weight class? Has it come to that? I hung up and went to the store, where I was waited on by an old man with thick glasses who looked like my Dad's accountant. He reached into a jumbled pile of uniforms and equipment and pulled out a slimy-looking mass of black rubber that danced around in his hands as if it was alive. "Here, try this on. It's the only one I've got."

"What size is it?"

"Heavyweight."

My God! Am I really in the same weight class as Mike Tyson?

"The sizes run small," the salesman explained, to spare my feelings. "It wraps and stretches all around you when you put it on."

"Then what happens?" I asked. "Do you just lose weight automatically when you put on one of these things?"

"No, no, no. You've got to run around, do calisthenics. Sweat off the weight."

I stepped behind a curtain into a tiny changing room and tried to squeeze myself into the rubber suit. For five minutes I hopped around like Superman in a phone booth after a heavy dose of kryptonite, forcing my feet, my legs and then my insurmountable butt into this clinging, constricting, all-consuming monster. For the next five minutes, sweating bullets, I fought a pitched battle to force my arms through the sleeves and stretch the back across my shoulders. When the battle was won, the creature's two halves—meant to be joined by the zipper—remained miles apart. Close to the boiling point, I stripped down to bra and panties and struggled to drag the zipper upwards, but no matter how desperately I pulled, I couldn't get it across my waist. Finally I staggered out of the changing room, dripping and slippery with sweat, and ordered the old man to look the other way. His glasses steaming over, he wrapped his arms around me from behind and tugged the zipper up with all his might. When it reached my neck, sealing off the last pocket of resistance between my skin and the outside world, I was startled by a giant slurping sound that was probably heard for blocks around. The old man leaped backwards and steadied himself against a shelf.

Gasping, I tried to pry the rubber off my chest, but it didn't budge. The suit was stuck to me like an enormous suction cup.

"I was afraid of that," the old man said. "Now you really have to lose that weight. It's the only way you're ever going to get out of this suit."

I started to panic. "Couldn't you cut it off? I mean, if you had to?"

"Not without peeling off your skin." He grabbed my shoulders and pointed me toward the door. "Now get out there and run. Twenty or thirty miles ought to do it."

I lurched toward the door like a robot. Run? I could hardly bend my legs. My body temperature had spiked to about three hundred degrees.

"And don't drink anything," he added. "That defeats the purpose."

18. Philanthropy

Staggering into the house in her rubber suit, Alice lurched into the bathroom before her parents saw her. With only two hours to go before the fundraiser, she climbed on the scale for the verdict on two days of jogging, calisthenics and starvation, and she could hardly believe her eyes: her weight loss target had been achieved! Delirious with dehydration and hope, she peeled off the rubber suit, showered and jumped into her Gallaher Catering uniform. There was no time to try on Tiffany's zebra-striped cocktail dress; she stuffed it in a shopping bag (along with the matching shoes, which Tiffany had never been able to fit her feet into) and flew out the door, arriving at the law firm just as the caterers started setting up. Andrew was there, supervising the preparations. She kept her head down and looked away whenever he glanced in her direction. She concentrated on her work: setting out trays of cold cuts, shrimp, ham, roast turkey and prime rib on the tables, stocking the bar with soda, beer and wine. Two days of working out without food and water had left her ravenous, like an escaped convict fleeing through the desert. She couldn't keep her eyes off the slices of salami or the crabmeat pastry puffs. She reached into the cooler for a beer but quickly set it on the bar when she saw her supervisor watching her.

At seven o'clock Tiffany arrived with Clea in her slinky new dress. She scowled once at Alice, then pretended not to know her. Andrew greeted Tiffany but he seemed to be with another woman, the wall-eyed midget who'd given a talk at the

Museum of Homeless Art. When the room had filled up, Alice shoved a platter of cold cuts and crabmeat pastry puffs and three cans of beer into her shopping bag and ducked into a ladies' room down the hall.

As the intern in charge of the fundraiser, Andrew had spent his afternoon decorating the large conference room across from Peter Wolf's office with pictures of starving children in Africa and brutalized women in the Middle East. None of the expected donations would benefit those groups, but (as Mr. Wolf explained) it was important to make the clients feel good about themselves as philanthropists. Starting at 6:30, Andrew stood beside Mr. Wolf greeting clients as they arrived in the reception area. First came the Poffenbargers (Mrs. Poffenbarger, *née* Campbell, was the great-grand-daughter of the inventor of tomato soup), then the Van de Kamps (of baked bean fame), then the desiccated scioness of the Philadelphia cream cheese fortune, Cornelia Rugtwit Hildebiddle. Bob Baskerville sent his regrets and promised an original Buster McCoy soot-and-spittle wall hanging for the next Beg-A-Thon. The clients had learned their estate-planning lessons well: all donations were in appreciated assets, for maximum tax benefit. Mrs. Poffenbarger, the tomato soup heiress, donated the actual soup can depicted by Andy Warhol in his famous painting (estimated value: $3.8 million). Miss Hildebiddle pledged a marble cheese board once used by Grover Cleveland to serve Philadelphia cream cheese at the White House (estimated value: $2.4 million). The Forepaughs (arriving with Melissa) brought a plastic dog bowl presented to Pickles by Kim Kardashian (estimated value: $1.8 million).

"Thank you all so much!" Peter Wolf said as he acknowledged the gifts in the crowded conference room. "All of your generous, tax-deductible donations will be featured in an upcoming Sotheby's auction. And your names will be engraved on the plaque in the building lobby."

Andrew had seen Tiffany slip in with Clea, and he was eager to chat her up in hopes of identifying the waitress at the Homeless Art reception. But as soon as Mr. Wolf finished talking, Melissa sidled up and dug her fingernails into his arm. The shoulders of her black silk jacket were sprinkled with dandruff. "Don't even think about talking to those two sluts at the bar," she said under her breath.

"One of them is my secretary."

"All the more reason not to talk to her."

Melissa led him toward a group of well-dressed older women barking at each other near the windows. "I know I'm not supposed to say this," he said to Melissa, trying to change the subject, "but I don't think I understand the whole charitable giving thing."

Mr. Van de Kamp, escaping from the women (who included Mrs. Van de Kamp), appeared beside Andrew just as he made this confession. "It's like this," he said, as if Andrew had asked him for an explanation. "Say you find an old cheese board in your attic. Who's to say whether it was used by Grover Cleveland? Who's to say it wasn't? So you have it appraised based on that assumption and find out it's worth a million bucks. Why? Because Miss Hildebiddle paid that much for one just like it at the last Sotheby's auction, in the belief that it was once used by Chester Alan Arthur. It happens that Stark Raven is your favorite charity, so you donate the cheese board to the firm and they sell it at Sotheby's for the appraised value. You get a million dollar write-off and the firm gets a million dollars in tax free income."

"So far so good," Andrew said warily. "But who buys this kind of stuff?"

Mr. Van de Kamp winked at Melissa. "We buy it from each other."

Just then Peter Wolf glided up, smiling at Mr. Van de Kamp.

"What do you mean?" Andrew asked.

"Think about it. Somebody buys the Grover Cleveland cheese board at Sotheby's for a million dollars. Say that's Mrs. Poffenbarger over there. She hangs onto it for a couple of years and has it reappraised. Now it's worth two million. She donates it to a museum and takes a write-off for two million. And now Miss Hildebiddle's Chester Alan Arthur cheese board—the one she bought for a million at the first Sotheby's sale—is worth twice what she paid for it. Maybe more: maybe two-point-four. She donates it to the firm and takes a $2.4 million deduction. "

"And"—Mr. Wolf added—"when the firm sells it at Sotheby's, the person who buys it pays $2.4 million. And that becomes the basis for the next appraisal."

"I'll never understand this," sighed Mrs. Van de Kamp, who had joined the group.

All eyes were on Mr. Wolf. "It's all legal and proper," he assured them.

In the ladies' room, Alice locked herself in a stall and squeezed into the zebra-striped cocktail dress. It wasn't quite as easy a fit as she'd expected (although the matching shoes fit perfectly). She slipped out to fluff her hair and touch up her makeup in a mirror. Then, still ravenous, she returned to the stall, where she gobbled the cold cuts and crabmeat pastry puffs and downed all three of the beers. That was a big mistake. Without the constraint of the rubber suit, her body sucked up the calories from the hors d'oeuvres and beer in a metabolic frenzy and immediately began to blow up to its former size. She felt her hips and breasts and shoulders tugging at the seams of the cocktail dress as she expanded to fill it. Her knees wobbled, her head swam, her armpits exuded an odor that was beyond the wildest dreams of any deodorant. Instead of a seductive 24-year-old in a zebra-striped cocktail dress, she felt and smelled like an actual zebra on the Serengeti plain. Stomping, rearing, possibly getting ready to stampede. Everything she'd achieved in the past two days was about to be trampled into dust.

Andrew turned his back on Peter Wolf and headed for the bar, involuntarily tugging Melissa along with him. He ordered two double bourbons and swallowed them like medicine. "What's the matter with you?" Melissa demanded.

"This is all a big scam," he said in a low voice.

"Of course it's a scam. Everything's a scam. Get over it."

"OK, here's how I'll get over it." He ordered two more double bourbons and bolted them down. Way over his usual limit, but he didn't care. He had nothing to say that required the use of his brain. Ten minutes earlier, as he listened to Mr. Van de Kamp, he'd glanced toward the bar and noticed a woman stooping behind it who looked like the waitress he'd met at the Homeless Art Museum. But that woman, whoever she was, was no longer in sight. Instead he saw Clea and Tiffany smiling and waving in his direction.

When he took a halting step toward them, Melissa seized his arm and dragged him back into Peter Wolf's entourage of philanthropists. The attorney was entertaining them with a video on his phone that showed his five children frolicking on the back of a giant Galapagos tortoise. "This tortoise was captured and brought to America by Herman Melville in the 1800s," he said. "We call him Darwin."

"How adorable!" said Mrs. Van de Kamp. (Presumably she meant the children; Darwin himself was grimacing bitterly, as if he wished he'd evolved into something carnivorous, so he could eat them.)

"Tortoises make great pets," Mr. Wolf went on. "They're quiet, intelligent, good with kids—and they live forever. With a tortoise, you don't face one of those heartbreaking scenes with your kids, as you do with dogs or cats, where you have to explain about dog years, cat heaven and all that."

"I've heard a tortoise can cost as much as a condo in Vail," Mr. Forepaugh observed.

"You're paying a premium because they're an endangered species," Mr. Wolf nodded, "just as you would with a wombat or an albatross. But with exotic pets you can reduce your risk by buying life insurance. The only company that sells it, Pet Life, happens to be one of our clients (it's a subsidiary of Third Millennium)."

"Do you hear this?" Mrs. Forepaugh elbowed her husband. "We need to get that for Pickles."

Mr. Forepaugh remained skeptical. "How do they make money selling life insurance on tortoises?"

Peter Wolf laughed. "How could they *lose* money selling insurance on a pet that lives four hundred years?"

"Sounds like a pretty good scam to me," Mr. Van de Kamp said admiringly.

"Pet Life is a non-profit," Mr. Wolf said, "so how could there be anything wrong with it?"

"All legal and proper," Andrew muttered as he grabbed another double bourbon and slipped into the crowd, taking advantage of Melissa's momentary inattention to escape across the hall into Peter Wolf's office, where only Hildegarde would notice his condition. But when he turned to close the door behind him, he confronted Mr. Van de Kamp, who emitted a low whistle as he caught a glimpse of the sculpture. The baked bean magnate's tongue was hanging out so far it clashed with his necktie. "Who is that piece of... art?"

"That's Hildegarde," Andrew said, trying to sound sober. "Vassily Plescinski, 1985."

"I'd like to pick up one of those for my office!"

"They come on the market from time to time." Andrew wobbled and almost fell over. "Plescinski did a whole series. Check the Sotheby's catalog."

When Mrs. Van de Kamp summoned her husband away, Andrew found himself alone with Hildegarde, who lounged on her pedestal like a mermaid on a rock. For the first time he noticed a small plaque on the edge of the pedestal. It read, *Gift of Bob Baskerville*. As Andrew leaned forward to examine it, he felt himself toppling forward and landed on his knees clinging to the pedestal just below Hildegarde's waist, thanking his lucky stars that no one could see him in this position.

"Hi, there!" a woman's voice chimed behind him.

Desperately he lurched upright and skittered away from the sculpture. When he turned around, breathless and dizzy, he realized—though he could hardly believe his eyes—that the voice belonged to the woman of his dreams, the waitress from the Museum of Homeless Art. She stood in front of him like a fairy-tale apparition, just as beautiful as he remembered her, though dripping with sweat and apparently on the verge of bursting out of a zebra-striped cocktail dress.

"Oh," he stammered. "Hi. I thought I saw you earlier. But—"

"You thought I was a caterer."

"Right. Amber, isn't it?" He said that even though she'd told him it was a fake name.

"It's Alice, actually," she smiled, wiping the sweat off her forehead. "Sometimes I dress up as a caterer. Just to see what it's like."

"I'm Andrew. Sometimes I dress up as an attorney and crawl around on the floor of my boss's office. I don't know why."

They both laughed at that. "I'm really an unpaid intern," he added.

"What a coincidence! So am I!"

She stole a glance into the hallway and lowered her voice. "I'm not supposed to be here, except as a waitress. If they catch me, will they throw me out?"

"No. I organized this fundraiser. I'll just say I invited you."

She thanked him with a mischievous smile. "Aren't you going to introduce me to your date?"

"Melissa? I came in here to get away from her."

"No," Alice said, pointing behind him. "I mean her."

"Hildegarde?" He jumped aside as if noticing the sculpture for the first time. "I hardly know her."

Alice tiptoed forward and took a closer look. "It's amazing how lifelike this is. It's like she's one of those frozen cave people."

"Yeah, she's from the stone age, all right. 1985. Whoever posed for this must be about seventy by now."

Alice noticed the plaque, and when she stooped down to read it her expression changed. "*Gift of Bob Baskerville.* What's this?"

"The sculpture was a gift from Bob Baskerville. He's—"

"I know who he is," Alice cut him off, suddenly pale. "Who did he give it to?"

"The firm. Instead of legal fees."

"You take money from Bob Baskerville?"

"What's wrong with that?"

When Alice tried to answer, she was silenced by an ear-piercing howl as a fierce, menacing presence whirled into the room. "You!" Tiffany shrieked, dancing around her like a crazed ballerina. "What are you doing in my dress?"

"You weren't wearing it."

"How did you even fit into it?"

Alice smirked at Andrew. "She's a lot fatter than she looks."

"And those are my shoes!"

"I'd like to see you fit your fat feet into them," Alice said, kicking them off.

Tiffany glared into Andrew's eyes. "Everything she's wearing, she stole from me. I wouldn't be surprised if she's wearing one of my bras."

"No chance of that fitting me!"

Infuriated, Tiffany reached out and seized the top of the dress, and after a fierce bout of tugging, shoving and name-calling, its ample décolletage deepened to a chasm. Alice threw her hands over her chest and ran down the hall as Tiffany stood laughing.

Her triumph was short-lived. The rumor of a peasant rebellion brought Melissa hurtling into the room. She clutched Andrew by the elbow and dragged him away. "What are these low-lifes even doing here?" she scowled, in a tone that was meant for Tiffany.

Hildegarde watched serenely from the pedestal with her usual enigmatic smile. Had she not held herself aloof from the human comedy, she might have noticed that Tiffany, stalking out soon after Andrew and Melissa, neglected to retrieve the zebra-striped shoes that Alice had discarded on the floor.

19. After The Ball

The morning after the fundraiser Andrew's tongue was three sizes too big, his skull five sizes too small. A savage drumbeat pounded inside his head. Only when he rolled out of bed and into the kitchen, where Patti had kindly left him a pot of hot coffee, did he begin to feel human again. He peeled his tongue off the roof of his mouth and tasted the coffee, fighting back images of a nightmare—or was it a recollection of the night before?—about an ogress, a vixen, and a beautiful serving girl. The serving girl—who called herself Alice—had risen before him like Venus from the mist. She fought with the vixen, who tore off her dress, and then the ogress—was she called Medusa or Melissa?—dragged him into a mob of philanthropists who tore him limb from limb in a Bacchic frenzy. How much of that really happened and how much had he imagined? As he sipped his coffee, reality grudgingly came into focus. Alice was real, sublimely real, the woman of his dreams. Melissa was the woman of his nightmares, conjuring the philanthropists to exact a furious revenge if he scorned her. And the vixen Tiffany hovered between them, at once blocking and lighting his way. He knew what he had to do. He had to continue the search for Alice until he found her and made her his own, even if it meant making Tiffany his unwitting guide. But no one— not Tiffany, or Clea, or least of all Melissa—could know the true object of his quest.

He slouched into work an hour late. Mr. Wolf was already in his office with the door shut. Clea sat at her desk paging through a pornographic magazine.

"Don't look at me that way," she said as he trudged past her desk. "I'm doing legal research for Mr. Wolf."

"Legal research?"

"He asked me to study this magazine to see if it has any socially redeeming value. Then I'm supposed to go in and talk to him about it."

As they chatted, Andrew noticed Alice's zebra-striped shoes on the shelf beside Clea's desk. "I'm glad you invited Tiffany last night," he said. "Even though I didn't get a chance to talk to her, because of that girl that attacked her."

"What a wack-job! Can you believe she snuck in with the caterers?"

"Unbelievable." He reached over and picked up the shoes. "You know, I feel really bad about what happened. Those are Tiffany's shoes, aren't they? Let me take them back to her so I can apologize. You wouldn't happen to have her phone number, would you?"

20. Running On Fumes

Alice Coggins

One night after dinner I was out on the stoop listening to my Dad plan his castle when Randolph trudged around the corner with his shopping cart, like a tired housewife after a busy day at the garbage dump. A few minutes later Mr. Reddy arrived with Dad's cigarettes and the three of them started arguing about the economy and why it never seemed to improve. Dad said things would get better when the stimulus from Free Lunch Day trickled down and created jobs. "Then why not have Free Lunch Day every day?" Mr. Reddy objected. "If it creates jobs, why not have it every day? Why not have Free Dinner Day too? And don't forget about breakfast—isn't that the most important meal of the day?"

For once in his life Dad seemed at a loss for words. I waited to hear him explain how Free Lunch Day created jobs. Unfortunately, at that moment my Mom banged on the window and called him inside. "You take it from here, Alice," he winked, leaving the explaining to me. "I'll be right back."

Randolph reached in his cart and pulled out a crumbling, yellowed *New York Times Magazine* he'd brought from his garage, which he opened to a drawing of robots lined up in a factory. "Back in 1963," he said, "when this magazine come out, they was worried about machines taking over all the work. The experts—this article quotes a lot of experts—said that by the twenty-first century the world's biggest problem would be folks having too much leisure time. You hear that? Too much leisure time!"

"Wasn't that just another way of saying everybody would be out of work?" I asked.

"No, they was talking about something else—too much leisure time. That's why they started the Potlatch. The government told the WPA: Find something for these fools to do! The WPA took everything people did to fill up their leisure time and turned it into a job. Sixty years later, they got everybody working like a dog."

"Nobody I know can find a job," I said. "All my friends are doing unpaid internships."

"But they work like dogs, don't they, even if they ain't getting paid?" Randolph beamed triumphantly. "Nobody has any leisure time. I don't even have leisure time. You know anybody who's got leisure time?"

I was sure I had him now. "My Dad," I said. "He's never worked a day in his life."

"House arrest ain't leisure time. You count incarceration in leisure time, we got the biggest leisure class since the French Revolution."

"The biggest industry in America," Mr. Reddy broke in, wagging his finger at Randolph, "is shoplifting from my store. The young people steal everything they can grab when I'm not watching them with my hand in my pocket pretending I have a gun. Candy, snack foods, soda, newspapers, cosmetics—"

"Is shoplifting one of the industries started by the WPA?" I asked Randolph.

"Could be," he shrugged.

"And when they're not shoplifting," Mr. Reddy pressed on, "the young people spend their time hanging around in front of my store selling each other illegal drugs."

"The WPA probably had a hand in that too," Randolph said.

"And then"—Mr. Reddy had a wild, distracted look in his eyes, as if he'd fallen completely under Randolph's spell—"there are allergies. In my village in India nobody had allergies. Now my children are allergic to everything under the sun: peanuts, tree nuts, gluten, milk, eggs, fish, pollen, mold, dust mites, cats, dogs, noise, their teachers, each other. And let's not forget obsessions. My wife believes that radio waves control her digestion, that the phone company records all her conversations with her mother, that aliens will snatch the children away if they wander outside..."

"Like I told you," Randolph grinned, tossing his *New York Times Magazine* into the cart, "it's all part of the Potlatch."

Randolph was crazy but he was on to something. Somehow, when nobody was looking, the whole economy—the whole society—had been retooled to consist of wasting time in ever more elaborate ways. If you were lucky enough to find a job, you had to work like a dog doing things that used to be considered fun, illegal or crazy. Not that you could expect to get paid—dogs don't get paid, do they? But how had this happened? Was it the WPA, as Randolph claimed? Globalization? Climate change?

Just then the only man besides Randolph who could have answered that question, a man who'd dedicated his life to wasting time and making it look like work—my Dad—came out the door. For some reason he was wearing the full-length yellow rubber fireman's coat he wore when he helped plug a water main break about fifteen years ago. "Hey, Alice," he said, handing me a slip of paper with a doctor's name on the top, "your mother needs you to drive out and pick up her migraine prescription."

"Now?"

"Without this prescription, I don't know if she'll make it through the night. And the only pharmacy that has it in stock is at Cottman and the Boulevard."

"Cottman and the Boulevard? That'll take me about an hour."

"I'd go if I could," he said, frowning at the ankle cuff under his fireman's coat. "You'd better get going." He handed me his keys. "Here, you can take the Cadillac."

21. Desperately Seeking Alice

Why had Alice's father suddenly appeared on the stoop in his full-length yellow fireman's coat and sent her on a pointless mission to Northeast Philadelphia?

When Ray had slipped into the house ten minutes earlier, he found his wife and Tiffany in crisis mode. Tiffany flounced around in the living room, modeling what to Ray's jaundiced eye looked like a hooker outfit—purple knee-high boots, black tights, short leather skirt and halter top—while her mother picked up his empty Coke cans and Fritos bags and sleep apnea hoses and straightened the pillows on the couch.

"Hey, what's going on?"

"Tiffany's got a live one," the mother said in an urgent tone usually reserved for appendicitis and cardiac arrest.

"What do you mean?"

"A boyfriend. He'll be here in a few minutes."

"Is that right?" Ray chuckled. "I'll put on a Sinatra record."

His wife picked up the bent hanger he used to scratch under his ankle cuff and waved it in his face. "Listen to me! You've got to get Alice out of here before the boyfriend arrives. Tiffany doesn't need any competition."

She handed him a prescription her doctor had given her a month before. "Go back out and tell her I'm dying of a migraine. She needs to get this filled for me right away, and the only pharmacy that has it is up at Cottman and the Boulevard."

"I don't know about this. Why not—"

"Stay out on the stoop," she cut him off. "Don't say a word to the boyfriend, not even hello. And send your two fellow lunatics on their way before he gets here."

She reached in the closet and pulled out the long yellow fireman's coat. "Here, put this on and zip it up so it covers your ankle cuff."

Ray seethed as he slipped into the coat. "Who is this guy, the King of England?"

"His name is Andrew," Tiffany said, adjusting her hair in the mirror. "He's a lawyer for non-profits."

"Why are you so big on non-profits?"

"Dad—"

"Do you think you'd be where you are today if I'd left the private sector when I was your age?"

"The private sector? You mean, like, crime?"

"Where she is today," Ray's wife said, "is in a crumbling row house with cockroaches and a leaky roof and no A/C." She twisted his sleep apnea hose into a noose and took a step toward him. "If you weren't under house arrest, I'd send you to live with your mother."

"My mother's dead."

"I know."

Andrew arrived at the Coggins house a few minutes after Alice drove off in the Cadillac. When he saw the man in the fireman's coat, he was afraid he'd arrived in the middle of an emergency. But the man (who, he quickly realized, was a deranged street person) acted like everything was normal. He stayed on the stoop, grinning foolishly, and when Andrew rang the bell he bowed and held the door for him. It was a shame, Andrew thought, that there weren't more programs for the mentally ill. He reached in his pocket for some change and shoved a quarter into Ray's hand.

"You're a lucky guy," the man said, looking directly at him for the first time.

Andrew smiled. "How would you know that?"

"It's not every day you meet a nice Neanderthal-American girl."

A pale, birdlike woman stood inside the door with a spray-can of air freshener aimed in his direction. Andrew had called Tiffany about fifteen minutes before, saying he was in the neighborhood and would like to stop by. Presumably the bird woman was her mother, though for all he knew she might have been another psychotic who'd wandered in off the street. She stepped back and led him down a short hall into a living room. The place smelled like cabbage and cats and canned ravioli.

"Is Tiffany home?"

She glared at the plastic bag he was carrying. "You bring your lunch?"

"Just a pair of shoes," he laughed.

"Have a seat." She pointed at Ray's Barcalounger. "Want something to drink? Diet Coke? Sprite?"

"Water would be great."

"Water?" She brandished the air freshener can suspiciously. "You want ice in it?"

"No, thanks."

"You don't like Diet Coke? You don't even like ice?"

"Diet Coke would be fine. With lots of ice."

"We don't have any diseases," she said, sending a blast of air freshener toward him. "In case you were wondering." She dimmed the lights and retreated a few steps into the kitchen. "Tiffany, you've got a visitor."

At this signal Tiffany swayed in from a back room in her high-heel boots, black tights, short leather skirt and halter top. She and Andrew exchanged friendly greetings, and she sat down on the couch across from him. "What have you got in that bag?" she asked.

He reached in the bag and pulled out the zebra-striped shoes. "Are these yours?"

"Oh! The shoes I lost at the fundraiser."

"Are they yours?"

"Sure, they're mine. These are my shoes, aren't they, Mom?"

"Maybe you ought to try them on," Andrew suggested.

Tiffany peeled off her boots and tried to squeeze the shoes onto her feet, a maneuver that required her to cross, uncross and recross her legs a dozen times. Even after all that effort the shoes reached only halfway to her heels. "See? Perfect fit."

"Maybe they're the other girl's," Andrew smiled.

"What other girl's?"

"She said her name was Alice."

"Mom, do I know anyone named Alice?"

"You must have known her," Andrew said. "You said she stole your clothes."

"Oh, there's a girl named Alice who used to work here."

"Scullery maid," the mother yelled from the kitchen.

"Take my word for it," Tiffany smiled, crossing her legs again and kicking off the shoes.. "You don't want to know her. You'd much rather know me."

With that introduction, she segued into a breathless advertisement for herself, like a living selfie illustrated with enough smiles, shrugs, pouts and poses to crash the social network. Try as he might, Andrew couldn't bring the topic back around to Alice. After forty-five minutes—at a signal from her mother—Tiffany made him promise that he would call the next day, yanked him out of the Barcalounger and rushed him out the door.

The homeless guy in the fireman's coat was still on the stoop. He greeted Andrew with his demented grin and jumped aside to let him pass. An absurd suspicion entered Andrew's mind. Could this lunatic be Tiffany's father?

22. Hell In A Handbasket

Hector was anxious to report the findings of his sex investigation back to Gwendolyn. Based on his field research at bars, clubs and social events, he had concluded that the stimulus package was probably unnecessary. At least in his age bracket, there was still plenty of sex; in fact that was all anybody seemed to think about. Clea and Tiffany, for example—two of the women he'd talked to at the Homeless Art reception—managed their lives entirely through various sex apps on their phones, which enabled them to hook up with the optimum number of men each night. But every time he approached Gwendolyn to propose a meeting, she would brush him off with a suggestive comment or the kind of joke specifically prohibited in the Bank's Compliance Manual. "Just keep up your research," she told him one day as he tapped on her door holding the pocket notebook in which he'd recorded his field data. "You need to go to more clubs. Have you ever been to Shazam? That's where I like to go on a Saturday night."

"No, I haven't been to that one," he admitted.

"I hope to see you there this weekend."

A low buzz to the tune of "Like a Virgin" followed him back to his cubicle, rising in intensity with each secretary's desk he passed. Then a hissing sound—"Psssst!"—brought his head spinning around. The secretaries lowered their eyes, though the humming continued. A nearby door stood open a crack, and inside (in what he'd thought was a supply closet) he could see Arbuthnot—the only other male employee of the Bank—peering out from behind a desk. "Come on in!" Arbuthnot whispered.

Hector slipped inside, closing the door behind him. The room was larger than he'd imagined, but empty except for the desk and a couple of wooden chairs. Arbuthnot sat at the desk hunched over a manila folder as if he didn't want Hector to see it. He wore an old-fashioned gray pin-striped suit—the kind men used to wear when there were still men at the Bank—that had frayed cuffs and coffee stains on the lapels. "What's going on out there?" he asked.

"It's just the secretaries," Hector said. "They make fun of me because I'm saving myself for Alice."

"Who's Alice? Someone who works here?"

"Just a girl on my block."

"Good luck with that." Arbuthnot flipped open the manila folder but kept its contents hidden by his sleeves. "The women here—from the Board of Governesses on down—like to pretend that sex makes the world go round," he said. "Even they know better than that."

"What does make it go around, then?"

"Money. At least that's what I learned at Wharton." Arbuthnot smiled—not to imply that he was joking, but the opposite: the answer was so obvious that anyone who doubted it was a fool. He needed a shave and seemed to be missing some of his teeth. "But for the time being, you can pretend to go along with the women and their fantasies. Humor them if you must. We men—and there are only the two of us here— have more important things to think about."

"Right," Hector agreed without knowing why.

Arbuthnot peeked into the file folder and squinted back at Hector with a twinkling eye. "But while we're on the subject of sex: Is the stimulus package working?"

Hector glanced down at his pocket notebook. "Based on anecdotal evidence"—he'd decided not to mention Clea or Tiffany by name—"aggregate demand has held steady over the past few weeks."

"Any bottlenecks in the supply chain?"

He shook his head. "If anything, velocity has increased."

"Consumer staples always do well in a downturn," Arbuthnot nodded. "But as for the rest of the economy"—he shrugged, as if he knew better than to expect an intern to understand such complexities—"we're very concerned."

"They say it's recovering," Hector mumbled. "According to data published by the Bank—"

"You can't believe what you read," Arbuthnot cut him off. "Especially data published by the Bank. The fact of the matter is, the economy's been going to hell in a handbasket for so long, nobody even knows what a handbasket is anymore. Do you know what a handbasket is?"

Hector sidestepped the question. "But what's the problem? I thought—"

"The problem is: Where is all the money going? We print it by the truckload—the money supply is now big enough to fill outer space—but as soon as it leaves here it disappears. Plain disappears. Like it's being sucked into a black hole."

"What could be happening to it?"

"I'm not supposed to say this," Arbuthnot confided, lowering his voice, "but we blame the public. Nobody does any of the things they're supposed to do anymore. They don't work, they don't save, they don't borrow, and they don't spend. Forty-three percent of the population can't be bothered to get out of bed in the morning."

"I didn't realize things were that bad."

Arbuthnot paged through Hector's personnel file. "I see that you had a double major in economics and medieval theology."

"With a minor in embalming," Hector added.

"Even so," Arbuthnot said, closing the file decisively, "with that background you ought to be able to figure out what the problem is. I want you to report back to me—directly to me; you needn't mention any of this to Gwendolyn or the others— a week from today. Is that clear?"

23. Food Stamp Day

Alice Coggins

Picking up various supplies for my parents seems to be my main purpose in life. The morning after I spent an hour driving up to the Northeast to get a prescription filled for my Mom, Dad sent me over to Mr. Reddy's store for his cigarettes. A bus marked "Gallaher's Travels" idled at the curb as dozens of senior citizens crowded into the store. Most of them were white, overweight and well dressed, if you consider blue hair with a size fifty lime-green pants suit well dressed. They lined up like they'd just stepped off a casino bus in Atlantic City, but they looked happier than the A.C. crowd. On Food Stamp day, I found out, Mr. Reddy's store was a much better bet than the slots.

I noticed Hector Lopez, the shy guy who always peeks out at me as I walk by his house, trying to help some Hispanic ladies who'd come with their kids to buy groceries. The senior citizens wouldn't let them near the door. "We've got a bus waiting," a geezer in a golf shirt told the women, blocking their baby strollers. One of the kids was screaming its head off. "Can't you keep that kid quiet?" the geezer's wife complained.

"He needs something to eat," Hector said.

"Tell him to get in line like everybody else!"

I felt a little guilty when Mr. Reddy waved me to the front of the line. "What are all these people doing here?" I asked him.

"It's Food Stamp Day," he said. "Once a month, poor people get food stamps on a debit card linked to a government account, and they come here to buy soda with them."

"But these people aren't poor," I said in a low voice. The man at the head of the line, scowling in a red sports coat and Phillies hat, swiped his debit card and waited for Mr. Reddy to register the purchase.

"Oh, yes! Some of them are so poor," Mr. Reddy smiled, "that they get ten, twenty, thirty times the usual amount of food stamps. Then they use the whole amount to buy as many cases of Coke, Sprite and other popular beverages as I can sell them."

The cash register spit out a receipt and Mr. Reddy handed it to the man in the Phillies hat. "Thank you, sir, thank you very much. Fifty cases of Diet Coke, twelve-ounce cans, twenty-four to the case. Thank you very much."

The man shuffled away and another man lunged forward to swipe his card. "But I don't see any cases of soda," I pointed out.

"Of course not," Mr. Reddy smiled. "I have no room here for thousands of cases of soda. The soda remains in the warehouse of Gallaher Beverage Distributors Inc., which is where the bus will take these customers next."

"To pick up their soda?"

"Of course not. No one can drink hundreds of cases of soda. They will go there to sell the soda back to Gallaher Beverage Distributors Inc."

"Sell it back?"

"For fifty percent of what I charged them for it, paid to them in cash. Then Gallaher Beverage Distributors Inc. can sell it again, and if they sell it to me, I can also sell it again. It's a win/win." Mr. Reddy bowed slightly. "I thank your father for bringing me this business. That's why I am pleased to provide him with free cigarettes." He handed the second man his receipt. "Thank you, sir. Thank you very much. One hundred and twenty cases of Pepsi-Cola, twenty-four sixteen-ounce cans." The man stumbled away, and a small, intense woman in designer sweatpants and a Ski Aspen T-shirt groped for the card-swiper.

The whole thing sounded like a scam to me. "But for the government—"

"It's a great blessing for the government," Mr. Reddy interrupted, reading my thoughts. "Because now I have twice as much money in my pocket, which I will save for retirement by buying government bonds. Gallaher Beverage Distributors Inc. also has twice as much money, to reward its delivery men who conserved valuable resources by not delivering the soda to my store. And my customers—thank you, madam, that's ninety cases of Mountain Dew, twenty-four twelve-ounce cans, thank you very much—will now have money to spend at Gallaher's Grand Casino (which is where the bus will take them after Gallaher Beverage Distributors Inc.), instead of consuming unhealthful soda which would make them even fatter and eventually cause heart attacks and increase health care costs by a far greater amount than the paltry sum the government must pay for the soda. Thus the customers are happy, the distributor is happy, the casino is happy, the government is happy, and I am happy. It's a win/win."

He handed me my Dad's daily ration of smokes. "Here are your father's cigarettes. Now he will be happy too."

"Until he dies of lung cancer."

"Correct," Mr. Reddy smiled. "How about another lottery ticket? The Mega Millions jackpot is up to 375 million dollars." He pulled off the next ticket and held it out.

"No, thanks. My Dad is sure he's going to win with the one he has. Why spend another two bucks?"

"This one's on the house."

When Mr. Reddy said those words, the discontent I'd heard rumbling behind me boiled over into pushing and shoving and shouted threats and waving fists. "I want that free lottery ticket you offered this girl!" the man behind me hollered.

"I want a free one too," the woman next to him growled.

"We're senior citizens! The lottery's supposed to be for our benefit!"

The mob glared back at me through their bifocals, their trifocals and their $10.95 Wal-Mart polaroids, and it was a hair-raising sight. I had a vision (which comes back to me sometimes in the night) of being torn limb from limb by men in plaid golf pants and old ladies in lime-green pants suits. But before I had time to panic, Hector Lopez leaped out from behind the snack display and snatched me safely into one of the aisles. The crowd quickly forgot their bloodlust and surged toward the checkout counter, waving their debit cards in an irresistible drive to convert Food Stamps into casino chips.

I found myself out on the sidewalk with Hector and the Hispanic women, who still couldn't get into the store. The kids were screaming bloody murder, but Hector didn't seem to notice. He's been in love with me ever since we took the same bus in the ninth grade. He gives me the creeps a little, but only because he keeps asking me out. He's actually a very nice guy. He's doing an internship at the Federal Reserve Bank.

"You saved my life, Hector," I told him. "How can I ever repay you?" It was what they call a rhetorical question, but Hector had an answer.

"How about lunch? Would you like to go have some lunch?"

We ate at an Italian place on South Street, just pizza and Cokes, and I paid my share, so Hector wouldn't get any ideas. He had the day off, but all he talked about was his internship at the Federal Reserve Bank. "What do you think is wrong with the economy?" he asked me as he bit into his pizza.

"Who knows?" I said, thinking of my family. "Maybe it's because everybody just wastes all their time."

"Inefficiency," he nodded.

"It's beyond inefficiency," I said. "Inefficiency means taking too long to get something done. What I'm talking about is not getting anything done at all. At least not anything worth doing. People have jobs, they work hard, but"—to my surprise, I found myself quoting Randolph—"it's all part of the Potlatch."

Hector looked like he'd seen a ghost. "The Potlatch?"

"Never mind, it's just an expression I've heard from... one of my Dad's friends."

"What—what does it mean?"

"It means"—I struggled to define it without sounding like a crazy person—"it means everything is just a make-work project to keep people busy with pointless activity."

He glanced around furtively and lowered his voice. "There was a woman at the Museum of Homeless Art who talked to me about the Potlatch. She said, 'If there's less of something, or more of something, it's because of the Potlatch.'"

"That sounds about right," I smiled. "If you believe there's such a thing."

"You don't?"

"Not really. My Dad's friend is sort of crazy."

Nervous beads of sweat glistened on Hector's forehead and he suddenly changed the subject. "Do you think there's less sex than there used to be?"

I couldn't help laughing. I thought I'd heard every come-on line hatched by the mind of man, but this took the game to a whole new level. Was this how they picked up girls at the Federal Reserve Bank?

Hector looked as innocent as the day he was born. "I'm serious," he said. "This is for an economic study I'm doing for the Bank."

"Is sex part of the economy?"

"Everything's part of the economy," he said, and he told me about the assignment he'd been given by his supervisor, whose name was Gwendolyn. He was supposed to go around to bars and night clubs to investigate whether sex had declined into a state of entropic deceleration.

"Entropic deceleration?"

"ED," he nodded. "The Board of Governesses is considering whether more stimulus may be necessary."

By this time I was laughing my head off. This had to be a joke—anyone but Hector could see that. He's such an easy mark. If this were one my Dad's scams, Hector would have lost his life savings in about thirty seconds. Somebody had to set him straight, so I figured it might as well be me. "I wonder if Gwendolyn is just messing with you," I said.

"You mean, all this could be a joke?"

"A joke, or maybe something else. Maybe she's interested in you."

"Interested in *me?*"

"Sure. You're a good looking guy."

We finished our lunch and wandered back down Passyunk toward home. A block from my house I was surprised to see Tiffany (who doesn't usually get up before 3:00) gaping at us from the other side of the street. She didn't smile or wave, just stared as if she thought we couldn't see her. I said good-bye to Hector in front of his house and walked around the corner past Mr. Reddy's store. The casino bus had moved on to its next destination. Mr. Reddy stood in the doorway sweeping up the coffee cups and candy wrappers left behind by the senior citizens. As I passed, he gave me a quirky sort of smile, as if he and I shared a secret.

By the time I got home I felt anxious, frustrated, a little depressed, the way I imagined Hector must feel when he worked on his sex investigation. Is this what it means to be an intern, I wondered—to be the butt of some elaborate joke playing on your innocence and inexperience, which you'll never be able to understand? Hector isn't the only one. Sometimes I feel like I'm being kept in the dark, the only person in the world who doesn't know some deep, dark secret that everybody else is in on.

24. Blind Justice

Andrew knew he'd dodged a bullet when Tiffany hustled him out the door. She was a temptress and he wasn't immune to her charms. And what kind of family did she come from? What if her father was the demented doorman in the fireman's coat? There was no way he'd even consider dating the daughter of that lunatic.

He tried to visualize the shape of his life and it wasn't a pretty sight: an amorphous, directionless blob, like a single-celled amoeba or a piece of roadkill pizza. The best he could hope for—if he couldn't find Alice—was a fatal accident or terminal disease that would at least spare him the indignity of marrying Melissa. In the meantime he consoled himself with his work at Stark Raven, which consisted mainly of figuring out ways to keep rich people from having to pay their taxes. Luckily he had his pro bono case, which not only kept him busy but provided a daily reminder that life could be much, much worse. His client, Eric Johnstone, age 22, had been arrested four months earlier and held on $100,000 bail, which his family couldn't pay. No one seemed to know why he'd been arrested.

Andrew drove up to a special "pre-trial detention facility" in Northeast Philadelphia that resembled a Holiday Inn surrounded by a razor wire fence, where he met his client across a metal table to which he was shackled in his orange jumpsuit. Eric was a long-limbed, slightly-built young man with a distant smile and a habit of dipping his head forward as he talked. When he did make eye contact with Andrew he showed the same hostility he showed the guards, as if Andrew, by trying to get him out of jail, was part of the system that put him there. "So, Eric," Andrew began, his pen poised over a legal pad, "why are you in here? I haven't been able to figure that out."

"You're the lawyer," Eric shrugged, looking away. "Ain't you supposed to know that?"

"What did you do?"

"I didn't do nothing."

Andrew tried to smile reassuringly. "You can tell me," he said. "Everything you tell me is confidential."

"I didn't do nothing. That's why I'm in jail."

Was he trying to be funny? Or just flaunt his attitude? "You're going to have to explain that," Andrew said.

"OK, man, I'll try to explain." Eric glanced at Andrew and his eyes darted away. "Maybe you can understand better than me. I was mixed up with a gang starting when I was fifteen, run by my cousin Raheem. It was just for show, like the peacocks at the zoo. We didn't do nothing, just strutted around in our gangsta gear to make sure nobody'd mess with us."

"No guns? No drugs?"

"Nothing. We didn't have guns, and I couldn't stand the drugs—they made me sick. One day we all got busted for hanging around on the wrong street corner. A crack pipe fell on the sidewalk—it was Raheem's, not mine. But I told the cops it was mine 'cause I was a juvenile with no record and I knew they wouldn't put me in jail. All I'd get was probation."

"You took the rap for Raheem?"

"Right," he nodded. "Raheem walked away and I had to spend my life in therapy. They put me in AA and substance abuse and anger management and every other kind of group but the garden club. I had psychologists and social workers beating up on me like no gang bangers I ever seen, until finally I got down on my hands and knees and begged them to stop— and when I did that, they said, now we know what your problem is. You got low self-esteem. That was more than I could take. Tell me I'm a street-fighter, a badass, a drug lord, a hardened criminal on his way to being Public Enemy No. 1—I can take that, even if my mama can't. But *nobody* in this town's gonna tell me I got low self-esteem."

Andrew started to laugh but stopped himself. This was no joke.

"For a while I played along," Eric went on. "Then last winter Raheem caught a bullet in the head outside a movie theater, and that was the end of the gang. My mama prayed all night and my pastor got me right with God. The next day I walk into the self-esteem improvement group and tell them I ain't never coming back. I got no anger to manage, no behavior to modify, and my self-esteem is just fine, thank you. The only thing I need is a job and I spend so much of my life getting counseled I don't have time to look for one."

Andrew laid down his pen and stared at Eric. "Then what happened?"

"The next day the cops come to my house." He leaned forward and bored his eyes into Andrew's. "You're under arrest, they tell me. I try to beat it out the back door but they got a guy out there to catch me. First time I ever been in jail. Let me go, I tell them. I didn't do nothing, that crack pipe was

Raheem's (he's dead now, so I don't mind snitching). Too late for that, they tell me. We're bringing you in on a probation violation, plus resisting arrest. You could be looking at seven to ten."

"Seven to ten years?"

"That's what they tell me."

"Did you ask for a lawyer?"

"Sure I asked for a lawyer. That was four months ago. When you gonna get me out of this hole?"

"I don't know," Andrew said. "This is my first case."

It was cocktail hour at the Ogleby condo. Andrew and Patti relaxed on matching leather sofas in the living room, sipping mojitos made with Dominican rum and mint leaves flown in from Mozambique. David stood on the balcony with his third scotch and soda, chatting with Achilles.

"I guess that's the downside of being a lawyer," Patti said. Andrew had just told her about his visit to the detention facility. "Having to associate with the criminal element."

"As far as I can tell," Andrew said, "Eric Johnstone is the only client I have who's *not* a criminal."

"Then what's he in jail for?"

"No one seems to know."

"He must have done something really bad. Otherwise why would they keep him there?" She stepped into the kitchen and poured another shot of rum over the ice cubes in her glass. "By the way, have you and Melissa thought about a date for the wedding?"

June 1, 2219, Andrew wanted to say—or some other date when he was sure to be dead. But what he said was: "We're working on it."

"I know this is short notice," Patti went on, gliding back into the living room, "but you've really got to have the wedding before the end of the year. For reasons I won't go into. But steer clear of the first weekend in November. The Man of the Year gala at the Health Center is on November 8, and we'll need to be getting ready for that. The Forepaughs have invited us to sit at their table—with you and Melissa, of course."

25. Party Time

Late that night, after Andrew and David had both gone to bed, Patti stood alone on the balcony, confiding her deepest thoughts to Achilles. That noble reptile—captured in the South Seas by Captain Cook, house-trained by Marie Antoinette (a refinement unfortunately lost in the tumult of the French Revolution), ridden as a child by Winston Churchill at the Hyde Park Zoo, sold into pethood at the end of the Second World War—betrayed scant interest in her soliloquy. Under Patti's ownership he had suffered the indignity of devolving into patio furniture, and if he could read her mind he would have learned that an even grimmer fate awaited him. She was desperately in need of money. If she earned no commissions before the end of the year, she'd already decided, Achilles's long and meaningless existence would have to be exchanged for a claim against Pet Life, provided that he could be dispatched without arousing the suspicion of the insurance company. How would they view a suicidal plunge off the 19th floor balcony onto the sidewalk below? He'd grown despondent, she would tell them. Old (300+). Infirm (never left the balcony). Had lost his *joie de vivre*. She made a mental note to have Andrew check the Pet Life policy to see if suicide was covered.

The crisis which had triggered these desperate musings was Andrew's increasingly obvious aversion to Melissa. And who could blame him? She was an awkward, unattractive girl, with her wall-eyed stare and her food fetishes and her obsession with that vicious little dog Pickles. But if Andrew didn't marry her—and soon—the proud race of the Oglebys, once synonymous with power and wealth, would go the way of the Habsburgs, the Romanovs and the Grateful Dead. Only a marriage to money—even money with a distinct odor of pet food—could save them from extinction. Oh, if people only knew how broke they were! David had squandered everything, literally everything, on his drinking and gambling and God knows what else. All that remained of the family fortune was tied up in non-profits, with the non-profits now under the control of Bob Baskerville. She and David were living on hors d'oeuvres carried home in doggie bags from receptions and fund raisers, running up bills they couldn't pay, falling behind in their condo association fees. If she didn't sell a unit by the end of the year, the house of cards would collapse. And all her dirty little secrets would come to light.

"If trophy wives were bred like Jack Russell terriers," she confessed to Achilles, "I'd have come from some puppy mill in South Carolina. Long before I met David, I did some things I hope no one will ever find out about. Not that I'm ashamed of them—I'm not ashamed of anything. But why should anyone find out? That was a long time ago, longer than anybody can remember. And look at me now: a hot blonde, a mover and a shaker in the real estate market, President of the Homeowners Association. But what about Andrew? Though I love him as a son, he can't be allowed to ruin the family, just because he's revolted by Melissa. There's obviously some other girl in the picture. Who would know about that? His secretary, of course—the secretary always knows. I met her at the Homeless Art Museum. What was her name? Clea? I'll give

her a call, see what she can tell me. And if there's any legwork
to be done tracking this girl down and knocking her out of
contention, I know just the man to ask. The beefy concierge
who desperately wants to get me into bed. Mike Malatesta."

That brought up another problem: the Wurlitzers. "How
did the Forepaughs find out the Wurlitzers live in this
building?" she asked Achilles (again without eliciting a
response). "What a fiasco! Though you can't really blame them
for refusing to move in next door to a whistleblower who blew
the whistle on their own cat food factory. They're a nice
enough couple, the Wurlitzers, though hopelessly naive in their
determination to bring children into this world, where people
are struggling to pay their gym dues and pool fees. But if their
presence here means the Forepaughs won't buy a unit, the
Wurlitzers will have to go—and the sooner the better. As
President of the Homeowners Association, I can practically
guarantee that they'll be out by the end of the year. All it will
take is a word with Mike Malatesta, then a quick conversation
with the Wurlitzers in the lobby, when the two of them are
together and no one else is around...

*"Rosemary and Rick! Did I tell you about the party you're supposed
to have? There's an unwritten rule—or is it in the covenants?—that new
people have to throw a party within their first three months and invite
everybody else in the building. It's a theme party, and this year's theme
has already been chosen—not that anyone knows it other than the
Management Committee: It's 'Fifty Shades of Grey.' Sounds a little
tame, doesn't it? I totally agree with you. The women here have all read
the books and seen the movies—most of us could have written them
ourselves—so obviously you're going to have to spice it up a bit. Neckties
are OK as far as they go—but let's face it, they don't go far enough. If*

you want to impress people—and at this stage you really need to impress people, your whole future in the building depends on it—I think you'd get a lot more mileage out of whips and chains. No substitute for the real thing, you know.

"I'll let you in on a secret: people in this building are a little bit hypocritical. They pretend to be very boring and conservative, but get them at a party—even the retired attorneys and the little old ladies who go around with walkers—and all bets are off. All clothes are off too, more often than not, and wait till you see what's underneath them: the huge, multi-colored tattoos—you have those, I assume?—and the piercings of every conceivable flap of flesh. If you're a little behind in that department, I can refer you to the tattoo parlor on South Street where everyone who's anyone goes. You'll need to dress right, of course, if only to have the right clothes to go without. The concierge, Mike Malatesta—he's the only one other than myself who's allowed to know what the theme is—can help you with that. I'd recommend a 'biker' theme to go along with the whips and chains: For you, Rick: a Harley-Davidson drive chain around your neck, skin-tight leather pants, open at the crotch; and for you, Rosemary: chain mail over bare breasts and a dominatrix outfit. You'll need a generous supply of duct tape and party drugs (ecstasy, crystal meth, that sort of thing), some edgy hors d'oeuvres (I'd recommend high-gluten, GMO-rich pastries stuffed with dolphin meat), and of course hard-core porn loops on the flat screen TV. Mike can help you with the details."

Achilles, cursing the twists of fate which had brought him to Patti's balcony from his ancestral home in the Galapagos Islands, closed his heavy lids and ignored the rest of her monologue.

26. We Are But We Are Not

Hector spent the week dreading his next meeting with Arbuthnot. On Saturday night he stayed home and watched Univision with his *abuelita*, rather than going out to Shazam to meet Gwendolyn, who (thanks to Alice) he suspected of having designs on him in violation of the Compliance Manual. He told himself that his assignment from Arbuthnot took precedence over the sex investigation. True, Gwendolyn was his supervisor, but Arbuthnot—though he wasn't on any of the Bank's org charts—seemed to outrank her. He could usually be found in the employee cafeteria, sipping coffee out of a styrofoam cup. One afternoon after lunch he signaled to Hector as Hector was returning his tray, and Hector followed him out into the hall. He led Hector around a corner to an unmarked door which opened to an unused office. Again Arbuthnot took a seat behind the desk and Hector sat across from him on an uncomfortable wooden chair.

"Have you made any headway on our problem?" Arbuthnot asked, pulling a yellow legal pad out of a drawer so he could take notes. "Where's the money going?"

"I think it's a kind of inefficiency," Hector said, "or lack of productivity. Waste."

"Waste?"

Hector thought back to his conversation with Alice, though he'd decided to avoid any mention of the Potlatch. "People are just spinning their wheels. Hanging out in bars, driving around, eating in outdoor restaurants. Chatting on their phones."

Arbuthnot glared back with vexed incredulity. "There may be a misunderstanding here," he said evenly. "You think you've discovered flaws in the economy. Actually, what you've discovered *is* the economy."

"But if... but if that's the economy," Hector stammered, "then what's the problem?"

"The problem, as I believe you've been told, is entropic deceleration. The system is losing energy, slowing down. If present trends continue, it will grind to a halt in five years. The stimulus package might work for a little while, but in the long run, the only thing that can save us is an act of God."

Hector felt his chest tightening, his stomach clenching, as he recalled something he'd learned in Economics 101. "But in the long run," he gasped, "we'll all be dead."

"Precisely. The best we can hope for—and we can only pray that it'll happen soon—is an earthquake above 9.3 on the Richter scale."

It's the Potlatch! Hector thought. What he's talking about is a natural disaster followed by a monumental make-work project. Should I act like I know what the Potlatch is? Should I say anything about the woman at the Homeless Art Museum and her shadowy organization—*Somos pero no somos: we are but we are not*—that's dedicated to destroy it?

Arbuthnot spoke before Hector could make up his mind. "There's a glimmer of hope in the most recent data," he said. "An uptick in construction supplies being shipped into the area. Marble from Italy, granite from Vermont, lumber from Idaho. Even a portcullis coming in on a ship from Scotland."

"A portcullis?"

"One of those spiky iron gates they put in front of castles."

"Somebody's building a castle?"

"Somewhere in Northeast Philadelphia," Arbuthnot nodded. "Last place you'd expect, isn't it? But it's good news for the economy."

On the way home that night, still troubled by his conversation with Arbuthnot, Hector stopped at Mr. Reddy's store to pick up a can of Goya black beans for his *abuelita*. As he paid for the beans, he noticed Tiffany, Alice's sister, standing a few feet away, her arms laden with plastic bottles of shampoo, hair spray, eye make-up and other Health and Beauty Aids. "I saw you with Alice the day you took her to lunch," she said with a knowing smile.

"Yeah," Hector blushed. "Actually, we just went over—"

"She's crazy about you."

"She is?"

"Head over heels."

"Next," Mr. Reddy said impatiently, though there was no one in line behind him.

There was a lilt in Hector's step as he walked home from the store. He handed the can of black beans to his grandmother, changed his clothes and consumed his dinner in a daze. *She's crazy about you. Head over heels.* Was his dream coming true?

After dinner he glanced at his phone and found a message from Andrew, who wanted to meet him downtown at a bar called the Red Rooster. He hopped on a bus and joined his friend within half an hour. It was one of those shadowy, low-ceilinged places where lawyers take their secretaries after work. Andrew huddled at the bar by himself with an empty whisky glass, jiggling a tumblerful of ice. He was drinking Jameson neat and seemed to be lost in thought. When Hector sat beside him, he waved to the bartender and ordered two more shots. "How's the investigation going?" he asked after a while. "Is sex going to survive the twenty-first century?"

"Seems to be going strong."

"Plenty of supply and demand, and all that?"

"Well," Hector smiled, "more demand than supply."

Andrew dropped an ice cube in his glass and savored a long sip. "Drives up the price."

"The price?"

"Metaphorically." He downed the rest of his whisky and waved to the bartender for another round. "Most guys would never pay for sex—they want it for free, like a cell phone. But it's not exactly free, is it? When you read the fine print in the service agreement."

Hector laughed and took the bait. "How's Melissa?"

"I'm looking for a better plan before I sign my life away."

The bartender set up two more shots, even though Hector had barely touched his first one. Andrew hoisted his glass in a solitary toast. "Actually, there's another woman I'm interested in," he said. "She might live in your neighborhood. Do you know anyone named Alice?"

"Alice?... No!" Hector stammered. "Alice? As in Alice in Wonderland? As in Alice Cooper? As in Alice's Restaurant? As in—"

"Okay, I get it. You don't know her."

"Right. Never heard of anyone named Alice."

Andrew stood up to leave. "Thanks for coming over, Hector. I've got to get going."

Andrew left Hector at the bar in the midst of a moral and existential crisis. Except for that time in the third grade when, to protect his dog, he'd told his teacher that his baby brother ate his homework, this was the first time Hector had ever lied about anything. And it was worse than that: he had deceived a friend, perpetrating the worst kind of evil: the sin of betrayal, which Dante punished in the deepest circle of Hell. His training in medieval theology told him he was damned, but economics offered a ray of hope. Everything that happens is for the best in a free market, where each person, in pursuing his own self-interest, is led by an Invisible Hand to promote the general good. He knew where the Invisible Hand was guiding him, and why: he wanted Alice for himself. And she was crazy about him. "Head over heels," Tiffany had said.

As Hector bolted down his Jameson—it was way more than he usually drank, but he was in a mood to celebrate—he felt an ominous presence on the barstool beside him. Andrew's place had been taken by the mysterious woman from the Homeless Art Museum, who belonged to some shadowy group dedicated to resisting the Potlatch. "The people you're working for at the Bank are evil," she said in a low voice without turning to face him.

"Are you talking about Gwendolyn and Maureen?" he gasped.

"This goes way beyond Gwendolyn and Maureen."

"The Board of Governesses? Arbuthnot?"

She touched his arm and leaned closer. "Some say the Bank is controlled by a race of malignant dwarfs whose sole aim is to protect their treasure hoard. That they have enchanted the population by giving them an infinite number of meaningless tasks to perform. That when the people awake from their trance, it will be too late."

Hector realized that he'd had way too much to drink. "What are you talking about?"

"Those who speak, don't know," she said. "Those who know, don't speak."

He turned to face her for the first time. She was older than he was, possibly in her mid-thirties. Her clothes were expensive but nondescript: a white blouse, a gray business suit, pin earrings but no other jewelry. Her dark eyes looked like they would never betray a secret.

"Why are you talking to me?" he asked her.

"We're recruiting interns all over the city to join in the resistance. You have nothing to lose but your paychecks."

He chuckled, maybe a little too loud. "We don't get paychecks."

"Exactly." She tossed a bill on the bar and stood up to leave. "Be careful. They will tell you anything. They will deny that we exist. They will deny that *they* exist. They will deny that *anything* exists."

"Who are you?"

"You can call me Maria."

"But who are you?"

"*Somos pero no somos.*"

27. The Law Is An Ass

Andrew's next hurdle in the Eric Johnstone case was a meeting with the prosecution team, consisting of Eric's probation officer (Kyle Rotundo, the son of a powerful judge), the arresting officer (an African-American police detective named Blakely), and an Assistant DA named Mabel Fernandez, who did most of the talking. The meeting was held in a shabby, windowless conference room in City Hall, with Andrew on one side of the table and the prosecution team on the other. A ceiling fan whirled over their heads like the propeller on a World War II vintage fighter plane, threatening to scatter the contents of their files unless they clamped them down with both hands. "For Eric Johnstone," Ms. Fernandez began, trying to peek into her file without letting it blow away, "we're looking for at least two years of jail time."

"Jail time?" Andrew gasped. "You haven't even charged him with anything!"

Cupping their hands over their mouths, Mabel Fernandez and Kyle Rotundo leaned closer and conferred like a pitcher and catcher on the mound. "Then you are prepared to accept our offer," Ms. Fernandez said, turning toward Andrew, "provided that we file charges against your client?"

Andrew couldn't help laughing. "That's ridiculous."

She peeked into her file again and squinted at the documents. "Mr. Johnstone attempted to lie his way out of the self-esteem improvement group by feigning high self-esteem. After belligerently informing the therapist that he had no need for the group and would no longer attend its meetings, he walked out and failed to return the next day. When police officers came to arrest him, he attempted to flee."

"Have you ever talked to Eric?" Andrew asked.

"Of course not."

"I have. There's nothing wrong with his self-esteem."

"Look," Detective Blakely interjected, "if the guy has such high self-esteem, what's he doing in jail? You think those are the best and the brightest in there?"

"All he needs is a job," Andrew pleaded. "He can't find one as long as he spends all his time going to therapy groups."

"You think anybody's going to hire an ex-con?" Kyle Rotundo, chuckled. He was Eric's parole officer, an oversized young man with the face of a friendly pit bull. "Dream on!"

"If Mr. Johnstone continues to be incarcerated," Ms. Fernandez said, with a confirming glance at her team, "he'll have access to the kind of professional help he needs. Once he admits to having low self-esteem, the prison's team of self-esteem improvement counselors can help bring it up."

"Well, then," Andrew said, "there won't be any plea. We'll go to trial."

"Go to trial?" A suppressed guffaw twittered among the members of the prosecution team as they shot amused glances at each other. "Did I hear you correctly?" Ms. Fernandez asked.

"Yes, I said go to trial."

"You're a new attorney—maybe you still don't know the ropes—so let me spell it out for you. We're offering your client twenty-four months, with credit for time served. That's a very generous offer for someone who can't make bail. The case backlog is longer than our computers can keep track of. If your client doesn't plead, his trial, if he ever has one, will be years or possibly decades in the future. Twenty months from now—and long after that—he'll still be rotting in that hellhole in Northeast Philadelphia."

"Hey, watch out!" Kyle Rotundo objected good-naturedly. "My dad owns that jail."

Andrew could hardly believe what he'd heard. "Your dad?" he cried, pawing madly through his file. "Your dad is Judge Rotundo, right? The judge who set the bond at $100,000, and is supposed to conduct the trial? He owns the jail?"

"Well, not exactly," Kyle Rotundo admitted. "The City owns the jail. My dad owns the contractor that operates it."

"It's all legal and proper," Mabel Fernandez explained.

All legal and proper? Where had Andrew heard that phrase before?

It took only a single phone call for Patti to enlist Andrew's secretary in her campaign to destroy Alice. Clea (who was secretly in league with Tiffany) told Patti where to find Alice: interning at Gallaher Catering, serving at fundraisers, living at home in South Philly with a pair of dysfunctional grifters who never left their row house; and the more Patti heard, the more incensed she became that Andrew would show the least interest in such a person. With Melissa hovering in limbo and her parents deliberating their next real estate purchase, this upstart rival for Andrew's affections needed to be tracked down and eliminated—a task which Patti, settling on a scorched earth policy, had assigned to the concierge, Mike

Malatesta. Mike was a thuggish lowlife who could drive the
Wurlitzers out of the building before the Forepaughs realized
they lived there. To enlist his aid, all she had to do was hint
that his efforts would be rewarded with a roll in the hay.

Mike knew it was only a matter of time before Patti would
give him what he wanted. In the gym one day, after she
noticed him peeking around a corner, she'd whispered that she
looked forward to seeing more of him as soon as she could get
Andrew out of the house. She was bored with her husband,
she said, and if Andrew married Melissa she'd be spending a lot
more time alone in her apartment. What could that mean, he
asked himself, but that she wanted to go to bed with him?
Sure, she was a little older than he was, but still as hot as they
come. All she wanted him to do was to follow some girl
named Alice and do "whatever it takes" to keep her away from
Andrew. To Mike, coming from South Philly, "whatever it
takes" meant he might have to rough somebody up, or worse.
Patti didn't know—nobody in the building knew—that Mike
had done time for stalking women after he graduated from
high school. Well, he didn't exactly graduate, but they didn't
know that either. No harm, no foul, was how he looked at it.
Oh, yeah, there was one other thing Patti wanted: she'd asked
him to help out the Wurlitzers, the new residents she'd taken
under her wing, with a party they were planning. Having
sorted their mail for a month, he thought he knew all about the
Wurlitzers. But Patti had let him in on a secret: they were
hosting a "Fifty Shades of Grey" party and inviting everyone in
the building, including blue-haired Mrs. Levine on the sixteenth
floor and old Mr. Whitbourne, who stumbled around with an
oxygen tank and tubes up his nose. And they needed Mike to

help them plan the party? No problem. He had some biker friends from the old neighborhood who'd supply the party drugs, along with the whips and chains. He'd bring the porno movies (though his collection was admittedly light on senior S&M). He'd already escorted the Wurlitzers to the tattoo parlor on South Street that Patti recommended, so when they took off their clothes at the party—apparently everybody would be taking off their clothes—they'd look like they stepped out of a Gothic horror comic. Hey, if that's what they wanted—and what Patti wanted—he was happy to lend a hand. "Don't tell anyone else about the party," she'd warned him. "It's a surprise."

Some surprise! he chuckled, wondering if he should bring a spare oxygen tank for Mr. Whitbourne. But at the moment his chief concern was this girl named Alice. He had to track her down and do whatever it took to keep her away from Andrew. Piece of cake.

28. Against The Odds

Alice Coggins

The Mega Millions jackpot is up to $400 million and my Dad's only worry is how he's going to spend it. Even his castle won't be able to soak up all that cash. He's ordered a pair of gold-plated thrones from India, a Las Vegas juke box, pinball machines, flat-screen TVs for all fifty rooms—but that hardly makes a dent. "How about a torture chamber?" Mom asks him. "What's a castle without a torture chamber? You could sleep in there." He's hired lawyers from the biggest firms (I think he might need them), a bodyguard service (them too), and a financial planner (probably not). On the strength of his spending plans, banks are lining up to lend him millions and local merchants say he's putting new life in the economy. Not that he has actually paid for anything, or ever will. His only asset is the two-dollar lottery ticket he bought from Mr. Reddy.

The odds against it winning, as of last night, were 667, 777, 999 to 1.

As for me, I'm not doing too well. My weight started ballooning at the Stark Raven fundraiser and hasn't let up since. I feel nauseous when I remember that night. What was I thinking? Did I really think Tiffany would let me get away with wearing her dress? I should definitely stop taking advice from Grandma—she's senile, practically dead, like everybody in that Health Center. I think the old guy who's always next to her, Armand, actually is dead but nobody's noticed it yet. Next time I visit Grandma I'm going to see if his brains are leaking out. (OK, Tiffany's right—I read too many zombie novels.) I can't believe how my statistics have deteriorated since the fundraiser: Weight: +19. Confidence level: -9,999. If my self-esteem goes any lower, rocks will start rolling away from me when I try to crawl under them. Short of being dipped in plastic to become one of those nude sculptures they have at Stark Raven, my odds of ever seeing Andrew again are about the same as for my Dad to win the lottery.

And now, as if just being me wasn't bad enough, I think Baby Boy Barkocy has got somebody stalking me, maybe Howie the psycho. My Dad says not to worry as long as I keep my mouth shut, but lately something's changed. Wherever I go, I sense cars creeping up behind me, footsteps in the darkness, figures ducking into doorways. Is it Howie or something worse—some anonymous killer dispatched to keep me quiet forever? I'm so scared I even let Hector walk me home from the bus. He seems different lately—like all the self-confidence that's been sucked out of me has been blown into him. But apart from that, I think he might be going nuts. As we walked past Mr. Reddy's store, he brought up that mysterious woman he met at the Homeless Art Museum—Maria, he calls her now—who's supposedly part of some group fighting the Potlatch. She dropped in on him again and told him a crazy story (which he believed) about the Federal Reserve Bank being controlled by evil dwarfs obsessed with guarding a hoard of treasure.

"Dwarfs?" I repeated, just to make sure I heard it right.

He nodded solemnly. I tried not to laugh, because I would've been laughing at him. "Hector," I said, "I can't believe you fell for that. It's like something out of *The Hobbit.*"

"That's what makes it so scary."

"But isn't this just another joke your boss is playing on you? Gwendolyn or whatever her name is? First the sex investigation and now this. You didn't show up at her favorite club and now she's getting back at you."

Hector wasn't convinced. "No, I think Maria may be right," he said. "The Potlatch is evil and the Bank is behind it. You're an intern too, Alice. I wouldn't be surprised if Somos tried to recruit you."

"Somos?"

"*Somos pero no somos,*" he said. "We are but we are not."

Maybe I'm a little paranoid from being stalked by a hit man (that'll do it every time), but Hector's vision of an evil conspiracy has been preying on me. Forget the malignant dwarfs, but couldn't the Potlatch be the reason my generation is getting screwed—a hidden government of rackets within rackets dedicated to keeping us busy with meaningless tasks so we don't see it for what it is? For all I know, the stalker who's after me was sent by the Potlatch, not by Baby Boy—or the Potlatch is run by Baby Boy, in his cleaned-up incarnation as Bob Baskerville, more dangerous than he ever was as a loan-sharking butcher in South Philadelphia.

I wondered what Randolph would say. He knows more about the Potlatch than anyone. "Does the Potlatch have secret agents?" I asked him one night out on the stoop after my Dad went inside. "You know, like spies or hit men or something who might follow you around to make sure you don't get out of line?"

"Sure they do," he said. "The Potlatch don't mess around."

"So if everything you do gets screwed up and your life's turning into a nightmare and you start to think there's somebody stalking you..."

"It's all part of the Potlatch."

29. The Set Up

Events unfolded quickly after that, with a logic as irresistible as Fate:

Patti hatching her plan with Clea, with Clea taking her cues from Tiffany.

Clea telling Andrew that she's heard Alice has a boyfriend.

Tiffany telling Alice that Hector and Andrew are friends, planting the idea that Hector could lead her to Andrew.

Tiffany offering to help Hector get closer to Alice.

"Alice is crazy about you," Tiffany tells Hector, "waiting for you to make your move. First you need to get Andrew away from her. All you've got to do is tell Alice you've talked to him about her, and he doesn't like her. He said she's fat and ugly and stupid."

"Andrew wouldn't say that."

"Of course he would. He's a rich snob who'd never go out with a waitress. Anyway he's engaged to Melissa."

Tiffany setting the scene in Rittenhouse Square, where Andrew, after an early lunch with Patti, will be steered toward a park bench where Alice and Hector are playing out their little drama.

All Hector has to do is follow the script, telling Alice: "Andrew loves Melissa and he's going to marry her."

Alice, as predicted, in tears.

"She's not crying because she loves Andrew," Tiffany explains to Hector in advance, "but because she loves *you*. This is when you make your move. This is where you reach out and wrap your arms around her. Show her that you love her."

Ray Coggins would have been impressed with this set-up, even envious, as he was with any elaborate con. It was plotted out in minute detail, each molecule bumping into each other molecule at just the right speed and angle to produce the desired effect. Just like the universe itself.

30. Pro Bono Publico

Andrew had grown increasingly despondent in his search for Alice. Clea and Tiffany must have known where to find her, but they met his questions with a stone wall of silence. Hector, not surprisingly, had no idea who she was. Gallaher Catering refused to divulge the names or phone numbers of its interns. Andrew had been reduced to attending fundraisers (sometimes three or four in one night) for nonprofits he'd never heard of—the Museum of Early American Spoons, the Police Malevolent Association, the Society of War of 1812 Re-Enactors (a shadowy right-wing group which has since been charged with plotting to burn the White House)—all catered by Gallaher Catering, but still no sign of Alice. When Melissa complained, he dragged her along with him, hoping to bore her out of his life (to his chagrin, she developed an interest in Early American spoons and signed up to participate in the bombardment of Baltimore). Every morning he fended off Patti's demand that he and Melissa set a wedding date before the end of the year. The day of reckoning could not be postponed much longer.

One morning Patti casually asked him to meet her for an early lunch at a French restaurant on Rittenhouse Square. "I... I have a meeting at the DA's office at 11:00," he stammered. "On my pro bono case. Afterwards I'll need to talk to my client."

"We wouldn't want to inconvenience the criminal element, would we?"

"It's not that, it's just—"

"Surely you can get out of your meeting by 11:30," she said. "Your client will still be in jail after lunch."

"OK, I guess so."

Her tone was ominous. "We have things we need to discuss."

Shortly before 11:00 o'clock, Andrew headed to City Hall for another propeller-driven conference with the prosecution team: Detective C. Blakely, Probation Officer Kyle Rotundo, and Assistant District Attorney Mabel Fernandez. When he arrived they sat huddled around Kyle's phone playing a Pokémon game. "Have a seat," Ms. Fernandez said curtly. "We'll be with you in a minute."

She flipped aside her wind-blown hair as she sat down. "We just wanted to give you one more chance to reconsider our generous offer," she said. "Have you discussed this with Mr. Johnstone?"

"Of course," Andrew said. "He and I agree that it would be in his best interest to go to trial."

"His best interest!" she sniffed. She cast her eyes at Detective Blakely, who nodded knowingly. "Of course you wouldn't expect a criminal to care how his actions affect other people."

"That's why he's a criminal," Detective Blakely observed.

"There's a word for that," Ms. Fernandez said, pointing her forefinger at Andrew. "Sociopath. These people are sociopaths."

"All he wants is to get a job," Andrew objected. "After all—"

"Has your client considered all the people who'd lose *their* jobs if we let this go on?"

"Cops," Detective Blakely said bitterly. "Prison guards. Cafeteria workers."

"Probation officers," Kyle Rotundo added. "Social workers. Substance abuse counselors. Anger management experts."

"Bail bondsmen," Detective Blakely said. "Bounty hunters."

"Self-esteem improvement specialists," Kyle Rotundo added.

"And let's not forget attorneys," Assistant District Attorney Fernandez said with a sly smile. "Prosecutors, investigators, paralegals, clerks, judges, magistrates, bailiffs, marshals, court reporters, jury consultants, process servers— and yes, even slimy defense lawyers like you."

"I'm an intern," Andrew objected, packing up his files. "I'm not even getting paid."

"And don't forget about my dad," Kyle Rotundo said with a smile as Andrew lurched to his feet. "You think he can live on his judge's salary?"

Andrew fled the DA's office in despair, unnerved by the realization that Eric Johnstone was doomed to spend a large chunk of his life in jail. If he pled guilty—to what crime was still unknown—he'd serve another twenty months; if he refused to plead, he could be incarcerated for years before his case came to trial. It seemed obvious to Andrew that the prosecution was taking advantage of his inexperience, but what could he do? Wasn't an inexperienced lawyer better than no lawyer at all?

Patti was well into her second martini when he arrived at the restaurant. She had ordered his lunch as well as her own—some kind of mussels, which she knew he hated. That was a bad sign.

"There's something you apparently need to be told," she said, wasting no time on preliminaries, "though it should be obvious." She downed the rest of her drink and signaled to the waiter for another. "If you're not getting married, you can't just go on living at home."

Andrew tried to parse her words as if they were a legal text. "But I *can* go on living at home if I do get married?"

"If you and Melissa get married," she smirked, amused at the attempt, "I'm sure her parents will set you up in a nice apartment in a less expensive building. I even know of one that just came on the market. But if you don't get married, you can't go on living at the most expensive address in the city without paying your fair share. I mean the mortgage, the monthly maintenance, the parking fee, the pool fee, the gym fee—"

"I don't use the gym."

"I do," she laughed. "Anyway, you get the idea. This is for your own good."

"Like some horrible tasting medicine."

"Exactly."

He poked his fork into some mussels and stirred them around without eating any. "How am I supposed to pay for it?"

"You have a job. You're a lawyer, in fact."

"I don't get paid, though."

"Of course not. Nobody your age gets paid. That's why they're all living at home."

Andrew spread some butter on a roll and ate it. "Have you talked to my Dad about this?"

"Your dad, bless his heart, is so clueless when it comes to money that he would let me sell you into slavery if I asked him nicely. Why do you think he's in nonprofits? He lost every dime we had at a casino in Atlantic City. There's a nonprofit for you."

She glanced at her watch and signaled to the waiter for the check. "Think about it," she told Andrew. "But don't think too much. I need a commission from the Forepaughs by the end of the year."

She paid the check but lingered at the table as if waiting for someone. To Andrew's surprise, Clea, his secretary, appeared at the door and walked over to the table. "Mr. Wolf wants to talk to you," she told him.

"Now?"

"Yes. Right now."

Patti stood up quickly and led Andrew outside, and the two of them followed Clea on the sidewalk that ran along the edge of Rittenhouse Square Park. Suddenly Clea stopped, and so did Patti, as they gazed across the iron fence to a young couple facing each other on a park bench about twenty-five feet away. Andrew followed their gaze and almost choked at what he saw. The woman on the bench was Alice, and she was with Hector—his best friend, who'd insisted he didn't know her! And it was far worse than a simple case of deception. Alice was in the throes of some powerful emotion. Hector leaned toward her and murmured something in her ear. Then he reached out and wrapped his arms around her, and she hugged him back fiercely.

"Isn't that your friend Hector?" Patti asked. "Who's that girl he's with?"

"I... I don't know."

"So much in love!"

Andrew followed Clea back to his office in a daze, where Mr. Wolf had already left for the day. That night he skipped the fundraiser he'd been planning to attend (it was the annual meeting of the League of Lithuanian-American Law Librarians, held in a booth at the Denny's on City Ave.) and called Melissa to suggest that they pick an early date for the wedding.

III.

31. Education

Education everywhere. Education—the city's biggest industry—flourishing in pre-schools, elementary schools, middle schools, high schools, charter schools, public schools, private schools, Catholic schools, Quaker schools, Montessori schools, Waldorf schools, vocational schools, dancing schools, art schools, driving schools...

Education everywhere. Disseminated by an army of teachers, counselors, coaches, athletic directors, principals, assistant principals, superintendents, professors, associate professors, assistant professors, adjunct professors, visiting professors, instructors, lecturers, teaching assistants, deans, provosts, secretaries, lunch ladies, custodians, bus drivers, nurses, security guards...

Education everywhere. Reaching its heights in junior colleges, community colleges, universities, graduate schools, trade schools, business schools, law schools, medical schools, engineering schools, nursing schools, library schools, dental schools, barber schools, clown schools, bartending schools, embalming schools...

Education everywhere. Surely the city's children and young people—the beneficiaries of this dazzling array of resources—must be the best educated in the world. Such, at any rate, was the proud hope of Rosemary Wurlitzer as she looked forward to starting her new job—her first job as a teacher—at the famous Desmond Gallaher High School in Southwest

Philadelphia. By all accounts it was one of the best schools in
the city, if not in the nation.

Teaching in an inner-city school had been Rosemary's
ambition since her first year of college. In the suburbs where
she grew up, everyone looked alike, lived in identical houses,
and had the same amount of money. Her social consciousness
was aroused her first week at UCLA, when she perceived the
injustice inherent in 1% of the students being able to afford
better phones than the other 99%, together with unlimited
data. The 1% also wore cooler gym clothes, drank Grey Goose
vodka while the poorer students drank Absolut, and spent an
extra three days in Panama City on spring break. These
privileged students—who on graduation would also claim the
best internships—lived in luxury high-rises with pools, gyms
and saunas when they weren't in Africa or Central America
building schools or educating the populace on the importance
of a gluten-free diet. The less fortunate students (including
Rosemary) had to subsist on a sickeningly glutinous diet
consisting entirely of beer and taco chips, purchased with
student loans they'd be repaying the rest of their lives. The
sheer injustice of it all infuriated Rosemary and brought her
into the streets when the poorly-paid adjunct professors called
a strike. The strike was orderly at first but it got ugly when the
paint on Rosemary's BMW was scratched and a gang of strikers
blocked the entrance to her dorm. More violence ensued—
several students' phones were damaged by the police—which
didn't end until the National Guard chased the adjunct
professors back into their shantytown along the river. These
experiences radicalized Rosemary in a way that was typical of

her generation. She resolved that she would become a teacher in an inner-city school, and that she would never, ever, live anywhere but in a first-class building with a doorman and a parking garage.

Even now she wondered if her marriage to Rick had been a mistake. He was a pot head from South Jersey with a dual major in pet care and industrial espionage, whose parents drove a Chevy Blazer and had plastic covers over their living room furniture. Before she married him, she made it clear that he would have to upgrade, which he did, to the point where he no longer felt embarrassed walking their Portuguese water dog in Birkenstocks and a Greenpeace T-shirt. But lately she'd felt the onset of a nameless *ennui*, or *nausée*, or some such French emotion, as she sensed Rick reverting to form and threatening the progress they'd made to the American Dream. Yes, they had plenty of money, thanks to Rick's brief career as a whistleblower at the pet food factory, and yes, she was excited about their new apartment in the Walden Towers, and yes— not that there was anything wrong with Aden, Jaden or Caden, other than exorbitant veterinarian bills—she looked forward to her first child, a boy named Hayden whose hoped-for conception through in vitro fertilization had been putting a strain on their marriage. Neither she nor Rick had any fertility issues using the traditional method of conception, and she was afraid that Rick was starting to enjoy his visits to the fertility clinic, where he'd taken a shine to one of the nurses, but Patti Ogleby, who'd been so kind in advising them on interior decoration and the unwritten rules of the building, had left no doubt in their minds that IVF was the only way to go. Recently Patti had informed them about the "Fifty Shades of

Grey" party they were required to host for the building residents, and again Rick seemed a little too enthusiastic— hanging whips and chains in their bedroom, asking her to dress up in that dominatrix outfit, dragging her to the tattoo parlor on South Street ("These things come off, right?") and letting that creepy concierge Mike Malatesta leave his hard-core porno movies lying around the apartment. She definitely needed to spend more time out of the house and away from Rick.

So naturally she'd been delighted when Dr. Morton Hauptfuhrer, the principal of Desmond Gallaher High School, had called and hired her, sight unseen, to fill an unexpected vacancy that arose when one of the English teachers left on pet adoption leave after the beginning of the school year. Dr. Hauptfuhrer had very kindly invited her to come in for a tour before she began her teaching duties. "How about Thursday at 9:30?" he suggested. "Late enough to avoid the early morning rush."

She was unbelievably excited and proud as she drove down the cheerless streets to the school. Suddenly there it was, a three-story brick building—Who was Desmond Gallaher? she wondered. Was he one of those old-time presidents, like Grover Cleveland or Chester Alan Arthur?—with a red tile roof. A little shabby, but nothing a little elbow grease couldn't fix. There were no broken windows, no graffiti, no drug dealers or gangs hanging around. Admittedly the school had a razor-wire fence around the perimeter, and a manned security gate at the main entrance, but those had become standard at inner city schools. Something caught her eye, and for an instant she thought she saw a sniper on the roof. But when she looked up, whatever she'd seen—probably a bird—had disappeared.

She sailed easily through the security gate, relieved to see that urban tensions hadn't turned the school into an Orwellian nightmare. Dr. Hauptfuhrer, the principal, greeted her warmly and took her on a tour of the facility, nodding to the security guards who idled at fifty-foot intervals in the halls. He was definitely old school: a pale, bespectacled man in a conservative suit and brightly polished shoes who beamed with pride at what he'd accomplished. "We run a tight ship here at Gallaher," he told Rosemary. "We have the highest test scores, the highest graduation rate, the lowest student/faculty ratio, the best safety record and the most attractive salaries and benefits of any high school in the city."

Rosemary had never been so impressed. The halls and classrooms were immaculate. The library books were filed neatly on the shelves. The spacious faculty lounge boasted leather sofas, flat-screen TVs and a Starbucks franchise; dozens of teachers relaxed reading magazines, watching TV or fiddling with their phones. Proceeding with the tour, Dr. Hauptfuhrer led her down a wide hallway where she met the cafeteria administrator, the coaching administrator, the compliance administrator, the computer lab administrator, the curriculum administrator—"And those are just the C's," he smiled. "We have a whole wing for the T's and S's."

Gallaher High was a dream come true. So orderly, so clean, so quiet. Almost eerily quiet. What was missing? Rosemary wondered.

The tour had brought them back around to the main security gate, where the guards clustered around a student who must have arrived a little late. He stood splayed against the wall, legs apart, hands over his head, as four guards patted him down and ran a sensing wand over his clothing and between his legs. When they'd completed this inspection they sat him in front of a retinal scanner and peppered him with security questions—"What's your mother's middle name? What was the name of your first pet?"—and made him recite the Gettysburg Address. The student—he was a skinny black kid in a Sixers hoody—was sweating and trembling but he made it through the ordeal. "He's clean," one of the guards told the principal.

"OK, take him in to be fingerprinted."

"Fingerprinted?" Rosemary gasped.

"It's been a tense morning," Dr. Hauptfuhrer explained. "We had to go into lockdown."

"Was there a riot? I don't see any—"

"We have a zero tolerance policy here at Gallaher."

"Zero tolerance of what?"

"Drugs, bullying, weapons, smoking, peanuts, tree nuts, envy, sloth, greed—there's a complete list on file in my office if you want to spend an hour reading it. You can thank the students for that. Believe me, it's been a much better work environment since we stopped letting them in."

That's why it was so quiet, Rosemary realized. "Where are the students?"

"In jail, mostly, if they haven't OD'd. At least we've managed to keep them out of here."

32. Fate

Rosemary was in tears by the time she got back to the Walden Towers, shaken by the cynicism of Dr. Hauptfuhrer, who insisted that Gallaher High, even without students—especially without students—was the best school in the city. True, it offered the most attractive salary and benefits, including (and this, he reminded her, was the only reason she got the job) pet adoption leave. As she drove home—having already decided, following Patti's advice, to adopt a tortoise—she couldn't help wondering how soon she'd qualify for that benefit, and whether she'd be entitled to pet sick leave and pet bereavement leave as well. A surge of guilt suppressed her questions; at any rate, she could ask them at her month-long benefits orientation training that would start in a few days.

She poured her heart out to Rick, who lounged on the sofa in the skin-tight leather pants (open at the crotch) he'd bought for the "Fifty Shades of Grey" party. "Don't worry about it," he counseled. "This is a colony, and we're the ruling class."

"That's not how I think of myself," she sniffled.

He tried being supportive, even hopeful that she could turn the situation around. "Maybe you could be a whistleblower," he said. "Sneak some kids in the back door, teach them how to read and write—"

"The way you slipped the mice into the cat food machines?"

"Hey, I was doing the cats a favor! Cats love mice, don't they? Anyway, what are you complaining about? I walked off with a cool 77 million."

Rosemary had to admit that Rick's job at Forepaugh Foods had worked out for the best. But now look at him! He was still a lowlife, squandering the $77,000,000 as fast he could—not on opera tickets or ski trips to Switzerland or donations to charities, which would have made them look good to the neighbors, but on pornographic video games and fantasy football pools and paint-ball weekends with his college buddies. At least he was going all out for the party, which would secure their standing in the building (though sometimes she wondered if he might be overdoing it, with that leather suit and the Harley-Davidson drive chain around his neck and all the time he was spending with Mike Malatesta and his biker friends). "You'll never make it into the ruling class," she said spitefully.

His eyes wandered to the Sotheby's catalog which had lain unopened on the coffee table since it arrived in the mail. "OK, I've got an idea," he said. "I'll start an art collection. You know, paintings and sculptures and stuff. Then we can donate it to a museum and get our names on a plaque. Will that satisfy you?"

Seven stories above the Wurlitzers, on the nineteenth floor, Patti Ogleby shared her triumph with Achilles, who (though indifferent to the conversation) was kind enough to hold her wine glass on his back as she gazed out over the city with both hands on the railing. "Alice Coggins has been sent back to the row house in South Philadelphia where she belongs," Patti told

Achilles. "Andrew's marriage to Melissa will put him in reach of the Forepaugh Foods fortune. If I can get the Wurlitzers out of the building before the end of the year, Melissa's parents will buy a choice unit and I'll have the money I need to keep me and David out of the poorhouse." She reached for her wine glass as she remembered Mike Malatesta, who, when not dogging Alice's steps to make sure she stayed where she belonged, was working hard to lure the Wurlitzers into social annihilation. "All things considered," she told Achilles, raising the glass in a toast to herself, "I think we're doing pretty well."

Andrew, just twenty yards away in his bedroom, felt anything but triumphant. Shaken by the scene in Rittenhouse Square Park, he'd considered all his options, including suicide, and decided that marrying Melissa was as close to suicide as he needed to come. The wedding wouldn't take place until Christmas, and perhaps the earth would be struck by a giant meteor before then. There was no reason to despair.

On Saturday night Melissa dragged him to see a Greek tragedy called *The Furies*, by Aeschylus. The Furies were a group of nasty goddesses from the Underworld who pursued Orestes in order to punish him for killing his mother Clytemnestra, who'd killed his father Agamemnon, who'd killed his sister Iphigenia (it was a long story, which Andrew pieced together from Wikipedia articles he read on his phone during the performance). They were depicted as winged monsters with their hair entwined with snakes; they carried whips, and when they caught their victims they tortured them and drove them mad. For Orestes (according to Wikipedia), the Furies were a manifestation of Fate. No matter what he did or where he went, he could never escape them. They would track him down and make sure he got what he deserved. (Aeschylus, as it happened, tried unsuccessfully to avoid his own fate. An oracle predicted that he would be killed by a falling object, so he spent the rest of his life indoors. Then one day, stepping out under a clear blue sky, he was killed by a falling tortoise dropped by an eagle in the mistaken belief that his bald head was a rock suitable for smashing tortoises.)

For Andrew the lesson was clear: Your fate, no matter how hideous or unimaginable it may seem, is impossible to avoid. His was Melissa.

33. The Grand Scam

Alice Coggins

I'll never forget that miserable day in Rittenhouse Square when I found out that Andrew plans to marry the Dandruff Dwarf. When Hector broke the news, I threw myself into his arms (I hope that didn't give him the wrong idea) and cried my eyes out. Since then I've done everything to make my life so unbearable that I can't stand to think about it. Despair is my only hope. I've signed up to work at fundraisers seven nights a week (including the upcoming Man of the Year Award dinner honoring Bob Baskerville). On a typical night I consume as many hors d'oeuvres as I serve, and bring the rest home in a doggie bag. During the day I pig out on the couch with my Dad, gobbling cold shrimp and stuffed grape leaves as I read zombie novels and watch afternoon game shows on TV. Gradually I've recovered a little of my self-respect—enough, anyway, to be as spiteful as Tiffany would be in my situation.

Now that I'm just like Tiffany, she's being incredibly supportive. "What's it to me," I asked her one day, "if Andrew wants to marry a scruffy four-foot-ten vegan with the face of a wall-eyed pike?"

"Yeah," she agreed. "When she told him she was a vegan, she probably made it sound like she was a virgin. I've used that trick. You stick your finger in your mouth like you're retching at the thought of food, and say 'I'm a vegan.' Works every time."

"You've posed as a virgin?"

"It's been a while," she admitted.

The two of us have fun singing "Like A Vegan"—*Like a ve-e-e-e-gan! Bingeing for the very first time!*—whenever the subject of Melissa comes up, which is surprisingly often. Tiffany hears all about Andrew from her friend Clea, who's interning as his secretary. If I didn't know better, I'd think Tiffany wishes she had something going with Andrew.

In my spare moments I keep a running tally of my failures and defeats. I've been rejected in favor of a bulimic cat-food heiress and reduced to cackling with my witchlike sister. I'm being stalked by two different psychopaths—Homicidal Howie and some dark-haired thug who ducks behind a corner every time I turn around. And Hector says some shadowy group called Somos has me in their sights to save me from the Potlatch, which is run by evil dwarfs (any relation to Melissa, I wonder?). For the past two weeks my rate of weight gain has been doubling every two days. By the time I'm fifty (if I live that long) I'll account for 75% of the mass of the universe.

Uh, oh. Do I sound a little crazy, making a list of everything that's wrong with my life? It's not a suicide note, not yet, at least. Just a rough draft. There's still plenty of space left at the bottom of the page.

One afternoon I sat next to my Dad on the sofa, helping him scratch under his ankle cuff while Tiffany stretched out in the Barcalounger filing her nails. Mom huddled over the kitchen table calculating her mileage and overtime for the week (since it's a no-show job, she's paid for the miles she doesn't drive to work and the extra time she spends not getting there.) "Something big's happening in the rackets," Dad said. "I got it from the guys down at the clubhouse. This is the Big One. They're calling it the Grand Scam."

"Another Baby Boy special?" I asked, mildly interested. "Or should I say Bob Baskerville?"

"I guess you should," Dad grinned. "It's in the nonprofit sector."

Tiffany gave us one of her know-it-all looks. "I told you that's where the money is."

"Nonprofits work like any other con," Dad said. "You put up a little cash to get the game started, and then you convince the mark—I mean the donor—to give you a matching grant, no strings attached. Naturally what you want is a lot more than a match—ten, twenty, a hundred times more, but what do they know? You're paying yourself a seven-figure salary as executive director, so it all looks legit. Pretty soon you've got billionaires lining up to make donations."

"So what's the new scam?"

"It's not really a new scam. Just sort of a consolidation of all the old ones under new management."

"A monopoly?"

"You could call it that. They're cornering the market on the nonprofits. Baby Boy's already got the Museum of Homeless Art, the Police Malevolent Association, the League of Lithuanian-American Law Librarians, the Society of War of 1812 Re-Enactors—"

"Those last two are small potatoes," I said. "I skipped their fundraisers."

"Nothing's too small for Baby Boy. By the time he's done, he and Gallaher'll own every nonprofit in the city. They've already got some of the biggies: UCLA, the Philadelphia

Orchestra (it'll be switching to an all-Sinatra policy next season), the Dwight D. Schopenhauer Health Center where your grandma lives—that's owned by one of Gallaher's insurance companies, Third Millennium Life."

That grabbed my attention. "What's going to happen to Grandma?"

"She's in good hands. You think a life insurance company wants its patients to die?"

"I know how that scam works," Tiffany smirked. She's an intern at Third Millennium Life.

"I'll bet you do," Dad beamed. "What a sweet racket life insurance is!"

"I know *all about it,*" she smirked again.

"Tell me," I said. "What do you mean?"

Tiffany started to answer, but Dad cut her off: "You don't need to know, Alice. You don't want to know." He shot a warning glance at Tiffany. "The bottom line for you girls is, if you want to cozy up to rich guys, you'd better start cashing in on these nonprofits while you still have a chance. They won't be serving fancy appetizers to the horsy set much longer."

"What's going to happen to all the money people have donated?" I asked.

He enjoyed a broad, satisfied smile. "Let's just say it's going to be put back into circulation where it'll do some good."

"Let me guess: Ponzi schemes? Con games? Scams and rackets?"

"Like Randolph says: It's all part of the Potlatch."

Later that night I cornered Tiffany outside the bathroom. "Do you know who this Baby Boy is who's taking over all the nonprofits?" I asked her. "He also goes by the name of Bob Baskerville."

"No kidding?" she said with admiration. "I met that guy at the Homeless Art Museum."

"He's a loan shark from South Philly who somehow got to be Man of the Year."

"So what?"

"I'm worried about Grandma. Is she going to be all right in that Health Center?"

"She'll be better than all right," Tiffany said. "She'll probably live forever."

"What are you talking about?"

"Like Dad said, it's a sweet scam. Practically everybody in that place is on life support. Third Millennium Life collects their Social Security checks and applies them to their life insurance premiums, which are, like, thousands of dollars a month. All those old people have policies in the millions. The premiums keep rolling in as long as they stay alive—if they died, Third Millennium would have to shell out billions in claims. So like Dad says, you think they're going to let those people die? Grandma couldn't be in a safer place."

She slipped past me toward her room. "And Alice," she said in that sarcastic voice she only uses for me, "in case you have some wacko idea of trying to do something about it, let me tell you, I overheard the attorney from Stark Raven—Mr. Wolf—talking to my boss on the speaker phone. It's all legal and proper."

34. The Eye In The Pyramid

Hector was walking on air.

From that moment in Rittenhouse Square when he told Alice that Andrew planned to marry Melissa, he knew that Alice loved him. She wasn't crying because she loved Andrew (Tiffany had assured him of that, and who knew Alice better than her sister?), but because she loved him, Hector. That was when he reached out and wrapped his arms around her. He showed her that he loved her. And she responded with a warm hug and an outpouring of emotion, the way his *abuelita* did sometimes when she just threw her arms around him and cried. At that moment he knew: she loved him. The details (he was still a little fuzzy on the details) could be worked out later.

He thought about Alice every second as he walked, on air, back to the Federal Reserve Bank. That afternoon it was hard to keep his mind on the weekly economic data, even though it was encouraging. The recent spate of orders for marble, granite and lumber—and the portcullis imported from Scotland—had signaled the biggest expansion of credit and general business activity in Philadelphia in many years. The data showed a significant uptick in orders for construction materials and supplies, especially tapestries, turrets, spiral staircases and dungeon equipment, as well as backhoe rental, all related to the castle somebody was building in Northeast Philadelphia. Unemployment in the building trades had fallen by a full percentage point. Commercial real estate prices were up 5% on the rumor that a major player was in an acquisition mode. Anticipating increased tax revenues, the Mayor had announced an across-the-board pay raise to city employees and several new entitlements, including gluten-free lunches for hunger strikers. There were even reports (as yet unconfirmed) that some employers were upgrading long-term internships (e.g., entry-level positions which had been filled by unpaid interns for over ten years) into minimum-wage jobs. It seemed that a faint glow of light might be appearing at the end of the tunnel. When Hector reported these data to Gwendolyn, she dashed off a memo to her boss, Maureen, to be forwarded to the Board of Governesses, expressing her cautious hope that the Bank's stimulus policies over the past ten years were finally bearing fruit. "But as far as sex is concerned," she told Hector, "I'm still not convinced that we're out of the woods. On that, I want you to keep gathering field data and report directly back to me."

At his 3:00 o'clock break, he hurried down to the cafeteria for a Coke, hoping Arbuthnot would not be there. He looked at Arbuthnot differently now that Maria (the woman from Somos) had warned him that "the people you're working for" were evil. She couldn't have meant Gwendolyn, or Maureen, or even (he hoped) the Board of Governesses. If her accusation fit anyone at the Bank, it would have to be Arbuthnot. He was tall, lean and muscular for a man his age, with close-cropped gray hair and a sensuous, cunning smile. His forehead was high, his eyebrows arching, his eyes deep and imperious. There was no escape from those eyes, which Hector sensed could control him like the strings on a marionette. But when Hector encountered Arbuthnot on the way back to his office—it was in an isolated area near the mail room—he was all sweetness and light, even bashful, as if he was embarrassed about something. "I've got a confession to make," he said. "I've been pulling your leg a little. Things aren't quite as bad as I made them out to be."

"You mean about the economy going to hell in a handbasket?"

"Oh, it's going to hell, all right," he laughed. "But as for needing to be destroyed in order to save it—"

"You mean the earthquake and all that?"

"Right. We have a Plan B. It's already in effect."

That was a relief—a little too much of a relief, as it turned out. Hector was so relieved, he decided that this would be a good time to see if Maria's accusations had any basis. "Is Plan B the Potlatch?" he asked.

Arbuthnot's eyes flashed with anger. "Who told you about the Potlatch?"

"People talk," Hector mumbled, looking away. He didn't want to name any names, especially Maria's.

"Okay"—Arbuthnot made an obvious effort to control his anger—"I'm only going to say this once, and then we'll never mention it again. Understand?"

"Right."

"The Potlatch is a myth. An urban legend like the aliens at Roswell or the shooter on the grassy knoll. A crackpot fantasy that undermines all our efforts at the Bank. Do you understand why?"

"I guess because—"

"Who would lift a finger to do anything if he thought life was utterly useless and futile?"

For a brief second—and for the first time in his life—Hector felt a glimmer of existential angst. Owing to his strict Catholic upbringing, his grandmother's abiding faith in *santería*, his own innocent nature, and his chosen course of studies, Hector had avoided the corrosive effects of modern thought, and Arbuthnot's suggestion that life, in all its variety and complexity, might be utterly useless and futile (how could anyone with so much owed on student loans entertain that notion *even for a second?*) and that only the Federal Reserve Bank guarded the public from a crippling despair—left him speechless and queasy.

Arbuthnot cut off his thoughts: "End of discussion."

An awkward silence filled the space between them. "What's Plan B, then?" Hector asked warily.

"Globalization." Arbuthnot spoke the word deliberately and categorically, as if it were the last word he would ever utter; then, seeing Hector's puzzled expression, he went on to explain: "We print money not only for this country, but for the entire world. So even if our economy flatlines and the percentage of people who don't get out of bed in the morning hits 100%, we can maintain our high standard of living by printing money for the rest of the world."

"I don't get it."

He turned around and headed down the hall. "Follow me. I'm going to take you down into the bowels of the Bank."

"No, that's OK," Hector hesitated. "I don't want to go down there."

"Come on," Arbuthnot said with an ingratiating smile, beckoning Hector to follow him. "It'll be a good learning experience for you." He stopped short in front of an elevator and pushed the call button. When the elevator doors opened, Hector didn't step inside. Learning experience or not, he wasn't interested in any kind of bowels: the bowels of the Bank, the bowels of the earth, the bowels of Hell. He didn't even want to hear about his grandmother's colonoscopy. But Arbuthnot, who had circled behind him, nudged him forward into the elevator, activating the "Down" button with a key. In a few seconds they landed at the bottom and the elevator doors slid open. "Wait'll you see the money supply," Arbuthnot said.

On a narrow catwalk about fifty feet above the floor, they circled the perimeter of a vast open room—it must have been the size of a football stadium—filled from one end to the other with overflowing bins of money, like the coffers of some mythical potentate. The bins moved on conveyers tended by tiny men in green uniforms. "We're so high up," Hector observed, "that those men look like midgets."

"They *are* midgets," Arbuthnot said. "Dwarfs, actually, or gnomes, as some people call them. They were brought in from the Zurich office. You don't want to look them in the eye."

"Why not?"

"Take my word for it. If one of them glances up at you, look the other way and spit."

Near the middle of the immense room—at about the forty-yard line, Hector guessed—he and Arbuthnot backed their way down a metal ladder to floor level, where they stood beside an open bin overflowing with currency. Arbuthnot grabbed a handful of bills and flipped through them like a deck of cards. "Looks like Monopoly money, doesn't it?"

Hector could hardly believe his eyes—it really did look like Monopoly money. "You mean the guy with the top hat and cane is on the thousand dollar bill?"

"Who did you think was on there? That's Grover Cleveland."

Arbuthnot gestured grandly over the king's ransom that filled the cavernous space. "This is what makes America great," he said. "All the other countries have to use our money. We can print as much of it as we want to, and spend it on anything we want—as long as what we spend it on is made somewhere else."

Hector began to feel some misgivings. "But isn't that—"

"And when we've bought everything we could possibly want, we know the other countries will send the money back to us by buying bonds that we'll never have to repay."

"Isn't that sort of "—Hector groped for the right words, not wanting to provoke Arbuthnot a second time—"I don't know, a Faustian bargain or something?"

"Why do you say that?"

"I mean, since everything's made somewhere else, nobody here has a job."

"I have a job," Arbuthnot sneered. "Those gnomes have jobs. *You* have a job, don't you?"

Apparently he didn't realize Hector was an unpaid intern. "Yes," Hector mumbled, "but... where does it all end?"

"It doesn't end," Arbuthnot declared with a fierce gleam in his eyes. "It goes on forever."

A gang of gnomes seemed to be marching toward them from the twenty-yard line. Arbuthnot tapped Hector's arm and together they clambered back up the metal ladder to the catwalk. In his hand he clutched one of the bills he'd removed from the money bin. Holding it in front of Hector, he pointed to the eye at the tip of the pyramid, and the words emblazoned on a scroll under it: *Novus Ordo Seclorum*. "What do you think that means?"

"I don't know," Hector said. "It's in some language I don't understand."

"Nobody understands it," Arbuthnot smiled. He released the bill and watched it flutter down to the gnomes assembled under the catwalk. "Let's keep it that way."

That evening as he walked home from the bus, Hector passed a builders' supply warehouse with a fenced area outside for storing lumber. A burly man in a red John Deere cap sat on a forklift moving a stack of two-by-six-inch pine boards about ten feet long. He set the lumber down beside the fence and Hector's eyes almost popped out of his head. The word **"POTLATCH"** was stenciled on the end of each board.

Hector stopped and grabbed the fence in both hands. "What are you doing with this lumber?" he demanded.

The fork lift operator let his lift idle as he considered whether to answer Hector's question or pick him up and add him to the woodpile. "Some guy's building a castle up in the Northeast," he finally said. "You got a problem with that?"

35. Lender Of Last Resort

Alice Coggins

One night I worked at a five o'clock cocktail reception and was home by nine. At about 9:30, my Dad was out on the stoop by himself having a smoke; I was in my room upstairs, trying to catch a cool breeze through the open window. I looked down and saw a black Cadillac Escalante with tinted windows gliding up to the curb. The driver jumped out and looked up and down the street. Then the passenger door opened and out climbed Baby Boy Barkocy, alias Bob Baskerville, stuffed into an expensive dark suit. The driver—I recognized him as Howie—followed him halfway to the stoop and fixed his eyes on my Dad. My Dad didn't act surprised. I think he was expecting them.

I stepped to the side so they couldn't see me in the window, but I could see them and hear every word they said. "I've been hearing rumors, Ray," Baby Boy said. "They say you're building a castle."

"That's right, Baby Boy," Dad said. "I'm building a castle."

"They say you're borrowing against the materials and supplies you buy on credit to build your castle, then lending out the borrowed money and using the interest you collect to pay for the materials." Baby Boy tilted his giant head as if he had water in his ears. "Am I hearing this right?"

"I don't understand, Baby Boy. Didn't you give me the go-ahead on lending?"

"Sure, Ray, but what I had in mind was a lot more financially sound. What you've got here is a house of cards."

Dad tossed his cigarette into the street. "It's been working out fine so far."

"It's risky, Ray. And there's another rumor that's got us even more concerned. They say you don't really have the money to build the castle. They say all you've got is a two-dollar lottery ticket with odds of a billion to one."

"The odds are better than that."

"Whatever they are, divide them into two bucks and that's what you've got."

"I'm sure my ticket's going to win."

Baby Boy stared back at Dad for a long time as he tried to figure out if Dad was putting him on. One thing about my Dad—he's never insincere. That was the key to his success as a con artist. He always believes what he's saying, no matter how ridiculous it sounds to everybody else. "I hope you're right, Ray," Baby Boy said. "But frankly I'm concerned. And I'm not just speaking for myself. The Boss is concerned, too. Very concerned. He's concerned that maybe you're engaged in unsound lending practices."

"It's not like that, Baby Boy. Nothing like that."

"Whether you lose your money or not, frankly he could care less. What he's worried about is risk to the organization. Systemic risk. You know what I mean?"

"Sure I know. It's not a problem."

Baby Boy smiled and nodded as if he confidently accepted this reassurance. "When I was in the lending business—some people used to call me the lender of last resort—I never loaned out money I didn't have. It's not right."

"I'm going to pay every penny I owe," Dad said.

"I had very low default rate, by the way." Baby Boy gestured toward Howie, who aimed his empty stare at Dad. "Howie can attest to that. He's a Wharton grad, did you know that?"

Baby Boy backed his enormous frame off the stoop without offering to shake Dad's hand. He trudged toward the car, then turned around to add what sounded like an afterthought. "I don't want to see you go under, Ray," he said. "That's why I wanted to make sure you're not hoping for a bailout." He smiled his friendly butcher's smile. "Because when we do a bailout, it's in somebody's boat about ten miles out from Atlantic City."

In my suicide note, or maybe in my memoirs, or maybe in a letter I'll leave with my attorney to be published in the *National Enquirer* in the event I meet a gruesome and hideous death, I'm going to tell the truth about Bob Baskerville aka Baby Boy Barkocy, the demon butcher of Wolf Street. Nobody would listen to me now, but by then (assuming Howie doesn't finish me off in the next couple of weeks) I'll be famous in my own right as the World's Fattest Woman. Then I can say whatever it takes to save my Dad from Howie and Grandma from the Grand Scam. I'm afraid of Baby Boy, afraid for myself and for my Dad, who won't stop building his castle until they drag him out and throw him in the ocean. Right now I'm working on a backup plan. I've signed up to waitress at the Man of the Year Award dinner on November 8, where Baby Boy will be the guest of honor. I've studied the program and have a pretty good idea of how the room will be set up. If I can get close enough to Bob Baskerville to slip a little rat poison into his coffee, I might be able to shorten his tenure as Man of the Year to about five minutes.

In the meantime I can't talk about this with anybody, especially Hector. He's a nice guy but he's a little crazy, at least on certain subjects related to his job. Hanging out with him probably isn't the best thing for my mental health. If you're already a little paranoid, spending an hour with Hector can make you want to lock the door and crawl under the bed. And as if I didn't have enough on my mind, I'm starting to realize that Hector thinks I'm in love with him. Talk about crazy.

We met at a bar called Del Giorno's, which used to be a bank until about ten years ago, when they converted all the banks to bars or coffee shops. The waiters and waitresses are ex-tellers who look at you like you're trying to cash a bad check. When I didn't have much to say, Hector wanted to know why I seemed so nervous and distracted. "I've got to be careful," I told him. "I'm being stalked, under constant surveillance...."

"Why? What's going on?"

I couldn't tell him about Baby Boy and his threats. "It's something I heard about from my Dad," I said. "The Grand Scam, they call it. Somebody—certain people—are scheming to take over... part of the economy, most of the economy, in fact—"

"It sounds like the Potlatch."

"No, this isn't the Potlatch. I'm not sure there's any such thing as the Potlatch."

"Listen, Alice, the Potlatch is real." Hector glanced around furtively. "I've seen the dwarfs."

This is where the crazy part always starts with Hector. The Potlatch, the dwarfs, the mysterious woman who's trying to lure him into the resistance. He snatched up our check, waving aside my offer to pay my share. "Officially the Bank denies that the Potlatch exists," he said, keeping his voice low. "But Arbuthnot—he's one of the higher-ups—took me down to the vault and showed me the money supply. It's what funds the Potlatch all over the world."

The waiter stood beside the table and counted out our change. Hector picked through it figuring out how much to leave as a tip. "I'm sorry, Hector," I said. "I've got other things to worry about. I'm afraid they're going to pull the plug on my Grandma at the Health Center. They're threatening my Dad if he doesn't stop work on his castle."

Hector spun toward me, his eyes gleaming like a madman's. "What did you say? Your Dad's building a castle? Is it up in the Northeast?"

"How did you know?"

He peered at me as if he thought I might be lying. "Did he order lumber from Idaho? Torture equipment from Spain? Is he the one with six backhoes digging a moat?"

"That's my Dad."

"The lumber's from the Potlatch. It says so right on it."

"Isn't that the name of a lumber company?"

I tried to stand up, but Hector reached out his hand and held me in my seat. "Alice," he said breathlessly, "don't let them stop him, whoever they are. The whole city is depending on that castle."

36. New Hope For The Dead

I need to visit Grandma and make sure they aren't getting ready to pull the plug on her.

If Baby Boy succeeds with his Grand Scam, what will become of the Health Center? I know Grandma's already worried about the Potlatch—"It's what keeps us alive," she told me once, "whether we want to live or not." Does that make it good or bad? And if Tiffany is right, there's nothing to worry about. Third Millennium is dedicated to making everybody live forever.

When I visit Grandma I always stop in the lobby to chat with the security guard, a cute black guy named Spencer Casey who seems as suspicious of the Health Center as I am. It's like the lobby of a first-class hotel: plush carpeting, a grand piano, hanging tapestries and a reception desk that must be fifty feet long. One day Spencer took me on a little tour and showed me the inner courtyard and the "function rooms"—that always sounds a little too biological for me, they're just large empty spaces with moveable walls where various events can be held. I'm familiar with such places from my catering work. In fact (though I didn't mention this to Spencer), it's in one of these rooms—the "Mother Teresa Room"—where I plan to poison the Man of the Year before he gets back out on the street.

When you take the elevator up to the 30th floor, where the private rooms are located, you notice an odd thing: there are no buttons for floors 2 through 29. You can only go all the way to the 30th floor. I zoomed up to the 30th floor and found

Grandma in bed as usual, now with a respirator controlling her breath.   Armand crouched in his wheelchair beside her. "Grandma?" I said softly, not wanting to wake her if she was asleep. "Are you awake?"

"Yes, Alice," she said without opening her eyes or even moving her lips.

"Is everything OK? Are you getting enough to eat?"

"I'm fine. Don't fret about me."

"Are you still worried about the Potlatch?"

"The Potlatch carries you along. Not to worry."

I slipped out of the room and found a staircase that took me down to the 29th floor, where a sign informed me that I was entering a *Restricted Area.* The whole floor was one giant room, a ward filled with beds jammed close together, each one holding an unconscious patient: men and women (usually you couldn't tell which) shriveled and speckled beyond recognition, stretched out under a tangle of respirators, monitors and IV tubes. The only sound was the gurgling and beeping of the machines.

"Impressive, isn't it?" said a voice behind me. "All these people saved from death."

I spun around to find a short, pear-shaped man wearing green scrubs and a gauzy head covering like a chef's hat. He sipped coffee out of a red ceramic mug. His name tag said *Dr. Mason.*

"But," I hesitated, "are their lives worth living?"

"Do you have any appreciation for what modern medicine has accomplished?" Dr. Mason asked, goggling up at me through his heavy-framed glasses. "When we defeated the scourges of mankind—malaria, smallpox, cancer, heart disease—we were able to add a few years to the average person's life. But for every disease we conquered, a new one would spring up in its place—toenail fungus, social anxiety disorder, the heartbreak of psoriasis, jock itch, dandruff, male pattern baldness, dust mite allergies, gluten phobia. Obscure maladies that used to be buried in the footnotes became mass murderers. We came to realize that our adversary was not some compendium of pathologies, but death itself."

"Death itself?"

"The conquest of death is a dream as old as humanity. Some of us haven't given up the fight."

He led me down the nearest aisle, past the rows of immobile patients like a general reviewing his troops. "Our interventions have necessarily grown more drastic and elaborate as the half-life of survival has shortened," he went on. "Medicine became focused on the last month of life, then the last week of life, the last day of life, the last hour of life, the interval continuously dividing by half in the race against death. Today we're dealing with the last seconds of life, and the horizon is still receding. It's like the race between Achilles and the tortoise. As long as we divide each last interval in half, and then in half again and half again, and so on *ad infinitum*, death can never win the race."

"But aren't these people dead?" I mumbled, barely able to talk. They were zombies.

"There is no death here," the doctor said. "You've got to have faith."

I had to get out of there. "Do you work for the Health Center?" I asked him as I headed toward the stairs.

"Not exactly," he answered. "I work for the insurance company. Third Millennium Life."

That was when I realized that Grandma was right. All these people—everybody in the ward, in all the wards—were already dead! They were being kept alive so Third Millennium Life, which owns the Health Center, could keep collecting their Social Security checks and their life insurance premiums and never have to pay any claims. And all the doctors and nurses and technicians and billing clerks were in on it.

I ran up the stairs to the 30th floor and down to Grandma's room. She was lying as I'd left her, stretched out flat on the bed with the respirator over her face, her head twisted to one side, her eyes closed, her hands folded across her chest. Old Armand crouched beside her bed in his wheelchair, wrists straining at the straps, glaring at me with an almost feral hostility as I patted Grandma's arm, rubbed her cheek, and finally shook her shoulder without any response. With a sickening sensation I realized that the only difference between Grandma and the dead people in the ward downstairs was that she had a private room. Her breathing just tracked the respirator; her hands were as cold as icicles. She must have been dead for a long time, I realized, though I was sure I'd spoken with her only a few minutes before. Did I really hear her say the things I thought I'd heard? Glancing down at Armand, hoping he could help me out, I realized that he was only slightly more alive than she was. My whole conversation with Grandma must have been a hallucination. Or could it—I asked myself in desperation—have been a vision? Some kind of supernatural visitation that might lend some kind of meaning to this nightmare? "You've got to have faith," the doctor had said, but I saw then—much as I wanted to pretend otherwise—that I had no faith in anything. The doctor's faith was an illusion—no, worse than an illusion, it was a deception, perpetrated by Third Millennium Life and the Gallaher machine. I burst into tears and looked down at Armand.

"Get the hell out of here!" he said.

Dad drew a big red circle around Wednesday, November 9 on the kitchen calendar. "That's the last Mega Millions drawing," he told Mom. "The day my dreams come true." She stepped over and circled the Wednesday a week later. "That's the day my dreams come true," she said. "You want an open or closed casket viewing?"

I'm afraid my Mom may be right. November 9—the day after Election Day and the Man of the Year Award dinner—is the day my Dad's illusions will be shattered. His lottery ticket will become worthless and he'll owe millions of dollars to various cogs in the Gallaher machine. He'll have to call in all his loans, most of which will never be paid. Gallaher's partner in the Grand Scam, Bob Baskerville (newly installed as Man of the Year), will not be amused. Dad's kneecaps (at the very least) will be shattered along with the dreams of a lifetime, and his poor mom, my Grandma, will be sent down to the zombie ward.

I'm desperate to buy more time, run out the clock, whatever. My only hope is to blow the whistle on Bob Baskerville to someone in the upper echelons of society who isn't part of the Gallaher machine, if such a person exists. Since Hector works for the Federal Reserve Bank, maybe he knows someone I could talk to. I have to be careful, though. I can't even mention Bob Baskerville's name until I'm sure I have somebody I can trust. And to be honest and fair, before I get Hector involved in this I have to tell him once and for all that I'm not in love with him. He's a dear soul but I'll never love him that way.

Hector seemed devastated when I broke the news. But when I told him about the Grand Scam, without mentioning any names, he agreed that I need to talk to someone in a position of power. "I know just the man you should talk to," he said. "He's an old-line WASP, definitely part of the ruling class with great connections. Big in nonprofits especially. It's going to be a little awkward, though."

"Why?" I asked. "Who is it?"

"Andrew's Dad. David Ogleby."

37. Smoke And Mirrors

Weekly economic data showed continued improvement throughout the region. Intense construction activity in Northeast Philadelphia had boosted sales of Italian hoagies, cheese steaks, potato chips, Flyers T-shirts, pickup trucks, six-packs and lottery tickets. Using standard economic models, Hector calculated that overall output would surge by ten percent in the coming year. He decided to ask Arbuthnot if an increase in the money supply should be considered.

Arbuthnot was characteristically evasive when Hector cornered him in the small unmarked office where they often met. He crouched behind the desk, fingers dancing over the keyboard of his laptop as he put the finishing touches on what must have been some important project for the Bank. "Money supply?" he finally said, glancing up from his work for the first time. "What are you talking about?"

"You know," Hector said. "What you showed me in the vault? With the gnomes?"

"Keep your voice down. Nobody is supposed to know about those gnomes."

"What I'm wondering is, with all that activity, is the economy going to need more money?"

Arbuthnot stood up and dodged around Hector to the door. He opened it quickly to make sure no one was listening outside, then snapped it shut and darted back to his chair behind the desk. "Since you're working at the Federal Reserve

Bank," he said, "there's something you need to know. It's about money."

"Money?" As an economist, even a junior one, Hector thought he knew everything there was to know about money. "What do I need to know?"

"It doesn't exist."

Hector suppressed a laugh. "Doesn't exist? But the Bank—"

"It has never existed."

"Well, there used to be gold—"

"Money didn't exist when it was gold, either. The gold existed, of course. But what made it more valuable than any other kind of rock? What made it *money?*"

Hector fumbled with his answer, struggling with a realization which had hovered at the edge of his consciousness since the beginning of his junior year in college. "People thought"—this new insight leaped in front of him, hideous and leering, but almost blinding in its certainty—"it was valuable." He knew his answer was absurd. He felt the way a young priest might feel if on the day of his ordination his father confessor informed him that God did not exist.

Arbuthnot smirked condescendingly. "I could show you documents here at the Bank that only a few higher-ups are allowed to see," he said. "Spread sheets tracing the flow of money through the banking system. When you study those, it's like trying to follow a thread through a labyrinth. You never come to the end."

"But I've seen the interbank accounts," Hector mumbled. "The monthly flow of funds reports, the—"

"The money in one bank exists only as credits on the books of other banks, which in turn exist only as credits on the books of other banks, and so on forever. You can follow the thread until eternity and you'll never find the money. Because it doesn't exist."

They sat in silence for several minutes, neither making eye contact with the other. Arbuthnot's revelation had been shocking, almost obscene. It hung in the air like a faint odor, never to be mentioned again.

Arbuthnot went back to his work on the laptop, running his fingers over the keyboard with an amazing facility. A follow-up question—the logical next question, it seemed—took shape in Hector's mind. "Then what about the Potlatch?" he finally asked. "Does it exist?"

"Something like that exists," Arbuthnot said. "Something that keeps everything going. You can call it the Potlatch if you want to."

"But what is it?"

For the first time Arbuthnot looked up from his work. "It's like the story of the blind men and the elephant," he said, smiling indulgently. "One blind man felt the trunk and said an elephant is the branch of a tree, another felt the tail and said an elephant is a rope, another felt the leg and said it was a pillar. That's how it is when you hear talk about the Potlatch. Some people see rigged elections and payoffs, and say the Potlatch is a political machine, an alliance of politicians and businesses and unions to manipulate events to their own advantage. Others see the police and the courts and the legal system—to them the Potlatch is a racket as old as the hills, set up to keep the powerless in their place. Others, with the economy in mind, see the Potlatch as a vast system of exploitation and waste, a monumental make-work project going back to the Egyptian pyramids. Others take a darker, more fantastic view and see a vast conspiracy of dwarfs or bankers or secret agents, a state within a state, while others see a cosmic dimension: it's the Tao, the Wheel of Life, Schopenhauer's Will..."

"God? Could it be God?"

Arbuthnot laughed. "Who am I to say? All I do is push the buttons."

38. A Close Call

Alice Coggins

Baby Boy's threats didn't faze my Dad. When I asked him if he was worried, he said no—if Baby Boy threatened him again he'd just call the Boss. He'd worked for Gallaher all his life and Gallaher would stand by him. Nothing was going to keep him from building his castle.

Then one night we're out on the stoop and the big black Cadillac Escalante cruises up to the curb. Same drill as before: Howie jumps out and looks up and down the block, then Baby Boy hoists himself out, slow as an elephant and sort of thoughtful, like he's coming to a funeral. Once on the stoop, he and Dad exchanged greetings without smiling—I tried to duck inside but he motioned for me to stay—and he put his enormous, ham-like arm around Dad's shoulder. "I talked to the Boss about you," he said in a low voice. "He's a little disappointed, Ray. He thought house arrest for life would keep you out of trouble, but now he wonders if that was the right decision. It's like you want to finish your life sentence on the early side."

"I don't get it," Dad said. "What's the problem?"

"Maybe I didn't make myself clear on my last social call. Or maybe you're getting hard of hearing. So I'll tell you again: You need to shut down the lending operation and stop building the castle."

"But they already dug the moat."

"Fill in the moat."

"You can't just fill in a moat. It's—"

"People fill in moats all the time," Baby Boy cut him off. "With dirt, sometimes cement. And you know what? Sometimes those moats don't go in circles, like the ones around a castle. Sometimes they're rectangular and about six feet long."

He removed his arm from Dad's shoulders and took a step backwards. "This is the last time you're going to hear this from me, Ray. Gallaher doesn't like castles and he doesn't like loan sharks who loan out money they don't have."

"I'll call the Boss," Dad said. "This is a misunderstanding. He'll back me up."

"A misunderstanding, huh?" Baby Boy smiled. "You know that squirt Gallaher hangs around with, Jerry something, with the gimpy leg? I'm telling Gallaher about you, and Jerry says, 'Who the hell is Ray Coggins, anyway?' And Gallaher says: 'I'll tell you who he is—he's a nobody, that's who he is. If he was any dumber he'd be a fence post. He's a Neanderthal who can't even be allowed out of the house.'"

My Dad looked paler than I'd ever seen him before. His lower lip was quivering.

"Gallaher said that?"

Baby Boy laughed as he recalled his conversation with Gallaher. "That guy's a laugh a minute! You know what else he said? 'If Ray Coggins wants to have an impact'—like I say, the guy's a comedian—'we could always add another dead man to the voter rolls. In a close election, one more vote could make all the difference."

Dad tried to keep his gaze steady as he wiped a speck of drool off the corner of his mouth. "I always vote the straight Gallaher ticket."

"Sure you do. But there aren't any close elections, are there? Only close calls. And you're having one right now, Ray. You're having one right now."

Baby Boy lowered himself to the sidewalk and plodded in the direction of the Escalante. "This is the last social call I'll be making," he said, turning back around. "After this it'll be strictly business." He gestured toward Howie, who perked up like a dog that hears its name. "Howie's our human resources manager. If we hear any more about castles or the lending business, he'll be coming over to activate your long-term disability package. Did I mention that he's a Wharton grad? He's got number crunching down to a science."

I had ducked into a shadow but Baby Boy's eyes found me out. "Your daughter has a cute smile, Ray," he said. "Nice teeth. When Howie comes over, be sure to ask about the family dental plan. I think it covers reconstructive surgery."

I felt sick to my stomach. Howie stared back at me with a psychotic grin. How could anybody that crazy have made it through Wharton? I'd catered some receptions there and knew how vain and driven its students could be—but could they be this bad? "I'll bet you were in the top of your class at Wharton," I flattered him, trying to sound casual. "What year did you graduate?"

"I guess I misspoke," Baby Boy said. "He didn't exactly graduate. He escaped."

"Escaped?" I mumbled. "From where?"

"The Wharton Institution for the Criminally Insane, in Wharton, Alabama."

At the mention of his alma mater, Howie threw his head back and let out a peal of insane laughter that echoed down the block.

"For you, sweetheart," Baby Boy said gently, "I've got one word of advice: Keep your trap shut while you can still open it."

I smiled and nodded as if I didn't want to barf.

"What's your name, by the way?"

"Tiffany," I whispered.

39. Disaster Of The Year

The Wurlitzers' "Fifty Shades of Grey" party, as Patti hoped, was the Disaster of the Year. The young couple welcomed their guests—toothless ex-stockbrokers who remembered the Great Depression, mustachioed widows leaning on four-footed canes, half-blind retired bankers and their wives who never left the building except for chamber music recitals and charity luncheons—to a scene that resembled a Hieronymus Bosch vision of Hell. Heavy metal music split the eardrums of those few guests whose eardrums could still vibrate, blaring over the sound of cracking whips, rattling chains and bloodcurdling screams. The caterers—heavily tattooed bikers and their Goth girlfriends, with metalwork dangling around every conceivable orifice—circulated with trays of hash brownies and life-threatening concoctions of mescal, tabasco sauce and grain alcohol, along with platters of uppers, downers and designer drugs that some of the guests shoved into their pockets, mistaking them for free samples of Lipitor. Porno movies for the senior set—the most popular being "Colonoscopy Queens Do Boca Raton"—cycled endlessly on the giant flatscreen TV.

Of course it was all in good fun, Rosemary reminded herself. Hadn't Patti assured them that the "Fifty Shades of Grey" theme was mandated by the Homeowners' Association? But some of the guests seemed to be taking it the wrong way. Blue-haired Mrs. Levine collapsed and had to be carried, or rather dragged (by two of the bikers), back to her unit on the sixteenth floor. Old Mr. Whitbourne, laboriously dressed in his best suit and tie, stumbled through the apartment with his oxygen tank, gasping desperately through the tubes in his nose. And although everyone in the building had been invited, Patti and her family were conspicuous by their absence. Bob Baskerville—whom the Wurlitzers had especially hoped to impress—had politely declined the invitation.

The Wurlitzers' fall from grace was sudden and complete. By the next morning, no one in the building would look at them, let alone speak to them—except Patti. Ever the good neighbor, she tapped on their door and offered her realty services in case they decided to sell their unit. Rosemary slammed the door in her face. Later Rick caught sight of her in the lobby and launched into a drug-enhanced diatribe, denouncing her in graphically obscene terms and vowing revenge.

One week later, the Oglebys relaxed on the balcony enjoying the unseasonably warm weather as they sipped their evening cocktails (a beer for Andrew, white wine for Patti, scotch and soda for David). "Can you believe this?" Patti asked her husband. "The Wurlitzers on the twelfth floor, who threw that outrageous party last week, are trying to make amends by donating some valuable art work to the Health Center. It won't do them any good, at least not in this building."

"What is it?" David asked.

"Who knows? Who cares? We'll see it unveiled at the Man of the Year dinner."

Patti was confident that the Wurlitzers would be out within a month, clearing a pathway to the sale of a unit to the

Forepaughs before the end of the year. There was one dark cloud on the horizon, however: Andrew had hinted that he might have misgivings about marrying Melissa. More specifically, he had suggested that he would like to postpone the wedding until the next ice age, when Hell was expected to freeze over.

A portion of the railing around the balcony had been removed by contractors as part of a construction project and was blocked only by yellow hazard tape. Patti set her wine glass on Achilles' back and knelt down to measure the distance between his front fin and the unguarded edge of the balcony. "I'm worried that Achilles might have suicidal tendencies," she said. "He's moved two inches closer to the edge of the balcony in the past month."

"Why would Achilles kill himself?" Andrew asked.

"Existential despair. His life is meaningless and utterly without purpose."

"He makes an excellent coffee table," David observed, setting his scotch and soda on the tortoise's back. "That's more of a purpose than most people have."

"Speak for yourself, dear," Patti said. She smiled at Andrew. "Growing up in the Galapagos Islands, he's seen evolution at first hand, or first claw"—she gestured distastefully toward the tortoise—"or whatever you call those things. And at some deep reptilian level he understands its basic paradox. The theory of evolution can only be true if life is utterly without a purpose. But that purposelessness must be unknown to the life forms that contend for survival. Each individual of every species must fight tooth and nail to prolong and replicate its existence. And who would do that—would you?—if you knew how meaningless it was?"

"I do it every day," David said, raising the drink back to his lips.

"Your father, for example," Patti said, glancing at Andrew, "who is well aware of how meaningless *his* life is, can hardly be lured off the golf course. If our ancestors were all like him, we'd be amoebas."

If I were an amoeba, Andrew thought, at least I wouldn't have to marry Melissa. But he knew that as a human, or even a tortoise, you have no choice but to love your fate. Being warned of his fate, Aeschylus unwittingly sought it out. If Andrew tried to avoid marrying Melissa, that would only make him more likely to marry her. He felt sorry for Achilles, struggling in his microcephalic way to find meaning in his meaningless life. It was heroic in its way, but in the end he would probably be killed by a falling Greek tragedian. "And this is why you expect Achilles to dive off the balcony?" Andrew asked Patti. "Existential despair?"

"I'm afraid so," Patti said. "It could happen any time, probably before the end of the year." She took a long sip of her wine. "Unless some major commissions come my way. In the meantime, would you mind checking the Pet Life policy to see if suicide is covered?"

40. Too Big To Fail

Alice Coggins

For a week after Baby Boy's last social call, I woke up every day feeling sick to my stomach. Not because of his threats against me—I've always thought Tiffany would look better with a different face (just kidding, Tiffany, in case you ever read this; trust me, I feel incredibly guilty about giving Baby Boy your name)—so much as his threats against my Dad. Baby Boy's visit unnerved him too. One afternoon I arrived home to the sound of breaking glass. It was one of those rare occasions when Mom was out on the stoop and Dad was inside. From the stoop we could hear him in the living room swearing his head off and smashing anything he could lay his hands on.

"What's going on in there?" I asked my Mom.

"He's getting in touch with his inner Neanderthal."

Actually it wasn't the threats that triggered his rampage. It was what Gallaher said about him: *He's a nobody, that's who he is.* To be banned from loansharking and forced to abandon his castle, to be scorned as a Neanderthal and compared unfavorably to a fence post, to be threatened by an escapee from the Wharton Institution for the Criminally Insane—those he could take in stride. But to be called a *nobody* by the man he worshipped as the Boss, when for so many years he'd thought of himself as a major *somebody,* one of the anointed few in Gallaher's organization—that was more than he could bear. My Mom was philosophical about his violence. If we had any crockery, he would have smashed it, but luckily all we have are those unbreakable plastic dishes my parents bought at Woolworth's when they got married. The breaking glass turned out to be Dad's collection of Welch's Grape Jelly jars decorated with Looney Tunes characters, which Mom has always wanted to smash. And it wasn't every day she got to see him humiliated and out of control. So from her standpoint it was what Mr. Reddy would have called a win/win.

I went inside and swept up the living room while my Dad moped on the couch, lost in his angry thoughts. By the time we finished dinner, he was back in his usual optimistic mood. He'd decided to use the fortune he planned to make from his lottery ticket to challenge Gallaher at the ballot box. The upcoming election, he said, would be the turning point for the Neanderthal Party. He had the campaign all worked out in his mind. An open challenge to Gallaher was out of the question: the only way he could win was to leverage the complacency of one-party rule. In the last city-wide election, only twenty-seven people had voted, all of them dead. Dad's plan—which I was supposed to carry out—was to distribute hundreds of absentee ballots to sympathetic voters, enough to win in every precinct, and file them just before the polls closed on election day. When the votes were counted, my Dad would rule the city, and Gallaher would be a nobody.

It was a brilliant plan, even if it shortened my life expectancy to about three days. Luckily I had a sound basis for claiming conscientious objector status from the Neanderthal cause. "I consider myself a Finn," I told him.

Tiffany disqualified herself on aesthetic grounds. "Don't take this the wrong way, Dad," she said, "but I can't support the Neanderthals. Have you ever seen their hair?"

He turned desperately to my Mom. "What about you, Hun?"

"If you can get me into a castle, I'll vote for the chimpanzees."

I desperately need to find someone in a high position, unaffiliated with Gallaher or Baby Boy, to support my guerrilla war against the Grand Scam—especially now that I've discovered the full horror of what goes on at the Health Center. Andrew's Dad is probably the last person I'd want to ask, unless Andrew himself introduced me. Hector claims Andrew said he wouldn't mind, but I don't know. It's a little too weird, definitely a last resort. I've got a better idea: I'll ask Hector to introduce me to someone at the Federal Reserve Bank. They're sponsoring the Man of the Year Award; one of their officials is even presenting it. Surely they wouldn't support the Health Center if they knew it was part of a scam by Gallaher and Third Millennium Life.

I decided to take Hector along on my next visit to Grandma. When we walked into her room, Nurse Jenkins was bent over Grandma adjusting her gown. "Hi, Hector," she smiled, and hurried from the room.

"Hi!" he called after her. "How are you doing?"

"You know her?" I was pretty surprised.

"I knew her in college," he said. "She was in one of my classes."

Grandma kept her eyes shut. For a long time she refused to speak because she suspected that Hector worked at the Health Center. "This is Hector," I told her. "He's my friend. He doesn't work here."

"How did he know the nurse?" she demanded without opening her eyes.

Hector and I both laughed. Obviously the old gal was still pretty sharp. There was something I wanted to ask her. "Why don't you have an IV, Grandma? All the patients on the ward downstairs have IVs."

"Armand keeps pulling it out, so they gave up," she said.

"But don't you need it?"

She opened her eyes and stared into mine. "They put poison in them. Possum juice, we call it. It paralyzes you so you can't move around and bother the nurses. Armand won't let them give it to me."

Hector smiled down at Armand in his wheelchair. I'd forgotten to warn Hector about Armand.

"Get out of here!" Armand shouted. "Get the hell out of here!"

Downstairs in the ward I showed Hector the rows of patients stretched passively on their beds. All of them had IVs, as I'd noticed the first time. Oddly enough, Hector also seemed to know Dr. Mason. "What do you put in those IVs?" he asked him.

"Curare," the doctor answered. "It's perfectly safe as long as they stay on the respirators."

"Are there more wards downstairs?" I asked him.

"Twenty-seven floors of them," he smiled, sipping coffee from the red mug. "Just like this one."

On the bus back downtown I tried to broach the subject of Hector introducing me to one of the higher-ups at the Bank, but he still insisted that I talk to Andrew's father. He didn't seem shocked to learn that the Health Center was owned by Third Millennium Life. "Don't you see what's going on in that place?" I asked him. "They've got those people on life support just to keep from paying death benefits. What would the Bank think of that?"

"I think they'd be in favor of it," he said. "They're big on the health care industry, because it creates so many jobs. The more people it keeps alive—"

"You call that living? Those people should be allowed to die with dignity."

"Alice"—Hector's eyes shifted away, as if he wasn't sure he believed what he was about to say—"you've got to look at the big picture. Third Millennium Life would go under if it had to pay death benefits on all those people. The whole financial system could collapse."

The bus pulled up to his stop in front of the Federal Reserve Bank. "That might happen anyway," I argued as he stood up. "What if the Health Center couldn't keep all those people on life support any longer?"

"Then we'd have to put Third Millennium Life on life support," he smiled. "It's too big to fail."

My Dad's working full time on the campaign, which means getting me to do all the work. I picked up an absentee ballot at

City Hall and made two thousand copies at a printer in New Jersey. "Now what we need are boots on the ground!" Dad announced at a strategy conference on the front stoop, attended by myself, Mr. Reddy and Randolph, who has put together a crack team of operatives who even sleep on the ground: the homeless guys who can usually be found panhandling outside the entrance to the Museum of Homeless Art. Not many of them wear boots—most wear sneakers (usually without laces), flip-flops, or plastic bags tied around their feet with rubber bands. Their mission, in exchange for a hot meal, is to get out the vote for the Neanderthal ticket. In spite of Dad's efforts to make the party more inclusive, Mr. Reddy politely but firmly refused an appointment to the high command. "I am not a Neanderthal," he said, bowing slightly. "Thank you very much."

Assembling the campaign staff has been the easy part. "The only problem is," Dad said one afternoon, as it dawned on him for the first time, "who are we going to get to vote for us?"

I didn't say anything. But I had an idea.

Later that afternoon Dad was in a more confident mood. He lounged on the couch enjoying Sinatra's rendition of "Call Me Irresponsible" as he scratched beneath his ankle cuff with the coat hanger. Tiffany sat beside him staring at her phone like one of the patients at the Health Center.

"I'll tell you one thing," Dad said to no one in particular. "Baby Boy's Grand Scam isn't going to work after the election. All the nonprofits are coming to me now. The Curtis Institute —you heard of that? it's a music school—they're trying to hit me up for a major donation. I told them, change your name to the Sinatra Institute and I'll think about it. Who the hell is that place named after, anyway? Tony Curtis?"

"Curtis Mayfield," Tiffany said without looking up.

"Another outfit that's begging for money," Dad went on, "is the Philadelphia Orchestra. It's like the Mummers, only with no banjos, and they don't march."

"Or wear feathers," I pointed out.

"Right. Can you believe they haven't even considered selling the naming rights? You've leaving money on the table, I told them. Do have any idea how much Ben Franklin paid to have the Parkway named after him?"

"And don't forget George Washington," I chimed in. "Think of how much he must have shelled out for D.C."

"For a whole state," Tiffany added, to sound smart.

"Right," Dad said. "That's what I told them. You could collect millions for changing your name to the Wells Fargo Band. When you've done that, come back and we can talk about donations. But you're going to have to get rid of those violins." He shook his head. "It's frustrating, dealing with these people. I'm thinking of starting a charity of my own that I can donate to, like Baby Boy did with the Homeless Art Museum."

"How about the Ray Coggins Museum of Crackpot Ideas?" Mom called out from the kitchen. "If you can find a space big enough to hold your collection."

41. Novus Ordo Seclorum

At the Federal Reserve Bank, Hector had a somewhat disturbing discussion with Arbuthnot. At their last meeting, Arbuthnot had finally admitted that the Potlatch existed, though he refused to say what it was. Now Hector wondered if Arbuthnot would consider helping Alice defeat what she called the Grand Scam. As he'd told her, the Bank probably wouldn't find anything objectionable in Third Millennium's management of the Health Center. Their mission was to keep the economy humming by managing aggregate demand. Who could say that keeping Social Security recipients on life support shouldn't be part of the Bank's tool kit for maintaining full employment? That was a judgment best left to the Board of Governesses. However, there had been something troubling about what he'd seen at the Health Center. He'd known "Nurse Jenkins" and the pear-shaped man who called himself Dr. Mason in college, when he was an embalming major. They had taken their degrees in that subject and gone on to work as interns at Gallaher Funeral Services Inc. What were they doing on the medical staff of the Health Center? He wondered if it had something to do with the Potlatch, and if it did, whether the Bank knew what was going on. He decided that at their next meeting he would question Arbuthnot more about the Bank's views on the Potlatch.

"The organization you call the Potlatch," Arbuthnot said with a sly smile, "has been with us since before the Egyptians built the pyramids." They sat in his minimalist office (Hector had read that the highest executives have the least cluttered desks), enjoying the coffee they had brought with them from the cafeteria. Hector, who was beginning to feel more comfortable with Arbuthnot, leaned back in his chair with his legs stretched in front of him. "In fact," Arbuthnot went on, "the earliest written records—cuneiform inscriptions baked into Sumerian clay tablets five thousand years ago—lay out the whole conspiracy and its future plans in graphic detail (luckily no one is able to read them)."

Hector pulled his legs in and sat up straight. "The Potlatch is a conspiracy?"

Arbuthnot's nod confirmed that this was correct. "It has operated under many names and disguises, under the careful direction of bankers from the Medici to the Bardi, the Peruzzi, the Fuggers, the Rothschilds, right down to the Morgans and the Warburgs and the Rockefellers in our own times. In America it has most often been known simply as the 'Bank.'"

"Are you talking about *our* Bank?"

"They say the Federal Reserve system began with a secret meeting in Jekyll Island, Georgia, in 1910. That meeting was only a subterfuge. The real meeting— a conclave of leaders of the Bank, which of course already existed—took place several miles away, on the Hyde plantation. The Jekyll Island group and the later Federal Reserve System, with its twelve phony regional banks, were an elaborate fig leaf to allow the Bank to radically redefine its reach and powers."

"I can hardly believe this," Hector muttered. "But it's worked out pretty well, hasn't it?"

"It takes time to get the kinks out of any new system," Arbuthnot said. "Admittedly, mistakes have been made."

"What kind of mistakes?"

"Well, you know. The First World War—that was a noble experiment, but it left a bad taste in people's mouths. The Great Depression—again, a miscalculation, but well worth the effort. We learned a lot. The Second World War, the Korean War, the Vietnam War, the Gulf War, the—"

"Wait a minute! Are you saying that the Bank was behind all those wars?"

"Let's face it, Hector," Arbuthnot smiled. "There are only two foolproof ways to prevent unemployment. The most popular one is war. You make things and blow them up."

Hector shook his head sadly. "War is hell."

"That it is. But there's no unemployment in hell, is there? Eternal torment can take up your whole day. War—I mean all-out war—can do that too."

"Well, it's the last resort, I hope."

"Not quite. There's one other option that used to be quite popular, but it went out of vogue in the 1860s. Some of the Governesses think we should bring it back—on a non-discriminatory basis, of course. This time it would be for everyone."

"The 1860s? You don't mean...?

Arbuthnot chuckled. "Have you ever heard of a slave who's out of work?"

42. Meet The Parents

Alice Coggins

It was a Thursday night and I had to cater a fundraiser at eight o'clock. It was a big event out at UCLA, the annual candlelight vigil for victims of circumstance, one of those hypersensitive affairs where you have to wear plastic gloves and a surgical mask when you handle the hors d'oeuvres (if they knew me better they'd probably make me wear a warning label: Caution: Lives in a home containing peanuts, tree nuts and wing nuts). Hector asked me to meet him at Del Giorno's—to "discuss something important," as he put it, which I was hoping meant that he'd found someone at the Bank I could talk to about the Grand Scam. Instead, when I sat down beside him at the bar I realized that the person next to me on the other side was Andrew. I wanted to run away and never be seen again. But when I swiveled toward him I had one of those déjà vu moments that come once in a lifetime: you can see what's coming as if you're watching it on your phone, your life flashing on the screen an instant before it actually happens: Andrew fighting back tears as he says he's dumped Melissa, he never really loved her, the only woman he ever loved was me—

All that passed in an instant, and then was gone before I was done swiveling. It wasn't déjà vu because it never happened. Just a ridiculous fantasy. I should have known I looked too thin on that screen.

"Congratulations," I said, forcing a smile. "I heard you're getting married."

"Thanks," he nodded. It was like I'd said I was sorry for his loss.

It was beyond awkward, but Andrew was really nice. I'm not sure he thought Hector's idea of my talking to his dad was such a great one, especially when I wouldn't reveal the topic. "Something really important," Hector said. "Like I told you."

"OK, sure," Andrew smiled. "If you want to meet my dad, I'll have you over."

"How about your step-mom?" Hector asked. "Will she be there?"

"The Queen of the Night? Oh, yes. She'll be there."

Andrew and his parents live in a fancy high-rise near Rittenhouse Square. The concierge (who looked at me funny, as if he knew who I was) called ahead and sent me up on the elevator. Andrew greeted me in the hall and took me inside to meet his step-mom. She has the kind of face that reminds you why plastic surgery is called plastic. I wondered if she came with instructions.

"Patti," Andrew said, introducing me. "This is Alice."

"Alice?" Patti asked. A pair of apple-sized lumps appeared in her cheeks, as if the mention of my name was enough to melt her Botox. "Aren't you the girl who crashed the Stark Raven fundraiser?"

"I invited her," Andrew said.

"Actually I was there with the caterers," I said.

That was the wrong thing to say. Her face seemed to be splitting apart at the seams. "And you're from"—she choked on the words—"South Philadelphia?"

"Born and raised," I confessed.

"She's here to see Dad," Andrew said. "Come on, Alice. He's out on the balcony."

Patti tried to block our path. "Where do you think you're going?"

"There's something Alice wants to talk to Dad about."

"Something private," I said.

"Private? In my house?"

Andrew stepped around her and led me out to the balcony. It smelled like the reptile house at the zoo, and I could see why. In the middle was a giant coffee table that turned out to be a tortoise. "This is Achilles," Andrew said.

The tortoise ignored me. "Hi, Achilles," I said anyway.

"And this is my dad."

Andrew's dad and I both froze when our eyes met. He sat in a cane chair with a drink in his hand. Neither of us blinked or looked away. I felt sick to my stomach.

David Ogleby was Half Nelson, the compulsive gambler and embezzler I'd met at Baby Boy's butcher shop seven years before. The college president who embezzled every last dime out of his university and then sold it to the mob. I'd come to warn him about the thug he'd let take over the city.

Neither of us said anything.

I was sworn to secrecy as far as Bob Baskerville's true identity was concerned, so I couldn't hint at the real reason I was there.

"Well, what is it?" Patti demanded. "What's so important that you came here to talk about?"

I realized that she didn't know anything about it. She didn't know who Bob Baskerville really was or who her husband really was. She didn't know why David Ogleby was such a pitiful ghost of his former self.

"Go ahead, Alice," Andrew said.

Andrew didn't know either.

"I'm so sorry!" I squeezed his hand and ran out the door.

43. Rock Bottom

When I escaped from Andrew's building, I kept running until I got to Penn's Landing down by the river. I thought about jumping in but the water looked too dirty and cold, so I headed to the nearest bar. I have no idea how many drinks I had, or how many burgers or french fries or desserts. In my defense, I thought it would be my last meal. When Baby Boy heard about my visit to David Ogleby, my days would be numbered. And the number would be in the low single digits.

I ubered home around 2:00 a.m. in a drunken stupor and crawled into bed. When I brushed my teeth the next morning—actually it was afternoon—my eyes filled with tears at the sight of the girl in the mirror, who'd apparently been beaten to a pulp, thrown in a ditch and left for dead. When I slipped out of the bathroom I was hoping no one would pay any attention, which is almost a sure bet in my family. Mom sat absorbed in her work at the kitchen table. Dad was on the phone with his moat contractor. Hearing familiar voices on the stoop, I poured myself a cup of coffee and wandered outside. The weather was dour and ugly, just like me. Randolph and Mr. Reddy were debating a report on Eyewitness News that said young people my age were fleeing the city in droves, moving to Canada, Brazil, even Russia, to escape the legacy of hopelessness and despair that has overtaken us after decades of rooting for the Eagles. Mr. Reddy, who is a hard liner when it comes to the Eagles, was outraged by this broadcast. To his mind, any hint of defeatism is grounds for deportation to New Jersey. When I appeared on the stoop, he saw more than enough hopelessness and despair in my eyes to arouse his suspicions. "Why is your generation leaving the city?" he demanded.

"It's not because of the Eagles," I said, looking away.

"The Phillies? That I can understand."

"It's not about sports." I wasn't eager to share the disasters of my personal life with these two men. But I wasn't about to hide my feelings, either, even if I didn't want them to know why I had them. Mr. Reddy noticed the tears in my eyes. Satisfied that they had nothing to do with the Eagles, he nodded and gently asked me to continue. "My generation has plenty to despair about," I said, trying to find some more general explanation for my emotions. "We're all going through the motions of being adults without growing up. We don't have real lives and never will."

"No one has a real life," Mr. Reddy smiled, trying to cheer me up.

"We're trying to make sense of the dysfunctional world our parents built for us. They've created this monster and they expect us to live in it."

Randolph gazed up the block, past the junk cars and overflowing garbage cans, toward an empty plastic bag that was tumbling along the curb. "What's wrong with it?"

"It makes no sense. Every day people are being born, suffering and dying by the millions. There must be a purpose to all this."

"The Potlatch don't have a purpose," Randolph said. "It looks like it might, because of the way it repeats itself. But it don't. It's blind chance, repeated over and over again."

"Purposefulness," Mr. Reddy nodded knowingly, "without a purpose."

"That's the Potlatch," Randolph agreed.

"The material world is an illusion," Mr. Reddy explained.

"That's reassuring," I said, wiping my eyes with my sleeve.

"We busy ourselves with false perceptions and meaningless activities," Mr. Reddy said, "in order to avoid seeing ourselves and the world for what they really are."

"Pointless," I said, hoping one of them would disagree.

"And illusory," Mr. Reddy added.

"Look on the bright side," Randolph smiled. "The Potlatch don't have a purpose, but it don't have cops or judges or prosecutors neither. If you don't mess with it, it leaves you alone. You can be as pointless or as pointful as you want to be. You can live on the street like I do, or in a castle like your dad's gonna be doing soon. That's the Potlatch. It keeps you busy, but it don't tell you what to do."

I found myself getting angry. For as long as I can remember, everyone's been telling me that life is a racket, a ponzi scheme, a meaningless make-work project, or even (in Mr. Reddy's case) an illusion. Isn't there anything that's real? Isn't there love and courage and compassion somewhere in this crazy world?

"Every thought we have," Mr. Reddy said, "every word we hear, tells us to want something, something we can never have and that would be harmful if we got it. I stand in my store and when I see people walking by I say to myself, 'Why don't those people come in and buy something? Why don't they feel a sudden craving for Coca-Cola?' But I know that Coca-Cola isn't good for them. It will rot their teeth and destroy their kidneys and eventually drive them insane, but still I wish it on them, so I can pocket a few pennies. If your father ever paid for his cigarettes, I would probably hope he keeps smoking until he dies of lung cancer. Since he doesn't, I hope he quits as soon as possible. I am a bad man, but I can't help it. Nobody can help it."

You're not a bad man, I wanted to tell Mr. Reddy. You're a good man if you only knew it.

And look at Randolph, who owns nothing in this world but a pile of junk in an abandoned garage, but can always spare a kind word for everyone. Even my Dad in his crack-brained way is so innocent and loving that he hasn't even noticed in thirty years of marriage that his wife can't stand the sight of him. That innocence, that sympathy, that love—that can't all be part of the Potlatch, can it? "I'm not ready to throw in the towel," I said as I headed back inside. "I still want my life to make sense."

"Keep them wheels turning," Randolph called after me. "Even if they ain't taking us nowhere."

44. The Holdup

After my meltdown on the stoop with Randolph and Mr. Reddy, I desperately wanted to escape from the Potlatch. Even if there's no way out of it, you have to live your life as if there is, don't you? And nobody can live your life for you. You have to do that all by yourself. I gave up on the idea of poisoning Baby Boy Barkocy. That would be like throwing in the towel. And besides, I had a much better idea.

It was the night before Election Day, and the night before the Man of the Year Award dinner at the Health Center. I had spoken with Randolph about the get-out-the-vote campaign, and he knew what he needed to do. I called Hector and asked him to set up a meeting at the Federal Reserve Bank the next afternoon, which naturally he agreed to do (I have him wrapped around my little finger). Then I stayed up half the night writing speeches—three of them—which I printed out on my Mom's computer.

It was two in the morning before I finally went to bed, and luckily I fell asleep as soon as I closed my eyes. I had a big day ahead of me. I had to hold up a bank, raise the dead, steal an election, and put the sting on the Grand Scam.

In the morning it was raining cats and dogs, like it always does on Election Day. "That's Gallaher's doing," Dad muttered as we gazed out the window sipping our coffee. "Keeps the turnout low."

"We'll see about that." I pulled on my raincoat and grabbed an umbrella. "Can I take the Cadillac?"

"Sure." He reached in his pocket and handed me the keys. "You got the ballots?"

"They're in the trunk. I should be back by eleven."

When I stepped outside, I noticed two losers I'd never seen before watching from across the street. They both wore Flyers jerseys, sunglasses and backwards Phillies hats as if they were trying to make a fashion statement about being a jackass.

"Tiffany?" one of them said as he came toward me. They must have been a couple of her boyfriends lining up for the early bird special.

"She's not up yet," I told him. "Come back after noon."

Fifteen minutes later I brought the Cadillac to a soft landing in front of the Museum of Homeless Art, where Randolph stood reviewing his troops. Some lounged on benches or leaned against the wall, while others sprawled under a leafless tree hiding from the rain under black plastic garbage bags. "Hop in," I told Randolph, clearing some junk from the front seat. "Tell your troops we march at three."

In another fifteen minutes we penetrated the Health Center parking garage, where we paused for a final review of our game plan. "You're sure about this curare thing?" I asked Randolph.

"Sure I'm sure," he said. "I read about it in *National Geographic*. Curare is the stuff the Indians in the Amazon jungle put on the darts they shoot out of their blowguns."

"But it's not a poison, right?"

"No, it don't kill you. It *paralyzes* you."

"So that's why—"

"It *could* kill you, if it makes it so you can't breathe."

"Right."

"So if you're paralyzed by curare, you better hope they put you on a respirator."

We waved at the security guard in the lobby (my buddy Spencer), took the elevator up to the 30th floor and snuck downstairs to the 29th. There was no sign of any medical staff, only rows and rows of patients stretched out motionless under their IV tubes and their respirators. We walked up and down the aisles disconnecting the IVs, but keeping the respirators plugged in.

At the nurses' station, I found a pot of coffee simmering on a hot plate. Dr. Mason's red coffee mug stood beside it, ready to be filled at his next break. I reached to the shelf above and found a bottle of curare, which I started to pour into the coffee.

"Oral administration of curare don't work," Randolph said. "Try these." He handed me a bottle of Valium tablets, which I dumped in the coffee. Whatever else happened that day, Dr. Mason could look forward to a relaxing afternoon.

"Are you sure the patients will be OK?" I asked Randolph as we headed down to the 28th floor.

"If they stay on the respirators until the curare's out of their systems—four to six hours—they'll be just fine."

"You got all this out of *National Geographic?*"

"That and the *United States Pharmacopeia.* Got a copy in my office."

We hit the wards on the 28th floor, the 27th, the 26th, all the way down to the lobby, without encountering any hospital staff. Who needs doctors or nurses when the patients are paralyzed or already dead? Still, we had to work fast so that when we came back that afternoon we'd have plenty of time to disconnect the respirators.

I dropped Randolph off at the Homeless Art Museum and hurried back to the house to prepare for the next stage of the operation. Just before noon I called the Probation Department and asked for Kyle Rotundo, who sounded even dumber than I remembered him. I needed permission for my Dad to leave the house. Kyle was stubborn at first, until I suggested that I'd gladly fulfill his most degrading XXX-rated fantasies if he'd let Dad out that afternoon. Luckily I had the presence of mind to give my name as Tiffany.

"Two hours," he said. "I'll give him two hours. Where is he going?"

"You don't want to know."

As Dad sat on the couch, I wrapped an Ace bandage around his pants leg so you couldn't see the ankle cuff. He wore the powder-puff blue polyester leisure suit he'd bought at K-Mart in 1993. I found his lottery ticket and tucked it into my pocket. "Where are we going?" he asked.

"We're going to hold up a bank."

He was so nervous he could hardly stand up, even with the cane I found in the closet. "Sweetheart," he hesitated, "I'm no Boy Scout—I've been in the rackets all my life—but I've never held up a bank."

"There's always a first time."

"What if something goes wrong?"

"Don't worry, Dad. You're too big to fail."

Getting inside the Federal Reserve Bank was ridiculously easy. The only guards were a pair of old ladies with thick glasses who couldn't take their eyes off a soap opera on the TV. They peeked in our bags and waved us right through so they could get back to their show. We took the elevator to a large conference room on the tenth floor, where Hector had arranged a meeting with his boss, Gwendolyn, and her boss, Maureen, and several other Bank officials. Dad limped in with his cane like a politician at a Fourth of July picnic, shaking hands as he introduced himself around the table.

Maureen, who seemed to be in charge, was a puffy-haired little woman who barely reached the top of her chair back. "We're very happy to meet you, Mr. Coggins. At the Bank—"

"Ray," Dad interrupted. "Just call me Ray."

"All right," she smiled. "Ray. At the Bank—"

"Maureen, isn't it?"

"Right," she hesitated. "You can call me Maureen."

"I like to be on a first name basis," Dad explained.

"Certainly. As I was saying—"

"My Dad is very modest," I interrupted. "But as I'm sure you know, he has single-handedly revived the economy in the Delaware Valley. His real estate and construction activities—I assume you've heard about the castle—are projected to result in 10% annual growth in the region."

"That's correct," Hector nodded.

I reached in my pocket, pulled out the lottery ticket, and laid on the table. "This is his only asset."

"I'm sorry," Maureen squinted back at me. "That looks like a lottery ticket."

"It is a lottery ticket."

"The jackpot's over $700 million," Dad said proudly. "That ticket's going to win."

"How do you know that?"

"Maureen," Dad said, leaning toward her, "I feel it in my bones."

Maureen seemed at a loss for words. She seemed even smaller than she looked before.

"And this is your only asset?" Gwendolyn asked.

"Well, I've got my Sinatra records, all vinyl, some hard to find. Unfortunately my collection of Welch's Grape Jelly jars with the Looney Tunes figures was destroyed—I've got an insurance claim pending on that, could be big bucks—but I guess, other than the clothes on my back"—he smiled as he pinched the sleeve of his polyester leisure suit jacket—"that's pretty much what you're looking at. But trust me, that ticket's not going to lose."

"No, of course not," Maureen said with a grim smile.

I had about five seconds to move in for the kill. "Maureen," I purred, "you know what would happen if that ticket lost. All the materials and supplies my Dad bought would rot on the ground, and would never be paid for. And the money he borrowed against them wouldn't be paid back. The castle would never be finished. Thousands of construction workers would be thrown out of work. They'd cut down on their beer consumption, default on their truck payments, stop going to McDonalds—"

"It's not a pretty picture," Hector summarized.

Maureen glanced at Gwendolyn, then at Hector. She avoided looking at my Dad. "Obviously we're concerned."

I made my face relax so it wouldn't look like I was smiling, or trying to keep from smiling.

"We're willing to sign the ticket over to the Bank before the final drawing, which is tomorrow."

"Without recourse," Hector added.

"Right," I said. Hector had explained that concept to me. It meant my Dad wouldn't be on the hook for anything. "We're not making any promises that the ticket will win. If it does, you keep the money. If it doesn't—well, we won't expect to hear about it. Nobody needs to know it ever existed, or what might have happened if my Dad still owned it."

A long time passed—it seemed like hours—when nobody spoke. "I think I understand where you're going with this," Maureen said warily.

"Here's the idea," I said. "We'll incorporate a new bank, with my Dad as president and sole shareholder, myself as vice-president and chief operating officer. You advance the capital for the new bank, say $500 million—"

"That's a bargain, by the way," Dad said. "The ticket's worth at least $700 million."

"—and the new bank will assume all my Dad's obligations and continue funding all his projects."

Maureen struggled to control her face, which looked like it was about to shatter into a thousand pieces. "Including the castle?" she mumbled.

"Absolutely, Maureen," Dad said.

I smiled reassuringly. "We're totally committed to finishing the castle."

The paperwork was completed within an hour. There were congratulations and handshaking and good feelings all around.

Maureen and Gwendolyn and the other Bank officials were happy: an economic crisis had been averted and a solid new financial institution had been born. Hector was a hero for bringing the situation to their attention. My Dad was the president of Coggins National Bank, with capital of $500 million, and I was Vice-President and Chief Operating Officer. Our future in the world of finance was assured.

Still, I had to get Dad home before his ankle cuff started beeping. And I had a lot to get done before the day was over. I'd committed myself to getting out the vote, and in just three hours I was scheduled to waitress at the Man of the Year Award dinner honoring Bob Baskerville. That award was sponsored by the Federal Reserve Bank, and Maureen was the Bank representative who would present it.

Before Dad and I left the conference room, I pulled Maureen over for a quick sidebar. "Maureen," I said. "I have one last favor to ask you."

45. Magic

Hector still loved Alice, but he was troubled by the Bank's bailout of her father. Ray Coggins was well known as the neighborhood crank, a petty crook who'd founded the Neanderthal Party. How had he accumulated so much debt that the Bank would agree to fund his bank with $500 million? And while Hector and Alice and so many others struggled with their unpaid internships, why should Ray Coggins, of all people, be the one to hit the jackpot? Was there any justice in the world?

After Alice had rushed her dad home following the meeting, Hector tapped on the door of the unnamed, unnumbered room where he'd often spoken with Arbuthnot. Arbuthnot sat behind the empty desk as if he'd been expecting him. Hector briefed him on the Coggins meeting and its outcome. "I just can't believe they gave that guy so much money," Hector said. "Why? With all the inequality of wealth and income—why?"

"Money makes the world go round," Arbuthnot grinned.

"I thought you said it didn't exist."

"Of course it exists. It's just not what you think it is."

Hector felt awkward being lectured on such basic concepts. "What is it, then?

"It's a magic wand that you can point at somebody to get them to do what you want," Arbuthnot said. "Work for me, marry me, build me a castle, sell me your house: in effect, all the desires of everybody in the world that can only be fulfilled by someone else. That's what money is—and the Bank controls it." His color was high, his eyes gleaming with maniacal intensity. "We control all the pushes and pulls of the human heart: desire and gratification, generosity and greed, labor and exploitation—that's what money is, and we control it all!"

"That's what the Bank does?"

Arbuthnot stopped to catch his breath and let his smile relax. "Not that this magic is easy to control," he said, more calmly. "If we release too much of it, people burn themselves out in a frenzy of consumption. If we release too little, they become depressed, hostile, resigned to the futility of life. Only the Governesses know how to keep these forces in balance. They spin out the threads of Fate so the machinery of the world keeps humming along at just the right speed. Without them—without the Bank—there would be heat death."

"Heat death?" What was he talking about?

"Some people might be shocked," Arbuthnot went on, "or pretend to be shocked, to hear us talking like this. But here at the Bank we don't have the luxury of being MC."

"MC?"

"Metaphysically correct." He lowered his voice and peered around as if for hidden cameras. "How much do you know about the laws of thermodynamics?"

"Not much. I mean, I took chemistry as part of my embalming curriculum—"

"Work can only get done when there is inequality. In a state of equilibrium, nothing happens. Imagine a world in which everyone had the same amount of money. The magic wouldn't work, would it?"

"No, I guess not."

"Money would be worthless."

At the Coggins home in South Philadelphia, Tiffany Coggins put on her Tommy Hilfiger top and her Guess jeans and headed out to her hair appointment at Mary Ann's Shear Madness three blocks away. As she stepped off the stoop, two men—wearing sunglasses, Flyers jerseys and backwards Phillies hats—jumped into a black SUV and followed her. When she rounded the corner, the van sped up, then screeched to a halt.

The men jumped out. "Tiffany?" one of them asked, blocking her way as the other, gliding up beside her, slipped a black hood over her head.

"Hey, what are you doing?" were her last words before they tossed her into the back of the SUV and drove away.

46. The Undead

Alice Coggins

Events moved quickly at the Health Center that afternoon. By the time I got back after dropping my Dad off at home, it had been five hours after I turned off the IVs. The curare had worn off. The patients were wide awake and squirming in their beds, flexing their muscles, twitching and moaning and kicking their feet, as if they'd awoken from a twenty year enchantment. The doctors and nurses were all unconscious from a temporary overdose of Valium.

Randolph arrived with his ragtag army of homeless voter assistants. I'd asked him to wear his best clothes, and he obliged by unearthing a double-breasted zoot suit from his garage that made him look like a 1940s gangster with red high-tops. He and his crew lugged the absentee ballots in from the Cadillac while I went around disconnecting the patients from their respirators. Without the curare in their veins, they didn't need them anymore. It didn't take much convincing to get them to sign the ballots. We sorted the ballots by precinct and Randolph supervised their delivery to the polling places. By five o'clock the election was over, though no one would know that until the polls closed.

The hard part was keeping the patients in their beds. Liberated from the curare drips and respirators, they twisted themselves upright, still drooling, their hair disheveled, their blank eyes bulging, and struggled to their feet, staggering in their flimsy ill-fitting gowns. They gathered into groups and wandered in circles through the wards, pressing into the hallways and stairwells as they marched forward like a troop of zombies. They stumbled down the stairs and into the elevators and began to fill the lobby. There was no holding them back.

I almost panicked—this could spoil my whole plan. Luckily I had changed into my Gallaher Catering uniform for the last time. In that guise I was able to convince Spencer, the security guard, that the invading zombies were a delegation of patients who'd left their beds to make a surprise appearance at the Man of the Year dinner. We herded them into the Bruno Bettelheim Room, the private function room adjoining the Mother Teresa Room where the awards dinner would take place. The two function rooms were separated by a sliding partition, which (I explained to Spencer) would need to be opened when I gave him the signal. In the middle of the crowd I saw my Grandma lurching along behind Armand's wheelchair.

The dinner was scheduled to begin in less than an hour. The guests and dignitaries began to make their way through the main entrance into the luxurious lobby. Peter Wolf, the attorney from Stark Raven, who would serve as master of ceremonies. Maureen, from the Federal Reserve Bank, who waved to me with a sly smile. The Poffenbargers, the Van de Kamps and various rich people I'd seen at other fundraisers. And then—oh my God, it was bound to happen!—the Forepaughs and their dwarfish daughter Melissa. And then came Andrew—I couldn't let him see me. Not yet. His step-mother noticed me and gave me the evil eye. When Bob Baskerville marched through the door with his psycho sidekick Howie, I grabbed Spencer's arm and pulled him around a corner into the hallway. If the awards ceremony was going to be a success, I explained, I would need his help. My entrance had to be carefully timed.

"As part of the surprise?" he asked, raising his eyebrows. He knew I was up to something, but he didn't mind. When you're a security guard, you probably get tired of making sure nothing happens.

"That's right," I said, clutching the three speeches I'd printed out the night before. "It's going to be a big surprise."

47. No Exit

The air seemed to be running out in Arbuthnot's windowless office. Hector felt himself gasping for breath, his temperature rising as he began to panic. "So that's what the Potlatch is, isn't it?" he said as if talking to himself. "The secret government that keeps this insane system running!"

"Whatever it takes to keep the magic working," Arbuthnot nodded. "Here at the Bank, our job is to keep the wheels turning, the mill grinding, the spindle spinning, the sand dripping through the hourglass—you get the picture."

"And this has been going on for how long?"

"The metaphors have changed, the names and institutions have changed, but it's been the same process, essentially the same organization, since time immemorial."

Hector stood up, wobbling on his feet, almost overcome with desperation. "But what does it all mean?"

"Don't ask what it means!" Arbuthnot laughed. "Meaning implies purpose. There isn't any purpose, but no one outside the Bank can know that."

"There must be some way out!" Hector lurched toward the door and tried to twist the knob, but it slipped out of his grasp. Somehow, without leaving his chair, Arbuthnot had locked the door behind him.

Arbuthnot laughed. "You want out?" He stepped to the door and easily opened it. "Go ahead! But let me tell you something: The more you try to dig your way out of the Potlatch, the deeper you bury yourself."

"How could that be?"

"Because all the forces opposing the Potlatch are also part of the Potlatch."

"But there's a resistance movement, dedicated to destroying it. A woman named Maria—"

"She works for me."

"What?"

"Surely you realize by now that if there's a group fighting against the Potlatch, it must be part of the Potlatch. You can't not be part of the Potlatch."

Hector's mind was reeling. "But what about Somos?" he gasped. *"Somos pero no somos."*

"We are but we are not," Arbuthnot laughed. "Did you forget my name? *Are-but-not."* He laughed again. "The 'H' is silent!"

Hector ran out the door, down the hall to the elevators, past the security desk and out through the Bank's main entrance. Dusk had fallen and the sidewalk seemed darker than usual. As he headed around the corner, two men threw a black hood over his head, tossed him into the back of a windowless van, and drove away.

48. Man Of The Year

Alice Coggins

I peeked into the Mother Teresa Room to get the lay of the land. On the dais Peter Wolf chatted with Mrs. Poffenbarger while Baby Boy Barkocy a/k/a Bob Baskerville entertained Maureen from the Federal Reserve Bank. The Man of the Year trophy gleamed on one end of their table. Andrew sat beside Melissa at a big round table nearby, across from his parents, the Forepaughs and the Van de Kamps. In the space between the tables and the dais stood a large platform draped with white cloth. This, I'd been told, was a sculpture donated by some people named Rick and Rosemary Wurlitzer, which was to be unveiled that night.

The Wurlitzers caused quite a stir when they arrived. They were in their late twenties, heavily tattooed and riddled with piercings, squeezed into skin-tight black leather suits. Rick wore a looped whip on his belt; Rosemary sported a necklace that looked like a motorcycle drive-chain. They commandeered their own table—the old ladies who were already there fled to another table—where they were soon joined by Randolph and some of the homeless guys, who guzzled 32-ounce tallboys of Bud Light and made lewd comments to the waitresses. I noticed Howie near the partition, frowning with his arms crossed in front of him.

My boss kept giving me things to do and I kept not doing them. After all, it was going to be my last night working for Gallaher Catering and I couldn't go into the Mother Teresa

Room until the time was right. After the coffee was served and Peter Wolf had introduced Mrs. Poffenbarger to begin the program, Maureen stood up and discreetly made her way out to the hall, and while Mrs. Poffenbarger worked her way toward the middle of her first sentence ("... and we are fortunate indeed in having assembled in one place—in the aptly named Mother Teresa Room—many of the most generous benefactors of our city, if not of mankind. People who, like Mother Teresa herself"—she nodded toward Baby Boy, who blushed modestly—"have sacrificed their personal comforts and concerns to alleviate the suffering of the sick and the aged, the lame and the halt..."), I darted up to the dais—with the three speeches in my hand—and slipped into Maureen's chair, right next to Baby Boy.

"What the hell are you doing here?" he rasped in my ear.

"I'm here to present your award."

"You're nuts!"

I laid my hand on his beefy wrist and leaned closer. "Let me lay out your choices for you," I whispered. "When I present the award, I'm going to give either this introduction, praising you as a benefactor of mankind"—I handed him the first speech—"or this one"—I stuck the second speech in front of him—"spelling out who you really are, with enough details to put you behind bars for the next twenty years."

"You're not only nuts, you're dead."

"It has been well said," Mrs. Poffenbarger droned on, "that there is no better indication of a society's basic decency than the way it treats its older citizens. In our city, and in the nation, the Dwight D. Schopenhauer Memorial Health Center stands at the forefront of enlightened elder care..."

"Including your plot to fold all the nonprofits in the city into the Gallaher rackets," I added. "Such as this so-called Health Center, which is really just a racket run by Third Millennium Life."

I could feel his temperature rising as he skimmed the two alternative speeches. "You'd better give this one"—indicating the favorable one—"if you want to keep breathing."

"If I give that one," I said, "I'm going to ask a little favor in return. This is the acceptance speech I'm going to ask you to deliver." I handed him the third speech I had drafted and he fumed and growled as he read it.

Mrs. Poffenbarger shot us a friendly smile in hopes that we would stop whispering. "Since forming its alliance with Third Millennium Life—an alliance made possible by the efforts of Bob Baskerville—the Health Center has achieved an almost unheard of survival rate of 99%. It is no longer our patients, but death itself which is passing away."

"Your survival rate just went to zero," Baby Boy hissed.

Mrs. Poffenbarger winced, assuming the threat was meant for her. "And tonight," she said, "through the generosity of the Federal Reserve Bank, we will honor our new Man of the Year, Bob Baskerville."

Thunderous applause. "But first," she said, waving her hand to silence the crowd, "we have another blessing to celebrate, a very special addition to the Health Center and our city's lively art scene made possible by the generosity of Rick and Rosemary Wurlitzer. The Wurlitzers have donated an extremely important work of art, which after tonight will stand (or perhaps I should say, recline)"—Mrs. Poffenbarger tittered with mock embarrassment—"in the Health Center lobby for all to enjoy: one of the highlights of the 1985 Vassily Plescinski series, 'Call Girls of the Early 1980s.' And now I will ask Mr. Rick Wurlitzer to step forward to accept our gratitude as he unveils this exciting sculpture."

Rattling his chains and tapping the cleats on his motorcycle boots, Rick Wurlitzer swaggered to the covered pedestal and faced the crowd with a defiant and surprisingly lewd grin. After the applause died down, he yanked off the canvas cover and jumped aside.

The audience gasped. The sculpture was similar to the one of "Hildegarde" in Peter Wolf's office—a life-size, utterly realistic, full-color reproduction of a naked woman lounging on a stone pedestal, so lifelike in every detail that you expected her to say something or maybe get up and walk away. Like Hildegarde, she had the look of a 30-year-old New York call girl, circa 1985, which is exactly what she was. Only this wasn't Hildegarde. This, as everyone could see at a glance, was Patti Ogleby.

Rick Wurlitzer gloated and grinned back at his wife, who laughed out loud. Apparently the couple had a score to settle with Patti. Patti tried to shrug it off, and shot a threatening glance at Mr. Van de Kamp, who joined in the laughter. The Forepaughs stood up with Melissa and marched out, followed by the Van de Kamps. David Ogleby sat frozen in his seat, stunned by the realization that his trophy wife was a woman with a past, and a very long past at that. She was eligible for Medicare.

"I can explain," Patti muttered. Her face seemed to be crumbling. Suddenly she looked her age.

Now the whole room was laughing. Patti jumped up and fled out the door, with David close behind her. Left alone at the table, Andrew looked like he'd just arrived from another planet. I signaled to Spencer, who stood in a corner near the partition. He pushed a button and the wall began to open.

On the dais, Mrs. Poffenbarger didn't miss a beat. "For most of you," she said, "Bob Baskerville will need no introduction. Former president of UCLA, founder and Chairman of the Museum of Homeless Art, benefactor of so many charities around the city, he is truly a man for all times and seasons, not just for this year..."

"You won't get away with this," Baby Boy hissed in my ear. "Whatever I say tonight, or you say, Gallaher will make sure it never takes effect. And you won't be around anyway. In case you don't know it, Gallaher owns this town."

"Not anymore, he doesn't."

The patients had been so packed into the adjoining Bruno Bettelheim Room that when the wall opened they began to overflow into our space. They staggered in slowly at first, eyes wild, mouths agape, filling the spaces between the tables like a phantom wait staff. At a signal from Randolph, the homeless guys opened the doors into the hallway, inviting another troop of gray-faced patients to squeeze inside. Some people in the audience tried to leave. They were blocked by the patients and pushed back into their seats by the homeless guys.

Baby Boy waved to Howie, but there was no way his pet psycho could reach the dais. "These are some of the patients who voted in today's election," I told him.

"But those people are dead!"

"Not as dead as the people who voted for Gallaher."

I could see the panic in his eyes. I spread both versions of my introduction in front of him and stepped to the podium, where I introduced myself as the Vice-President and Chief Operating Officer of Coggins National Bank. "On behalf of the Federal Reserve Bank, I'm proud to have the honor of presenting this year's award," I said. "But before I introduce our new Man of the Year, there's another item I'd like to mention. As you all know, this is Election Day. And for the first time, through a coordinated get-out-the-vote campaign, many residents of the Health Center were able to cast absentee ballots for the candidates of their choice."

Randolph appeared beside me in his zoot suit and handed me a sheet of paper. "The returns are just in," I announced, scanning the paper. "It's a solid defeat for the Gallaher machine—which operates the Health Center—and a landslide for the Neanderthals."

One by one, almost soundlessly, the patients began to applaud, flapping their wizened hands together, lifting and lowering their creaky knees and bunioned feet, whistling through their toothless smiles as they welcomed the downfall of the Gallaher machine. The assembled guests—gathered to honor the Health Center and its owners—suddenly looked as ghastly as the patients. But when they saw Bob Baskerville rising to be introduced, they must have assumed that all was right with the world. And besides—I saw some of them glancing around in terror—there was no way they could make it out of there alive.

The Mother Teresa Room echoed with applause. Turning toward Baby Boy, I waited to see which version of my introduction he would choose. All eyes were on him, including those of the patients, who seemed intent on devouring the contents of his enormous bald head. He snatched up both speeches, crumpled one in his fist, and handed me the one he wanted me to deliver. His eyes warned me not to go back on my promise.

I folded the paper in half and laid it aside. "I had a long speech prepared," I said, "outlining the many accomplishments of our new Man of the Year, some of which would surprise even those who know him best. But as Mrs. Poffenbarger observed, this is a man who needs no introduction. And so without further ado, I give you Bob Baskerville, our new Man of the Year."

The crowd roared and Baby Boy flashed a winning smile as he stood up with my ten-page surrender document in his hand.

"I'm as eager as you all are to hear his acceptance speech."

49. Snapper Soup

Hooded, gagged and hogtied, Tiffany writhed on the floor of the black SUV as it juddered through the broken streets of Philadelphia. When at last it came to a stop—in an abandoned truck shed in an old industrial section of the city—her captors bundled her out in the dim light and stood her up in front of the man who'd ordered her capture. That man was Howie, who, as they dragged her hooded form toward him, could hardly contain the insane anticipation of what he would do to her.

She kept her eyes closed when they pulled off the hood, too terrified to witness her own fate, but she could hear him panting, smacking his lips, pounding a blunt instrument into his palm.

"You got the wrong girl, you idiots!" he screamed.

"You said Tiffany. This is Tiffany."

He lashed out at his assistants and they tossed her on the floor in front of him. He loomed over her, enormous in his Hannibal Lecter T-shirt, his muscles bulging in full tattoo sleeves the length of both arms. In the last moments before he bent down to wrap his massive hands around her throat, she opened her eyes and caught a glimpse of his broad chest, his sensuous mouth, his usually vacant eyes gleaming with psychotic rage.

"You're kind of cute," she said.

* * *

Five days after the Man of the Year dinner, Andrew's parents asked him to bring his new fiancée over to the apartment for cocktails. Technically they had already met Alice, though not in her capacity as fiancée, and no mention was made of any previous meetings. Melissa and her parents were likewise not mentioned. At first they sat on the balcony, where a gap in the parapet had been opened (Patti explained) as part of a renovation project, and blocked with yellow tape. Achilles, though facing the gap, displayed no interest in the renovations or the rest of the conversation. He even seemed bored with his duties as a coffee table. It was chilly, and Patti wore only a sleeveless white sequined dress that left most of her torso bare, so after a while they all went inside and sipped their drinks around the fireplace, where Patti built a raging fire. She wanted to make sure the happy couple knew that she and David approved of their engagement. "You have our blessing," she told them. Alice chuckled to herself. Was Patti the kind of person who should be issuing blessings?

Outside, a sinister trio had convened in the shadows of the Walden Towers: the building's most prominent resident, Bob Baskerville (more admired than ever after his magnanimous acceptance speech at the Man of the Year dinner), his driver Howie, and Howie's new girlfriend Tiffany, who sported a death's head tattoo on her cheek and two black eyes. The three of them gazed upwards at a balcony on the nineteenth floor, easily recognizable because of the yellow hazard tape marking a recent break in the railing. "That's the apartment," Bob Baskerville said. "with the lights on. In a little while they'll come down the elevator and walk out that door over there"—

he pointed to the building's main entrance—"and then over here to the parking garage. As soon as they step into the garage, hit them with this." He handed Howie a .38 caliber automatic pistol in a brown paper bag.

"Right," Howie said.

"You know what she looks like, right?"

"Who?"

"Tiffany's sister. The one who came to the butcher shop."

"Right."

"Her first, then her boyfriend. Hit the parents if they come out with them."

Tiffany goggled at Howie, blinded by love and strung out on the huge quantities of methamphetamines, opiates and hallucinogens he had fed her for the past five days.

"Right," Howie repeated. "Alice. And her boyfriend Andrew."

Alice and Andrew watched the fire crackle in the fireplace as they chatted with Patti and David. Patti reached the poker into the fire, adjusting the logs. "I don't know what we'll do," she said. "No one in the building will talk to me. The Wurlitzers have taken over the Homeowners Association."

"We'll probably have to move to a trailer park in New Jersey," David said.

"Anyway, we're very happy for you," Patti said. "Who would have thought we'd have a banker for a daughter-in-law?"

"We're desperate for money," David added, in case Alice had missed the point.

"Can't you get Social Security?" Alice asked. "Or food stamps?" In her new role as a banker, she had little sympathy for financial sob stories, especially from old people with poor credit histories.

Patti smiled and changed the subject. After Alice and Andrew had said their goodbyes and headed for the elevator, she turned to David and sighed, "Well, we're not going to get any money out of her. I guess it's Plan B." David nodded.

She pulled the red-hot poker out of the fire and headed toward the balcony

"Achilles!"

On the sidewalk below, Tiffany had wandered twenty feet from Howie and Bob Baskerville to contemplate her reflection in a shop window. Was that girl really her? she wondered. What was that thing on her cheek? Then as she glanced up at the balcony with the yellow tape on it, an amazing sight took hold of her attention. A woman in a white sequined dress stepped forward with a red-hot poker and bent down with it. And then what appeared to be an enormous turtle lurched off the balcony and plunged toward the sidewalk, landing smack on top of Howie and Bob. "Only 'smack' isn't quite the right word," Tiffany later told the police. "More like *Kaboom!*" The explosion was felt twenty blocks away and triggered an orange terror alert. Tiffany was splattered with a disgusting bouillabaisse of reptilian and human remains that ruined her Guess jeans and Tommy Hilfiger top. Emergency teams sifted through the wreckage for three days, holding out the hope that the Man of the Year and his driver had survived, but they were never seen again. The death of Achilles was ruled a suicide and covered by Pet Life, which became insolvent as a result. As soon as they received the insurance proceeds, Patti and David moved out west to start a new life.

Alice and Andrew were still in the elevator when the explosion hit. They felt the tremor but continued to the lobby and stepped outside without noticing the commotion around the corner. Strolling several blocks to an excellent seafood restaurant, they both enjoyed a cup of snapper soup.

50. Ever After

Alice Coggins

We moved up to the Northeast a few days after the awards dinner. Living in the castle, it's hard sometimes to remember what life was like in the old neighborhood. In a lot of ways nothing has changed. My Dad still loves my Mom, and she still hates him. Being President of Coggins National Bank is a perfect job for him, since it doesn't involve working for a living. He watches Flyers games and listens to his Sinatra records and steps out to the drawbridge when he needs a smoke. Mom has kept her no-show job but complains a lot about the commute. I gave up my internship at Coggins Catering Inc. (formerly Gallaher Catering Inc.) so I could spend my time running the bank. Everybody's happy about Andrew and me, even Andrew's parents, who run a non-profit brothel in Las Vegas.

Looking back on that night at the Health Center, I can see that it was some kind of turning point. The changes Bob Baskerville announced in his acceptance speech (which I wrote) have clinched his reputation as a humanitarian second only to Mother Teresa. He may win the Man of the Century award when they give it out a hundred years from now. All the nonprofits he and Gallaher controlled are now run by the beneficiaries. The winos have taken over the Museum of Homeless Art—you can see them out on the lawn most afternoons passing around a bottle of Night Train as they plan their next Beg-A-Thon. Third Millennium Life went belly up when the patients at the Health Center, freed from their respirators, soon found new digs (so to speak) in the cemetery. Of course Bob Baskerville—I mean Baby Boy Barkocy—didn't mean for any of this to happen. When he delivered his acceptance speech (with me standing beside him to keep him on script), he thought he'd have plenty of time to undo the damage before the new policies took effect. But Fate, moving a little quicker than usual (thanks to a prod from Patti's poker), caught up with him and Howie in the form of Achilles the tortoise. Desmond Gallaher had a heart attack when he heard about the election results and soon found lodging at Coggins Funeral Services Inc. (formerly Gallaher Funeral Services Inc.). Along with the former patients at the Health Center, he has remained on the voting rolls so he can do his civic duty as a member of the Neanderthal Party in future elections.

I'm sad to say that the last time anyone saw my Grandma or her friend Armand was that night at the Health Center. In the jubilation following Baby Boy's speech, the audience fled as the patients surged through the halls and crowded the lobby. With a sudden burst of energy, Armand stood up from his wheelchair and took Grandma by the hand. "Come on, baby!" he said as he led her toward the door. "Let's get the hell out of here!"

One night about a week after the awards dinner Tiffany woke us up banging on the portcullis, drugged out and heartbroken after seeing her new boyfriend Howie blown up by a falling tortoise. She looked pretty weird in the eyes, like maybe she'd already spent too much time with Howie. We put her down in the dungeon. It's got a straw pallet, a slop bucket and a fully-equipped torture chamber. Torture equipment is a lot like gym equipment, only with leather straps so you can't escape.

She'd been down there a couple of days when Kyle Rotundo, my Dad's probation officer, came to the door. He was here, he said, to collect on the debt Tiffany owed him— the fantasy fulfillment she (meaning I) had promised him on the phone so he'd let Dad go to the meeting at the Federal Reserve Bank. I'd forgotten all about that. The look on Kyle's doglike face (he was actually panting) told me he had some pretty animalistic plans for my sister. "I want my pound of flesh," he said. "Or—how much does Tiffany weigh?"

"About 130," I lied. How often do I get a chance to claim she weighs more than me?

"OK, then, I want my 130 pounds of flesh." His eyes gleamed with a wild surmise, like when a dog starts humping your leg.

"She's down in the dungeon," I told him, unlocking the cellar door. I hated to do it, but now that I'm Vice-President of Coggins National Bank, I look at things a little differently. A deal's a deal.

I went back in the kitchen, where Andrew sat with my Dad explaining the latest changes in the banking code while Mom, banging a cleaver on her cutting board, chopped up onions to make cheese steaks for dinner. After about fifteen minutes we heard the most horrible screaming and squealing and howling cries of pain and pleas for mercy coming up from the cellar. "Bloodcurdling" is the only way I can describe them. Mom and Dad glanced at each other and shook their heads. Andrew was on the verge of being sick.

Then the cellar door opened and Tiffany sauntered out holding Kyle on a leash, naked and on all fours. He was whimpering like a puppy.

"You know Kyle, don't you?" I asked my Mom. "From the Probation Department?"

Mom leaped at him, brandishing her cleaver within an inch of his nose. "I want my husband released and out of the house!"

"And out of this ankle cuff!" Dad said.

Tiffany tightened the leash and Kyle's eyes bugged out. "Whatever you want!" he whined. "Whatever Tiffany wants!"

"There's a young man in your dad's prison," Andrew said, taking the leash from Tiffany. "Eric Johnstone. Do you remember him?"

I forgave Tiffany after that and let her live upstairs. Kyle asked her to marry him and I hope she accepts. She lost her internship when Third Millennium folded but now she's doing hair and makeup at the funeral home and she loves it. As part of our deal with the Federal Reserve, my Dad's bank took over all outstanding student debt and immediately forgave it, freeing Andrew, Hector and everyone else from their bondage as interns. Andrew quit Stark Raven and now he devotes himself to pro bono work. He hired Eric Johnstone as a paralegal after he was released from jail. He's a bright kid and we're hoping he'll go to law school.

Randolph has become a celebrity, selling his paintings all over the world through galleries in Paris, London and Tokyo. He sports a spiffy new Burberry coat and new red high-tops, but still prowls the alleys with his shopping cart collecting pizza boxes, old paint cans and jugs of used crankcase oil. *Art News* lauded him as a modern master who's given "mixed media" and "found materials" a whole new meaning. To offset the income from his painting, he donates junk from his garage to the Museum of Homeless Art, with Andrew's tax advice. "All my life I thought I was a bum," he told us. "Now I realize I was just a nonprofit."

"That's where the money is," Andrew said.

Randolph laughed. "It's all part of the Potlatch."

But is that right? I wondered. Is everything part of the Potlatch?

Hector was abducted the night of the awards dinner and driven around in the back of a van until he passed out. When he awoke in a strange house he expected to see Arbuthnot and the malignant gnomes menacing him with cattle prods and face-shaped cages full of rats.

Instead he found himself alone with Gwendolyn, his boss from the Federal Reserve Bank. She explained that he was spirited away to protect him from a dangerous madman named Arbuthnot who had infiltrated the Bank (and who has since been sent back to the Wharton Institution for the Criminally Insane, in Wharton, Alabama). What happened after that is a little vague. Hector is sort of shy and modest, and I couldn't get him to tell me everything that happened. All I know is that the next morning when he walked into the cafeteria and the secretaries started singing "Like A Virgin," Gwendolyn told them, "Not anymore!" Hector says they're going to get married in June.

As far as the Potlatch is concerned, I probably ought to let Mr. Reddy have the last word, since he looks at things from the cosmic perspective. The last time I visited him, I told him how well everything had turned out and he reminded me that all the aspirations of human life are futile. I didn't argue with him— what would be the point? But it seems to me that if you take the long, cosmic view you're making a big mistake, like canceling your cable service because it doesn't run forever. If the world's an illusion, why not sit back and enjoy the show? It's a fairy tale world, where (at least for a while) you can live happily ever after. But there are no curses, no evil dwarfs making you dance to their tune. Everything's up to you. Maybe life's a big Potlatch, and there's no point in resisting because, in the end, you die. I get that. But in the meantime, it doesn't have to be a racket. There's love and beauty and compassion (even sometimes for Tiffany), excitement, ambition, achievement, and all the rest of the things that make life worth living. And what if Mr. Reddy's right, and it's all an illusion? What difference would it make?

THE END

About the Author

Bruce Hartman lives with his wife in Philadelphia. He is the author of *A Butterfly in Philadelphia* (2015), the first book of a projected "Philadelphia Trilogy" of which *Potlatch* is the second entry. His other books include the techno-dystopian comedy, *Big Data Is Watching You!* (Swallow Tail Press, 2015), and four mysteries, *The Philosophical Detective* (2014), *The Rules of Dreaming* (2013), *The Muse of Violence* (2013), and *Perfectly Healthy Man Drops Dead* (Salvo Press, 2008). For more information, please see his website and blog, www.brucehartmanbooks.com.

www.ingramcontent.com/pod-product-compliance
Lightning Source LLC
Chambersburg PA
CBHW020243180626
46810CB00006B/2338